PRAISE FOR *OPPOSITE SULLY'S GYM*

Opposite Sully's Gym is a perfectly paced slow-burn mystery that's also one of the best crime novels I've read in years. Patrick Bird reminds me a lot of Howard Engel's great PI Benny Cooperman but with a darker and grittier edge.

— WAYNE ARTHURSON, Crime Writers of Canada Award–winning author of *The Red Chesterfield* and the Leo Desroches series

Alexis Stefanovich-Thomson has spun an absorbing mystery out of one of the most unlikely chapters in Toronto's history. *Opposite Sully's Gym* is a compelling page-turner that takes you into the city's shadows, finding intrigue in the local connections to an earth-shaking assassination.

— ADAM BUNCH, author of *The Toronto Book of the Dead* and *The Toronto Book of Love*

One of the most riveting thrillers I've ever read. Stefanovich-Thomson deftly [takes] the reader back to 1968, following the assassination of Martin Luther King Jr. The Toronto setting is beautifully observed, with vivid descriptions of the rooming houses, the police service, current events, and even the cars and mores of the time.... Stefanovich-Thomson ratchets up the tension like a master, unfolding twist after twist, to an absolutely unexpected final chapter. The best book I've read this year.

— MELODIE CAMPBELL, award-winning author of *The Silent Film Star Murders*

Opposite Sully's Gym is that rare mystery that combines a dark, suspenseful whodunnit with a vivid, engrossing historical setting. I haven't been so wrapped up in a novel since Walter

Mosley's *Devil in a Blue Dress*. Alexis Stefanovich-Thomson is a terrific writer!

— ASH CLIFTON, award-winning author of *Twice the Trouble*

Stefanovich-Thomson follows his Edgar-nominated debut with this taut, skillfully crafted novel set in the turbulent Toronto of the late sixties. Equal parts murder mystery and historical thriller, [the novel] perfectly captures the paranoia of the era and the grit and grime of Toronto's streets, factories, and rooming houses. Well paced and witty, *Opposite Sully's Gym* is a love letter to the great PI stories of the twentieth century, when all a detective needed was a keen mind and a good pair of shoes. In Patrick Bird, Canada has, at long last, our answer to Lew Archer.

— J.J. DUPUIS, author of the Creature X Mystery Series

Move over Chandler. Move over Hammett. Here comes Stefanovich-Thomson. Writing in the mode of the noir genre, Alexis has woven a dark tapestry that is threaded through with passages of exquisite beauty. Add to that thoroughly engaging characters (Who can forget Flavia?) and a compelling story and you have an outstanding book. I look forward to more Patrick Bird stories.

— MAUREEN JENNINGS, author of the Murdoch Mysteries series

Opposite Sully's Gym is a layered delicacy of classic noir fiction. The taut plot filled with suspense is structured around wonderful prose reminiscent of Ross Macdonald. This is a character-driven novel where the time period and setting carry equal weight to the main character. If you love classic noir, *Opposite Sully's Gym* is not one to be missed. Alexis Stefanovich-Thompson is definitely an author to watch.

— DAVID PUTNAM, author of the bestselling Bruno Johnson series

A rare and wonderful find: a novel set in Toronto in the late 1960s that weaves the real-life story of James Earl Ray hiding out here with a flawed hero we want to keep reading about.

— ROBERT ROTENBERG, bestselling author of *One Minute More*

In *Opposite Sully's Gym*, Alexis Stefanovich-Thomson works a noir twist into a notorious real-life moment to great effect. Taut, gripping, and utterly compelling, this is historical suspense of the finest calibre and a must-read for fans of hard-boiled detective fiction.

— TOM RYAN, bestselling author of *The Treasure Hunters Club* and *We Had a Hunch*

Opposite Sully's Gym is a layered, slow-burn noir that blazes to a stunning and unexpected climax. Stubborn and compelling wannabe PI Patrick Bird wends through the vividly realized streets of 1960s Toronto in a mystery that respects the classics while carving out something gritty, humane, and unforgettable.

— AMY TECTOR, author of the Dominion Archives Mysteries

OPPOSITE SULLY'S GYM

PATRICK BIRD MYSTERY SERIES

The Road to Heaven

Opposite Sully's Gym

A PATRICK BIRD MYSTERY

OPPOSITE SULLY'S GYM

ALEXIS STEFANOVICH-THOMSON

Publisher and acquiring editor: Meghan Macdonald | Editor: Shannon Whibbs
Cover designer: Laura Boyle
Cover image: man: shutterstock/Asia Evtyshok; taxi: Unsplash/Ross Sneddon

Library and Archives Canada Cataloguing in Publication

Title: Opposite Sully's gym / Alexis Stefanovich-Thomson.
Names: Stefanovich-Thomson, Alexis, author.
Series: Stefanovich-Thomson, Alexis. Patrick Bird mystery ; 2.
Description: Series statement: A Patrick Bird mystery ; 2
Identifiers: Canadiana (print) 2025019967X | Canadiana (ebook) 2025019970X | ISBN 9781459755888 (softcover) | ISBN 9781459755895 (PDF) | ISBN 9781459755901 (EPUB)
Subjects: LCGFT: Detective and mystery fiction. | LCGFT: Novels.
Classification: LCC PS8637.T4335 O66 2026 | DDC C813/.6—dc23

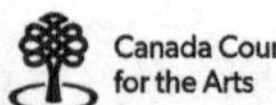

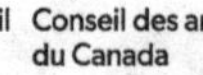

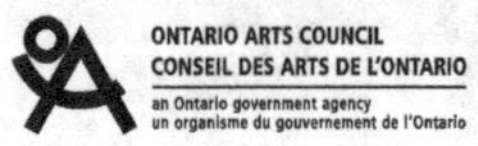

We acknowledge the support of the Canada Council for the Arts and the Ontario Arts Council for our publishing program. We also acknowledge the financial support of the Government of Ontario, through the Ontario Book Publishing Tax Credit and Ontario Creates, and the Government of Canada.

Printed and bound in Canada.

Dundurn Press
1382 Queen Street East
Toronto, Ontario, Canada M4L 1C9
dundurn.com, @dundurnpress

For Ava and Lev

Before ...

TWO WHITE MEN sat in the Dodge Dart in the strip mall's parking lot watching the oncoming traffic: the transport trucks and family sedans, the commuters and tourists, the station wagons and lone men in pickups with dogs hanging their heads out the window. Gaffer, behind the wheel, was the older of the two, thinner, and with less hair. He pushed his wire-framed glasses up his nose and stared at the road that rose to meet the bridge, leading, almost due north, over the river to America. In the passenger seat, Raul took the second last bite of a hamburger; mustard, half a pickle slice, and chunks of raw onion dripped from what remained in his hand onto the greasy paper on his lap. A clump of relish clung to the bottom of his moustache; his lank hair hung long on either side of his thin face covering his ears completely. When he opened his mouth to push in the last piece of lunch, two sharp eye teeth showed. He closed his full lips and chewed, crumpled the empty paper, dropped it into the bag lying on the seat, and tossed it out the window onto the asphalt.

"That was stupid," said Gaffer.

"Eating makes you sleepy." Raul hadn't finished chewing his food, and it showed when he talked.

Gaffer's face tightened and he jerked his glance back to the road. Raul cranked the window up, angled his body on the bench, lay his head against the glass, and closed his eyes. The air grew a little warmer.

Gaffer sat facing the line of vehicles, slowing, stopping, and lining up for customs before crossing into the United States, but his gaze was directed at the traffic coming the other direction, down the long ramp and entering into Canada. The sun passed behind a white cloud and the shadow raced along the road, onto the lot, over the parked car, and up the bridge linking Windsor to Detroit.

"You don't make sense, Raul. You insist on coming out here when you know it's not safe, and then you do stupid things like —"

"What's not safe?"

"Your being here. Calling attention to us by throwing litter out the window. You're looking for trouble."

"There's no law against two citizens sitting in a car watching traffic. You want me to pick it up?" Raul wasn't watching traffic; his eyes were still closed. He scratched at the lonely patch of hair beneath his mouth. "No law against it."

"Except you're not even a citizen."

Raul sat up and looked across the front seat. "No? What do you know about my citizenship?"

Gaffer shot a glance at Raul, who now wore a pair of aviator glasses, blocking his expression, rendering him still more distant. They reflected and distorted the interior of the car and the world around them — the dashboard, the gear shift coming out of the steering column, Gaffer's knuckles on the wheel, the clouds drifting on the blue of the sky — but they remained directed at the figure in the driver's seat.

Gaffer's eyes couldn't hold the gaze and returned to the road. "There's a cab," he said.

Raul didn't look. The yellow taxi rolling down the ramp from the bridge had a top-light that read CHECKER CAB; the same logo was on the door and a Michigan plate hung on the front bumper. It drove past them without slowing.

After a moment Raul said, "Is it him?"

"No."

"You sure?"

"It was just two black girls in the back."

"You know, Gaffer, after Montreal, I never believed you had a sense of humour, but I might change my mind yet."

"I don't want to talk about Montreal."

"No? Enough of those Frenchie girls? You should've been down in Tijuana with Jimmy and me, then you'd have something you really didn't want to talk about. Jimmy liked those *señoritas* so much he put them in the movies."

Gaffer's lip curled slightly.

"He'll be here soon," said Raul. "Keep the faith." He pulled the sunglasses from the bridge of his nose, held them open in one hand, and stared into the stream of traffic. Without the glasses, his eyes were small and dark in his pale face. The light turned red up the road; the groans and wheezes of eighteen-wheelers braking travelled through the air.

Gaffer looked at his wristwatch and then out the window.

"Nervous Nellie," said Raul. "What's done is done. You got the place in Toronto?"

"I know a place that can work. For a start, at least. He'll be on his own once I get him settled. I'm not sticking around to hold his hand."

"Sure. I don't want to know anything about it."

"You told me already. That's why it doesn't make sense for you to be here."

"No? I just got to say congratulations to our boy. Do a little personnel management — give credit where credit is due. Everyone likes a little recognition for a job well done, and no one can say Jimmy didn't do his job as well as he could. A pat on the back, and I'll be gone."

Gaffer didn't say anything. The traffic was moving again. Another cab was coming down the ramp from the bridge, and he sat up a little straighter as it approached.

Raul drew his lips into something that might have been a smile on a different face. "Jesus, you're going to give yourself a heart attack jumping at every hack that comes rolling by. Relax. He'll be here when he gets here."

The taxi cruised past and, through the open window, the face of an old man with stringy white hair, a thin neck, and blotchy skin appeared and was gone.

"Do you think Jimmy's going in for disguises?" asked Raul.

But Gaffer didn't answer; he was staring at a second taxi coming hard on the heels of the first. The sun caught the slanted front window of the car, the glare hiding the passenger inside. The cab slowed, turned into the parking lot, and pulled up at the strip mall's convenience store. Seconds passed.

The back door opened and a man stepped out of the taxi. His brown hair was curled at the ends, and his unshaven face had patches of stubble beneath the chin. The driver exited the car, pulled a duffle from the trunk, and dropped it on the asphalt. The two exchanged a few words as the man paid with U.S. bills. The cabbie returned to his car and the thud of his door echoed in the empty lot. The man standing in the parking lot wore a plain white shirt; with one hand he held a checked jacket over his shoulder, and bending down, he picked up the bag with the other. The cab revved its engine and backed out of the parking spot. The newcomer walked toward the convenience store, as the taxi swung onto the roadway, back to America.

"That's him," said Gaffer. "It's James." But the passenger seat was already empty. He flicked his gaze back to the parking lot. It was empty, too. The door to the shop was closing slowly on its pneumatic brake. Gaffer was alone in the Dodge, waiting. His eyes shifted back and forth between the road and the convenience store. His hand went to the door handle but returned to the steering wheel where he held it still on the vinyl covering.

The store's door swung outward and the man from the cab, now wearing his jacket, stepped through, his bag hoisted over his shoulder. He sauntered over to the beige Dodge and popped open the passenger door. "Gaffer. Aren't you going to open the trunk for my bag? Fucking taxi gives better service than you."

"Where's Raul?" asked Gaffer, getting out of the car. "I wish you wouldn't call me that. It's not my name."

"What? You earned it, up in Montreal." There was a pause as they stood staring at each other before he continued, "No fucking 'Hello, how are you? Everything okay? Fuck, Jimmy, you're amazing. You did it when no one else in the world could.' None of that? Raul told me thank you from the whole fucking nation: The United States of America thanks me." He spoke with a drawl, but it didn't take the edge off his words.

Gaffer fumbled the keys, and they fell onto a line painted on the parking lot's blacktop. He stooped, picked them up, and opened the trunk on the second try. He raised his wary eyes to look at the new arrival. "It's good to see you, James. You've made us all proud. Really proud."

"And now to Toronto." You could hear every letter when he said the city's name. "You got a place set up for me?"

"Where's Raul?" Gaffer asked again.

"In the store. Fucking talking to the guy behind the counter."

"Get in the car. You shouldn't be standing out in the open. I'll find Raul, and we'll get out of here."

James sat in the passenger seat, where Raul had been a minute before. Gaffer went into the store: canned goods, breakfast cereal, chocolate bars, potato chips, cigarettes behind the counter, cleaning products lined up on a shelf, a pot of coffee stewing on a ring, girlie magazines on a rack, gift cards, plastic toys, toiletries. But no Raul. He circled the central island once more and looked into the parabolic mirror hanging from the ceiling, but he was the only customer.

"I help you with something?" asked the man behind the counter.

Gaffer looked at him, looked at the funhouse mirror, and said, "No."

He returned to the car. "Raul wasn't there."

"Isn't that just like him? Always fucking disappearing. 'Specially when you need something. At least I got my money." James waved a fan of colourful bills at Gaffer. "But it looks like we're playing fucking Monopoly."

"But where did he go?" said Gaffer. "Put that away."

"Who the fuck cares? Take me to Toronto."

"But doesn't he need a ride?"

"His loss. Your job is to get me to the city. Let's get going."

Gaffer started the Dodge and turned it onto the service road. At the first traffic light, he turned to ask James a question, but something held him back from forming it. The light turned green, and they drove in silence. By the time they were on the highway, his passenger was asleep, his snores providing a background rhythm for the ride. Gaffer stared into the distance as the road unrolled before him and the city approached. He had so many questions. He wanted to know James's story. But he was glad he'd held his tongue, glad he hadn't asked. It was better not to know what had happened on April fourth in Memphis, just two days earlier, when James Earl Ray had pulled the trigger and assassinated Dr. Martin Luther King Jr.

I

THE MARGARINE WAS losing its colour as it melted into the heat of the toast when Rose came into the kitchen in her waitress uniform. Her hair, still wet from the shower, curled over her shoulders.

"How's Mrs. Bird this morning?" I swallowed a mouthful of coffee from a mug advertising the union local at Massey Ferguson.

She frowned. "Where'd that come from?"

"The mug? I took it as I was heading out the door; thought the union should give me something, after all the nothing they gave me when I needed them."

"Maybe," she spoke slowly, choosing her words with care, "if you'd stuck around and got to know them a little better, they'd have helped you out more at the end."

"What's that supposed to mean?"

She turned to the fridge, swung the door open, looked inside, and closed it without taking anything out. "You know what it means, Patrick." It's never good when your name gets used as punctuation. "We had a deal."

She was right, but I didn't like having it thrown in my face before I'd finished my coffee. I'd asked her to marry me three times, and it was only on the third occasion that she'd given me the conditional yes — the condition being that I was working. And now I wasn't, and that had been the case on and off since our honeymoon, a predictable weekend in Niagara Falls — romance with the pounding of the water in the background and a great cloud of mist hanging over it all. And then back to the city for Monday morning, when Monday mornings meant something, more tired than when we left, the ache of love deep in our flesh.

"What are you bringing that up for now?" I said. And then I figured it out: it was the twenty-seventh and before long the calendar would be turning from May to June, and the rent would be due. These conversations came like clockwork.

"We'll make the rent." There was more confidence in my voice than I felt.

"That's not what this is about."

"We could take in a lodger if things get tight."

"I'm not living with a stranger."

The vehemence of her response surprised me. "It wouldn't be forever. Just until I got steady work."

"I told you no." She put her hands to her face and sucked in the sob before it came out; but I could hear it in her voice when she said, "And that's why I made you get a job and keep it before we got married because I was afraid this would happen. We're not playing house anymore. This is real."

I sat in silence, a swirl of steam rising from my coffee.

"You promised, and now you have nothing to say? Can't you do something? Anything."

I pushed my chair back, stood, stepped across the narrow kitchen, and took her in my arms. She shoved at my chest, trying to release herself from my embrace. My hands wrapped around her back.

"That's not what I meant," she said, pushing out of my hold and meeting my eyes with hers.

I stepped forward again.

"Stop. I'm late."

The clock on the wall, the circular face inside an elongated star, a wedding gift from an aunt I didn't really know, said ten to nine. "You don't start until eleven, do you?" If she was on the breakfast shift, she was past late.

"Don't you understand anything?" This time the tears did spring to her eyes. "I'm late. My period."

That kind of late. I looked at her, seeing her through fresh eyes, so sweet and gentle, so strong and crazy, and I forgot about the job I'd thrown over at Massey Ferguson, and the one before that at the used car lot, and the one I didn't count because I'd only done three shifts working security overnight at the Royal York, and my first real one with the detective agency that had ended so badly I never wanted to remember it. I forgot about the work world with all its demands, all the smiles turned upside down, and for a moment it was just me and Rosie and the life we'd created together and now, maybe, the one growing inside her. And I looked at her, stuck in the moment, unable to say anything, feeling the flush of unnameable emotion rush up from my heart and wrap its tendrils around my neck and then onto my face. The tears were in my eyes, too.

"What are we going to call him?"

She laughed as we stood in our clench, which had somehow come back together without either of us trying.

"It's just a week or two, Pat. Slow down. I need to see the doctor. We don't know for sure yet. But I feel different. I feel this time it's real."

"We deserve one. God knows we've been trying hard enough."

She laughed. "Maybe. We'll give it a couple more days and then I'll make the doctor's appointment."

I stepped back from her and put my hand on her stomach; it felt the same as it always did, soft and round and warm. Our eyes met once more; hers were smiling and mine were smiling back. "But you should be sitting down. Resting up. Taking care, in your condition."

She gave me a playful push on my chest. "Stop. But you can make me a coffee if that's how you feel about it." She pulled a chair out and sat at the table her mother had passed down to us with its red outlines of crescents on its Formica top, pudgy boomerangs, overlapping in a random array.

I lifted the kettle, weighing it in my hand to figure out if it had enough water or not, decided that reheated water wasn't good enough for my Rosie now she was pregnant, poured the contents down the sink, and turned the tap for some fresh.

I was still smiling when she said, "That's why I'm worried about work. Because I'm going to have to stop waitressing at some point, so it's important that you have something. Something steady. You're going to be the breadwinner when the baby's born."

"I'll get there. I promise."

If I said it enough times, maybe it'd come true. Now the job at Massey Ferguson, unionized and all, looked better than ever. But I wouldn't be going back there: my habit of burning bridges in retreat — full flaming, Molotov-cocktail, torch-throwing infernos — saw to that.

Rose blew her nose into a Kleenex from the box, rolled it inside her sleeve, and said, "I feel it. Or at least I feel like I can feel something. Maybe not physically yet, but an emotion, an intuition. It's hard to explain. I guess we'll have to wait and see what the doctor says. This time feels different."

There was a pause, and I felt like Rose wanted me to tell her where I was going to look for work today; except I wasn't, because her mother had recruited me for some unpaid labour.

"I'm helping Flavia this morning with the missing tenant." I never knew what to call her: to Rose, I called her Flavia; to her face, I called her Mrs. Gentilini; and in my mind, I called her my mother-in-law. None seemed quite right for the place she occupied in my life. She was a short Italian woman, the wrong side of the halfway marker, well put together for her age, strong and tireless; her English wasn't bad, and her heart was good — and sometimes between the two a few wires got crossed up, and that could lead to some confusion and excitement.

"Not again."

"Yeah."

"When did this happen?"

"I don't know for sure. She called yesterday when you were at work and asked me to help out. Someone disappeared three weeks behind on the rent and she wants me to —"

"You're not going into the room? That's —"

"— take a look around and see if I can help her figure out where he is and whether she can recoup some of the missing money."

"I wish she'd up and sell."

Flavia didn't have the ideal temperament to run a boarding house. Plenty of patience is needed — and she didn't have much — but given her situation there wasn't a lot of choice. The house on Ossington, the one where Rose and her sister grew up, proved too big for the family after the girls were gone, so Rose's father, Joe, when he retired, once his knee stopped working the way a knee's supposed to, had the idea of chopping the house up and renting the rooms while converting the basement into a contained apartment for Flavia and himself. It was smart; they had everything they needed: kitchen, bathroom, a home, and an income. And it would have worked, except for the heart attack that struck eight months later, taking him away and leaving the widow to manage the house full of tenants on her own.

Now Flavia, who had lived her life in Toronto like she was still in Calabria, speaking Italian whenever she could, not knowing the city beyond the four blocks around her house, not driving a car, and not having much of a social network beyond family, was asked to do a whole lot more. To her credit, after the tears, the hearse, the grave, and the veils of the funeral passed, she rolled up her sleeves and showed a determination not to be denied. Any tenant who took her accent as a sign that she didn't understand was quickly disabused of that notion. She managed what she could and wasn't beyond asking for help when needed. She still thought of me as the detective, although that was at least four jobs back, and occasionally called upon me to search for missing tenants or knock on apartment doors and look tough when the rent was overdue. I wasn't working; helping out was the least I could do.

"Did you talk to her about selling?" I asked.

"No. Not unless I want a slap up the side of my head. We'll be taking her out of there on a stretcher."

"Don't say that."

"I suppose not."

"It shouldn't take too long. Flavia says the tenant's gone, so I'll —"

"Is she sure?" said Rose. "She shouldn't get so involved in their lives. It's too much. She should just say 'Good riddance,' cut her losses, and move on. He's gone because he doesn't have the money to pay; chasing after him doesn't make any sense."

The kettle whistled, and I turned back to it, pouring the steaming water, clear and clean, into the cone where it churned up the grounds, swirled, settled into a murky brown, and dripped through the filter into the mug below.

"Which one is it?" asked Rose.

"The guy on the top floor. The photographer, I think."

"Jack? He's been there since the beginning. I thought he was the steady one. Not like that cabbie? He's so shifty. I hope he'd up and leave; there's something about him that gives me the creeps."

"I don't think I've met him."

We did our best to stay out of the running of the boarding house, to know as little as possible about the people who lived there but inevitably were drawn back into the vortex in an effort to support Flavia.

"You've got to find a real job. It's great you're helping Mama out, but she doesn't pay. And she'll be the first to run you down for not working. Especially when we tell her about …" She glanced down at her stomach.

"Slow down. We don't need to tell her yet."

"She's my mother. She's going to know at some point. She asks every time we see her. See if she doesn't drop a hint for you today. And if she has any suspicions, she'll ask Tina, as well." Tina, Rose's younger sister, had jumped the family hierarchy and given birth to twins six months ago, creating unnecessary grief for Rosie and me.

"Let me work on this. I'll help her today and then tomorrow is my first day looking for work for real. I'll get something. I promise. Something good."

But the joy of Rosie's news threatened to fade against my lack of prospects and my ability to screw up whatever job came my way. It was time to grow up, to leave the ideals of childhood behind, to — as St. Paul said — put away the childish things now I was a man. I could grit my teeth, and work all day, every day, for the rest of my life. Holding a job didn't have to be so difficult; everyone else just got up and did it, some of them even with a smile on their face. It didn't help that the guy I got compared to most often in the family, Tony, Tina's husband, my brother-in-law, Italian, proud parent of two little girls, had a steady gig as a mechanic at a suburban garage.

"Okay. Just get there. I need it. I'll feel better when you have work and it's steady. I'll know you can take care of me and ..." We looked down at her stomach at the same time, and, seeing the other do the same, laughed at our expectations and joy. "We don't even know for sure yet," she said. "We should slow down."

The coffee had stopped dripping through the filter. I gave the milk a sniff before pouring it in; clouds roiled in the darkness of the mug as I placed it on the table in front of Rosie.

FLAVIA'S HOUSE ON Ossington was just a little above Queen Street; it was the southernmost of three row houses on the west side, almost directly opposite Sully's Gym. Standing two-and-a-half stories tall, it was narrow and pointed with bay windows overhanging the sidewalk on the first and second floors and a dormer sticking its nose out on the third. I rang the bell, heard the chime inside, and waited for my mother-in-law. The bolt clicked, and the door swung open to reveal the strong white teeth of a broad smile that dropped immediately upon recognizing me.

"I thought you were someone coming to see about the room," she said.

There was a handwritten sign, reading ROOM TO LET, done in marker on a piece of cardboard, that Rose had made a year ago to help her mother out. Flavia kept it stored vertically between the fridge and the counter and brought it out as necessary; currently, it was stuck in the window cut in the front door.

"No such luck," I agreed.

"And now," she continued, "not one, but two."

"Two?"

"Already one was gone. Paul. The new one. Such a quiet man. Just stay quiet in his room. He left. I don't tell you because I don't like to bother you and Rose with my problems. At least he paid up and told me he was going. But that's two weeks now. Two empty rooms."

"But all paid up? So, no problem there?" Standing on the stoop, I peered into the gloom of the windowless hall. The days were getting longer — it was almost the end of May — but the mornings still held a chill. I stomped my feet to give my mother-in-law the chance to take the hint.

But instead of inviting me into the house, she glared at me. "No problem? No problem. What do you think? That money just comes from nothing? It must be nice. No problem. Yes, I have a problem."

"But Paul was all paid up? That's what I meant."

She looked at me with the same dark eyes as her daughter, relented, and stood back: "Come in. You're letting all the cold air into the house."

I pushed into the hallway, thinking of Rose and the baby that might be inside her, and tried to recalibrate my blood pressure to cope with my mother-in-law. It was one thing to quit paid work, but you couldn't quit family. Flavia banged the front door shut behind me; footsteps came down the stairs, and I looked into the darkness to see a tall brown man in a pressed white shirt descending toward us.

"Good morning, Mr. Yusuf," said Flavia.

"Good morning," he said.

"Mr. Yusuf's a good boy," she explained as he rounded the newel and headed to the back of the house where the communal kitchen was. "He's a student. Studying to be a doctor."

"Good for him," I said. Her statement felt like a comment on my shortcomings.

"He studies at the university."

I'd already cheered for him once; I wasn't going down that road again. "What about the guy who skipped out on the rent?"

Flavia gave me a shush and flashed her dangerous eyes; we wouldn't be discussing poor tenant behaviour in the public arena of the hallway. "Come with me downstairs." She pushed her thick figure past me in the narrow passage leading back to the kitchen, where Yusuf had something bloody and red dripping on a cutting board. He rearranged it on the wood, and its new position revealed it wasn't a hunk of raw meat but a pomegranate half, the seeds and juice spilling out. Flavia yanked my arm, and we turned through the doorway and down the uneven steps to her basement apartment.

"Nice boy, very clean," she commented. "He eats fruit for breakfast."

"And he pays his rent?"

"It's not funny to pay the rent," she said in a low voice, letting me know she didn't appreciate my humour.

"Fair enough. Let's talk about the tenant that left without paying."

"Two weeks behind on the rent. This week makes three."

"But he's gone?"

"Maybe, he didn't say anything to me. No one has seen him for the past month. No one."

"You're sure it's a month?"

"No. But it's almost a month." I opened my notebook, my pen hovering over it as I tried to figure out what was going on here. There was an elastic quality to Flavia's sense of time compounded and confused with the amount of money owed.

"What's his name?"

"Jack Turner."

"And what did he —"

"He was my best tenant." Flavia blinked twice. "He has the best room: the whole top floor, two rooms. He's been renting since the first day. He was the first we rented to. Joe and me." The roller coaster of Flavia's emotions had crested and now we were coming down fast, racing down the steep incline, and a slow drip started from her eyes and nose. A white pocket square appeared from inside her housecoat and dabbed at the wet spots on her cheeks. She angled her head away from me to make a discreet snuffle in the handkerchief; seeing her in distress, when usually so strong and proud, was as disturbing for me as it was for her. "He was such a good tenant, and now this. It's too much. Too much. I can't do this anymore."

She sat down on one of the kitchen chairs, vinyl cushioning over a steel frame, so she could focus on her grief, the loss of Joe, and the weight of responsibility. Her hands started up, describing the emotions more vividly than language could: the overwhelming nature of the work, the sorrow of going it alone, the grief at the loss of her husband, the loneliness of a woman getting older and trying to manage in an uncaring world, the trials of a landlady, the perfidy of tenants, and the ultimate fear of financial ruin.

I searched around and summoned up some empathy from somewhere just above where the toast was settling in my stomach, stuffed my doubts about where the responsibility for missing tenants might actually lie back where they belonged, and did my best: "It's okay, Flavia. We're going to find him. He'll turn up."

"You're the detective." She wiped her eyes with the handkerchief.

"I was and I can be again. I'll help you find Jack." Getting money out of him would be a whole other matter.

"You can find him?"

"I hope so. But let me ask you some questions. Did he have a job?" I already knew, but wanted to get her talking to help her dig herself out of the morass she'd stepped into.

"He was a photographer. He made a darkroom on the third floor. In the extra room. For his pictures." She wrinkled her nose to show she was not fully supportive of a profession that was neither nine-to-five, nor providing a steady paycheque. "He had the best room. The most expensive — the double room. And now no one's paying for it."

"When was the last day you saw him?"

"I don't know. A long time now. Long time. I saw him … no." She stood, crossed the room, pulled a calendar from the local butcher off the fridge, and returned to her seat. She scanned the boxes on the grid that represented the units of life and pushed a thick finger onto the previous Saturday. "Here. The eighteenth. I was coming back from the bakery, and I met him coming out the door. Right at the front step, and I said hello, politely, as I don't like to talk about the money on the street. But he brought it up. 'Good morning, Mrs. Gentilini,' he said. He always called me Mrs. Gentilini — his parents brought him up to show respect. He was a good boy." She frowned at her confusion. "'I know I owe you a week's rent,' It would be two on the next day, 'but I'm in a rush right now. Running. Bus to catch. But I'll get it to you soon and square it up.' And then he disappeared down the street. No next day. No catch-up. I never see him again." She raised both hands above her head, and her eyes followed them but there was no heaven above with mercy, just the basement's slightly discoloured ceiling tiles.

"But that's only a week ago."

"More than that."

"Maybe ten days at the most."

"But nothing since then."

"Have you tried his room?"

"I climb all the stairs, all the way up there every day, and knock on his door. But nothing. But now you're here. We go up together and ..." She produced a loop of keys from inside the pocket of her flowered housecoat and jangled it in the air.

"We're going into his room?"

"He owes me money. And not me. I don't go into the tenants' rooms. That's what you're here for: a detective can go into people's rooms."

It was what I'd expected: Rose's words, warning me to be careful, and my new responsibilities as a father bumped inside my head before I snapped back to the present situation. "And what are we going to do in his room?"

Her eyes bulged as she marvelled at my innocence: "Look for my rent money. You're the detective."

There was noise overhead as we heard Mr. Yusuf on the first floor: the squeak of a chair against the tiles, the quiet scream of water in the pipes as he filled the kettle, and the sound of heavy footsteps as he moved around the kitchen.

"Did Jack have any friends in the house? Or any friends who came over?"

"Came over? What sort of house do you think I run? My own family asks me if friends come over. No friends. He can go out to do that. Not in my house."

"No, you don't understand."

"I understand," she said. "I speak English. No one came over."

"Was he friends, for example, with Mr. Yusuf or your other tenant, the new one, the nice clean boy who paid all his rent up front?"

"I don't know," she'd worked herself up from her earlier shakiness to a slow-burning frustration, and with Jack's whereabouts unknown, I seemed to be the only target within range. "I don't know who's friends and who's not. Him and Danny."

"Danny?"

"The taxi driver. In the room on the first floor."

"Okay, let's go over the rooms one more time so I can understand who everyone is: You have Danny, the taxi driver, on the first floor." She nodded her head. "Jack, the photographer who's disappeared, on the top floor." She nodded again. "And then on the middle floor, there's Mr. Yusuf, the medical student, and Paul, the nice boy who paid ahead who is also gone and ..."

"... and Miss Shirley."

"Miss Shirley?"

"The nurse. Good job. Steady. Helps people." But she seemed unwilling to add either of her favourite adjectives, nice and clean, to her description of the building's lone female resident.

"And Danny and Jack were friends, maybe."

"Maybe," she conceded, adding cryptically, "They're both from Canada."

The conversation was tiring, and the big hoop of keys lay between us on the table. It didn't seem like my mother-in-law would offer coffee, so I suggested we go up to Jack's room to look around.

"I've been waiting all this time. Why you ask only now?" Flavia was up from the table and pushing me in front of her, up the first set of stairs so we could emerge into the half light of the hallway, above ground again. Yusuf sat at the kitchen table, a textbook open, as he worked his way through a colourful plate of fruit, the pale green and orange of the melons, the pomegranate seeds red teardrops against the white china.

"Up, up, up," chanted Flavia from behind me.

And up, up, up, we went. The second floor had another interior hallway, lit by a dim bulb, shut off from the daylight by four doors: Paul's unrented room in the front, Yusuf's beside the washroom door that stood ajar, and Shirley's in the back of the house. And then up one more flight of narrow stairs, the bare wooden treads worn from use, growing concave under the ongoing parade of footsteps, of Flavia's daily pilgrimage to knock on Jack's door, the banister smooth from the many hands that had run carelessly along it over the years. Rosie had had her room up here; her palm had skimmed this rail as she climbed the stairs in her youth. She was safe at home, or on the bus to the Skyline where she worked, and away from this. And Jack? He could be here, right now, ready to pay the rent or work something out; or he'd done a bunk and stiffed Flavia with three weeks unpaid. Either way, the world would keep turning.

At the top was a small landing, a short hallway alongside the railing over the stairwell, and two doors. Flavia, short of breath, gave a long sigh at reaching the summit, and pointed at the farther door, to the front of the house. "That's his room, where he sleeps. This" — she indicated the door beside me with her requisite frown of disapproval — "is the picture room." The window behind us faced out onto the flat roof over Shirley's apartment; the bottom sash was propped open by a short piece of dowelling. My mother-in-law, conscious of the chill in the morning air, creased her brow and removed the prop; the window, painted one time too many, stuck. I stepped in and helped her close it.

She muttered in Italian under her breath. "Here." She thrust the ring of keys at me, holding out one with the number four written in black ink on a piece of tape stuck to its head. As we moved along the narrow hallway, beside the balustrade, to the front room, a quiet settled between us; somewhere below a door opened, and footsteps sounded. I knocked twice, waited, and when enough time had passed, I put my hand around the knob, twisted, and met resistance.

"The key," said Flavia, and although I was focused on the door in front of me, I could imagine her dark eyes rolling. "It's locked. I told you already."

It was a cheap mechanism, the keyhole right in the knob; the key slid in, the teeth gripped as it turned, the motion swivelled the handle, there was the click of disengagement, a push from me, and the door swung open. The room faced eastward, but the morning light was fighting a losing battle to get through the heavy drapes hanging in the front window. Flavia gasped over my shoulder as the apartment's disarray became apparent: dresser drawers wrenched from their tidy slots, clothes littering the floor, the mattress slashed, its stuffing dusting the disaster like volcanic ash; photographs off the wall, their images torn and crumpled, the glass in shards, the frames splintered; paperbacks ripped from the single bookcase, their spines cracked, as they lay scattered at unlikely angles, their pages loose and torn, the down pillow slit and the feathers spread unevenly across Flavia's best room.

"My room. My house." My mother-in-law wavered between outright rage and perceived persecution. "You catch him, Patrick." She sputtered, stopped and started again: "I need to talk to Jack. Why would he do this to me?" She stepped past me into the room and used her foot to poke at a wooden frame broken beyond repair. Deftly, for her age, she wedged the toe of her slipper under the picture and flipped the broken frame over; a black-and-white photograph of a naked model posed with long hair and hands acting as fig leaves stared up at us. Flavia shuddered and placed her foot on the photo, further shielding the girl's nakedness. "Disgusting."

She reached for another frame and pulled it from the rubble. The glass, while cracked, still held, and Flavia shoved it at my midsection. I jerked out a hand in reflex to intercept it before one of the shards pierced my belly, got my thumb on the wood of the frame, and took the broken picture from my mother-in-law's grasp. A long sliver popped out and fell to the ground where it bounced onto the chaos. Feeling safer now the frame was in my hands, I turned my attention to the photo itself. It was a standard studio portrait of a young man shot in three-quarter profile: dark hair worn slightly longer than the norm, a patchy beard trying hard — maybe too hard — eyes turned strangely upward as if to heaven, and a distant smirk dancing on his lips.

"That's him," said my mother-in-law. "That's Jack. The one who owes me money. Find him."

"YOU WANT ME TO ..."

"Find him. He owes me money." There was high contrast in the way Flavia saw the world, and at moments like this, her innate directness pierced any language barriers. "He's ruined my room. My best room." Her tears were gone; she was moving past self-pity and entering into anger and vengeance. "You will find him."

And squeeze every last cent out of his poor, tired body.

"Go and find him." She jabbed her finger at his face in the photograph. "Him. Look: long hair, dirty face." She indicated the studio portrait where Jack's beard stood out as a challenge to Flavia's sensibilities.

"And this photo? Was it hanging on his wall?"

"I don't come up here. I leave the tenants alone. They pay the rent. I don't bother them."

"I'll tidy up here and see what I can find, but first we should look in the other room."

My mother-in-law shuddered at the idea that the next room might have suffered a similar fate. At one point this space had been converted into an upstairs kitchen. Rose always laughed that she was the only girl she knew who'd grown up with a sink in her bedroom. It was a small square space with a sloping ceiling cutting into one wall, and a window Jack had sealed off with blackout sheeting. The destruction here, if anything, was worse, because instead of clothes and bedding and framed photographs on the walls, this room contained the enlarger, the safe light, and the chemical baths. The blackout plastic had been ripped off the window and lay like a child-size body bag on the floor. The sunlight spilled through the window, where no light should come; the clotheslines drying photos above the old kitchen counter had been ripped down; film lay curled, twisted and bare, ruined and unspooled; the chemical baths overturned and slopped, their almost evaporated puddles staining the linoleum; the neck of the enlarger bent beyond repair; the thin shards of the red light bulb scattered in fragile fragments. And all in the destructive light of day that poured in through the window and had already killed the images on the exposed film. While the bedroom looked like the remains of a hurried and desperate search, the dark room was pure violence and destruction. It felt personal, an attack, not the by-product of a frantic hunt. In the go-go-go of the morning, I'd forgotten Rosie's condition; it surfaced in my memory like a revelation. This was her room, where she'd dreamed young dreams and stretched her teenage yearnings out into the universe. Heat burned in my chest and flushed on my neck, and the morning chill fell away.

I stepped into the room, wary of the ghosts lurking in the corners. Flavia unleashed a torrent of words I couldn't understand. There were too many syllables chasing one another in rapid succession to be four-letter words, but whatever they were, I shared the sentiment.

"Someone looks like they weren't too happy with Jack." The voice was too loud in the hush of the moment, too deep for Flavia, and too conversational for my emotional state. "What the hell happened here?" He was a tall man with thick sideburns running down the sides of his face and a moustache drooping over his upper lip. He craned his neck out to look over my shoulder into the room.

My mother-in-law frowned. "Mr. Danny, what are you doing up here?"

"Came to see Jack. My first morning awake after a stretch of ten days of nights. Came up to see if he wanted to play gin rummy."

"He's not here," Flavia said. My mind caught up: here was Danny, the taxi-driving first-floor tenant.

"Sure doesn't look like it," he agreed. There was an awkward pause while the three of us stood in the cramped space on either side of the doorway. "Who's your friend helping you out?" His eyes flicked in my direction.

"Friend ...?" Flavia was struggling to keep up with Danny's vernacular.

He had a deck of cards in his hand, so if he were lying about the gin rummy game, he'd at least bothered to make it plausible.

"I'm Mrs. Gentilini's son-in-law. Patrick Bird."

He raised his eyebrows. "The famous Patrick Bird? Maybe I should say infamous?"

"What's that supposed to mean?"

"Don't think I don't know. I read the papers. You're the one that got himself all tangled up in that Linklater case a couple of years back?"

"What do you know about that?" I turned away from the room and stepped into the door frame where the card player stood. While my name had featured briefly in a few of the newspapers, it hadn't benefitted anyone for my role in that earlier case to get much publicity: I was hardly a celebrity.

"Being a taxi driver, you hear a little about a lot." He wasn't fazed by my approach, and stood in the doorway, not giving an inch, boxing out my mother-in-law behind him.

"Well, what do you know about this, then?" I said.

"Go away. Back downstairs. We need to clean," said Flavia.

Danny didn't heed her command, which might have scored him points in my book at one point, but not right now. "Photographers," he said stepping into the room with an air of authority, "when something goes wrong, nine times out of ten it's either pornography, blackmail, or a combination of the two. Which angle are you working?"

"I'm not working ..." The sentence wound down without me finding a suitable escape route. It wasn't how I wanted to advertise myself. "I'm not looking at it from any angle. I told you. I'm Mrs. Gentilini's son-in-law, helping her out and looking to find the rent money that's —"

"Not his business," Flavia called from behind Danny's figure, framed in the doorway. "No talk about tenants' business."

"Sure made a fucking mess of the place," Danny commented, masterfully ignoring my mother-in-law. "Bedroom the same?" And without waiting for an answer, he sidestepped Flavia in the narrow confines of the hall and pushed into the other room. His low whistle sounded along the hallway. "Someone was looking for something."

"Get him downstairs," hissed Flavia. "He can't be in Jack's room. It's not right. They're —"

"Yeah," said Danny, returning, smiling broadly. "We're not supposed to be in each other's rooms." He had the ability to act as if Flavia didn't exist. "What kind of way is that to live? I pay my rent. I can be where I want and can have who I want in my room. And Jack's my friend. If he invites me up to his room for gin rummy, so be it."

"Nobody invited you," said Flavia. "We're going downstairs."

"It's been this way ever since that little Jamaican girl moved in here," he continued. "Lock up your doors. No talking to each other. If you find yourself across the kitchen table, look away and think pure thoughts. The joys of co-educational life."

"He was your friend?" I asked.

"You talk downstairs," said Flavia, sticking to the script.

"You're already down two tenants," said Danny. "If you want me to stay, you should tone it down. Try being a little less emotional. We're not in the old country anymore."

Flavia unleashed a torrent in her mother tongue and stormed down the stairs.

"These Italians sure are hot-blooded," said Danny, leering at me. "But then you'd know all about that."

"She's my mother-in-law," I said.

He waved a hand to dismiss my concerns.

"I don't want to hear you call her names is what I'm telling you."

"Then you can follow her back down those stairs, too."

"Listen, tough guy." I stepped closer. "If he was your friend, you can help and find him. It doesn't exactly look like he left in good circumstances. Instead of fighting Mrs. Gentilini and me, try a little co-operation."

"Co-operation?" He laughed. "You sound like those goddamn student leaders up in Yorkville. Playing piano, pontificating, and singing, and all the time thinking about their future, not our present. Co-operation my ass."

He hadn't budged. My second step had brought me into his space, and we stood in the too-close proximity of an uneasy stare down. I was pretty done with Danny and his belligerence, barging in, taking shots at me, insulting my mother-in-law, and refusing to leave. The guardrail over the stairs down to the second floor was behind him and cut at the level of his thigh; a well-timed shove would, at the very least, put him off balance, but if offered with a little more force would put him right over the edge. Maybe I was getting older and wiser — it seemed impossible that I was immediately more mature now, following hard on the news of the baby — but a brake inside restrained me from doing something I couldn't take back. Danny, despite his boorishness and insults, was my only connection to the missing man. Perhaps, also, I saw a shadow of myself in his determination to rub the world raw against his rough edges. He was older, a warning to me of the place where people who couldn't work with others ended up: bitter, stuck behind the wheel of a cab, working nights while their families grew up in their absence. Stepping back and stepping down, the ignoble retreat, was hard to manage with grace. It was one thing to attempt an accord; it was another to show weakness to a bully.

Without moving, I tried a peace offering of sorts. "You said with photographers it was either pornography or blackmail: which one do you figure Jack for?"

"You've got to listen, Pat."

"Patrick."

Danny's eyes seemed to smile but his mouth stayed closed. "Keep your ears open. I said nine times out of ten. And I think Jack's the tenth case: it wouldn't have been either with him. He isn't that type."

The tension leaked through the window and into grey light lurking between the close-packed row houses; the space between us widened without us being conscious of moving our feet, and I was able to respond. "How do you figure that?"

"I know him."

"That's all you've got."

"It's enough for me."

"Okay. But I never met the guy. Maybe you can help me out."

"He isn't that type. He takes photos. He does some freelance work for the newspapers, but his main interest is documentary, pretentious. Even artistic. Thought he was creating a record of modern life, a chronicler of our times. Lots of people, I'm not one of them, so don't get the wrong idea, feel like the world is on the edge of a golden age — the times they are a-changin' and all that kind of crap. Not me, but you can see how these idealists get themselves worked up. Sell themselves some optimism." He took a step away from me as he spoke, and the barometer between us moderated.

During the pause I got my question in: "So if it's nine times out of ten, what's the tenth case?"

But Danny had climbed up onto his soap box. "Jack just has too much naïveté and optimism to go for any of that smutty stuff, let alone trying to squeeze a dollar out of someone. He isn't opportunistic like that. He's a sweet kid. But stupid. I mean, the world looks more like the apocalypse than the age of Aquarius from where I'm sitting. This war in Vietnam, assassinations, police brutality, riots, repression —"

"So what's the tenth case out of ten?" I tried to break through his pontificating.

"Jesus, Patrick. I'm not doing your job for you." Danny smiled for the first time; I saw why he didn't do it too much. "The tenth case is when you take a picture, and there's something in there, someone in there, that you don't realize; your photo has meaning for someone else that they don't want out in public. A camera is a dangerous thing. It doesn't lie. Once you've got that image of the secret and you can reproduce it at will, the other side's only choice is to search and destroy. Stick with me and you might get this solved."

He was back at the other end of the short hallway, staring into the bedroom. "It checks out. You see what they've done to these rooms: search and destroy. They're looking for something. Someone's opened drawers, gone through the clothes, one by one, taken them out of the dressers and dropped them on the ground, they've looked behind the frames, they've searched in the mattress. There must be a picture and the negative that someone was looking for — that they wanted bad."

Danny liked the sound of his own voice. He looked back down the length of the small hall to make sure I was following along. "Someone's somewhere they shouldn't be: the prime minister's coming out of the bathhouse door. The mayor's sticking some snow up his nose. Who can tell? But also, they're pissed off." He was beside me now, sticking his head into the darkroom, inquisitive, getting a good view of everything. "Angry as all hell. Look in here: they smashed everything that'll break. Really took it out on the photographic equipment. Won't be using that again, that's for sure. They can't find what they're looking for, so they rip the whole place apart. Vindictive. They're sending a message. We're coming for you. Look out."

His take made sense, at least from what I could see. "Do you think Jack knows he has a photo that's incriminating, that someone else wants?"

"If he didn't before, he does now."

"But if he's the way you describe him, if he's not opportunistic, if he's not trying to turn it into a roll of cash, why doesn't he just give the photo over to whoever wants it, and life goes on?"

"That's the sixty-four-thousand-dollar question, isn't it? The obvious answer is that even if he didn't want to profit from the photo, maybe he had some reason for keeping it. People get funny that way — principles, getting stuck on something, getting righteous, and all that bullshit — thankfully it's not one of my faults."

"You want to help me tidy this up?"

"No, thanks. Your job not mine. You play?" He flashed the deck at me, pulled a worn set of cards out and made a fan in the air.

"Not me."

"I'm not surprised." One-handed, Danny collapsed the fan and fitted the cards back in their cardboard box. He strolled back to the head of the stairwell.

"Wait. I have a couple more questions."

"There'll always be more questions," he said. "I need a coffee right now. My shift starts at noon, so I'm out of here about 11:45."

"I thought you had today off?"

"I'm off nights. But still working. You don't drive, you don't get paid. And I've seen what your mother-in-law looks like when she doesn't get her rent. Time for my coffee. Time to start doing your own thinking." He disappeared down the stairs.

I moved to the bedroom, sifting through the detritus, pessimistic that I would find anything when I didn't know what it was I was looking for. More garbageman than detective. One pile for the trash — the stuffing from the mattress, the broken wood of the frames; one for clothing; and one for personal items — playing cards, paperbacks, postcards, and souvenirs; and the last for items I might want to keep, an address book, and the photographs themselves.

The picture of the naked woman had somehow made its way back to the top of the pile, and I paused, my eyes lingering on the model with her long hair and strategically placed hands. It wasn't exactly pornography, or exactly art. It had the commercial air of tasteful smut that would hang well on the walls of an Annex home with pretensions to bohemia. The girl's face tilted slightly down, allowing her hair to cascade over her shoulders, but her eyes were up and looking straight out at the viewer. It wasn't quite Mona Lisa, but her expression was, for lack of a better word, enigmatic. There was a smile, but it was challenging, vulnerable, and something else that I didn't have a word for. Was she the key to the missing photographer? Jack might not be a pornographer or a blackmailer, as Danny suggested, but things could happen when a young woman was down to her birthday suit, even if it was in the name of art.

IV

THE BEDROOM WAS as tidy as I could make it without garbage bags to pile the mess into — an old steamer trunk I'd found in the closet was filling up with the stuff to keep, and the remainder was piled into a craggy mountain. I put Jack's address book in my coat pocket, paused for a second, and folded the photo of the model into my notebook. It already had the crinkles and creases of mistreatment on it, one more crimp wouldn't hurt. With the first stage of cleaning completed, I went down the elongated spiral of staircases and hallways from the third floor to my mother-in-law's basement apartment.

She was still angry at Danny, muttering curses in Italian under her breath as she sat at the kitchen table. "You see the way he treated me?" she asked. "How he talk to me? I should put him out on the street. Teach him a lesson."

"He was rude," I agreed. "But maybe you want to wait until you fill the other rooms."

"I don't like waiting," she snapped, with more self-awareness than she typically showed.

"It's going to be all right." I paused, in the awkwardness of our relationship. "I'll tidy up the room if you let me know where to find a few garbage bags. We don't want to pick a fight with Danny right now. He was friends with Jack and might be able to help us find him."

The idea of finding Jack and recouping her losses seemed to perk her up. She put a pause on the grumbling, bustled around the basement, and came up with a small army of cleaning products: dusters, rags, mops, chemical powders, disinfectant spray, bottles of bleach, and stiff-bristled scrub brushes. She began to instruct me on how they should be used, the requirements for grade-A cleaning, and what would constitute an acceptable level of maid service. My natural reaction must have showed as my head made an almost imperceptible shake left and right and the grim set of my mouth signified no; that only raised her ire, threatening to reignite her anger. I retreated and for the second time that morning, found myself biting my tongue, listening to her stern directions, and nodding in agreement.

With the caddy of cleaning supplies in one hand, and a mop and pail in the other, I left my notebook and Jack's address book on her kitchen table. A simple sweep wasn't going to meet Flavia's cleaning standards. As I came up the stairs to the second-floor landing, the door directly in front of me that led to the back bedroom cracked open an inch, and the white of an eye showed in the sliver of darkness as if it were floating in space like that strange image the Americans put inside the pyramid on their dollar bill. And then it was gone and the door pulled shut. Shirley, the Jamaican nurse, was interested in my work, too. Everyone in this little rooming house wanted to know what was going on. My hands were full, so I soldiered on, around the newel post and past Yusuf's doorway, but as soon as I had my back to Shirley's room, I heard the creak of the door opening a narrow inch, and felt the eye on me again. I was tempted to swing around quickly into the final set of stairs and catch it framed in the crack, but there was no value in scaring her. My head was down, my eyes on the steps, as I mounted the staircase and climbed out of Shirley's sightline. The nurse was interested; if she was interested enough, she'd come and find me.

On the third floor, I started with the bedroom, dumping the broken frames and shredded bedding into the garbage bags. The mattress was a writeoff. More than a bag would be needed to contain its problems. I'd have to figure a way to drag it down the two flights of stairs without leaving its entrails scattered through the house. In my thoughts I'd built this work up to something real; I'd hoped I'd be doing some sleuthing again — and Flavia had jollied me along — but the task was strictly cleaning. Still, the spare parts of a man's life could pique some curiosity and get the rusty gears turning a little. It was clear — even if Flavia was still holding out for a miracle return — that Jack hadn't made a midnight move; he hadn't packed his bags, boxed up his prized possessions, folded his clothes into the old shipping trunk in the back of the closet, packed his photographic materials carefully in tea towels, hoisted it all on his back and slunk into the night. No, something unexpected, sudden, and, judging by the state of the room, violent had happened; someone had surprised him, causing his disappearance.

Flavia, bless her mercenary heart, was focused on recouping the lost rent and making him pay, squeezing the dollars out of his absent body. But there was more to it than that. It was possible he'd come back. Maybe there'd been a disagreement, a rough-and-tumble altercation, a bunk into the night, hiding out, staying with friends, or returning to his family's home; then his enemies had come and trashed his home in retaliation — maybe they'd taken what they were looking for — or maybe it wasn't found. Maybe the violence was simply wanton and vengeful, and not a purposeful search as I'd first imagined. And now the storm had passed, perhaps Jack could return — in which case he didn't need me to clean the mess — he could do it himself.

My thoughts, which threatened to become as hopeful as my mother-in-law's, were interrupted by a second visitor; the residents of the rooming house were curious to know what was happening in Jack's rooms. Shirley, the nurse, stood at the threshold of the room, looking at the scene of destruction. Short, with dark skin, a round face and delicate features under a steep forehead, her eyes met mine. She looked like she was about to ask a question but remained unmoving.

"You must be Shirley," I said.

She nodded.

"I'm Patrick. I'm Mrs. Gentilini's son-in-law. I'm helping her tidy up."

"What happened here?" she asked, stepping into the room and putting a hand on her midsection, just above the thin belt cinching her starched dress.

"Yeah. That's the question, isn't it? I'm trying to figure it out." She didn't offer anything, so I continued, "Did you know Jack?"

"No. I don't see him much."

"But you must have seen him around the rooming house. In the kitchen. On the stairwell."

"No, I work. I'm out working most days. Today, too. Soon." She turned quickly and her footsteps retreated across the wooden boards of the landing. Once out of sight, she stopped and asked me, "Is he coming back?"

"I don't know. That's what I'm trying to figure out."

And then, in explanation, she said, "I ask only because I have a friend who look for a room."

"Okay," I spoke to the empty door frame, "You'd best talk to Mrs. Gentilini about that. I'm just helping out with ..." My answer faded as I heard her footsteps descending the stairs. Another encounter, more perplexing than illuminating: there was something about Shirley's eye peering out through the crack in the doorway, her need to see what the rooms themselves looked like, her refusal to become engaged in conversation, her denial of ever knowing the missing man, and the poorly disguised look of fear that didn't jibe with the explanation she provided for her questions.

I loaded the last of the personal items into the steamer trunk: socks and underwear, faded jeans, a paisley shirt, pulp paperbacks with garish covers, a ceramic Buddha that doubled as an incense holder, notebooks with sketches and locations, pens and pencils, a few letters and envelopes, a grimy deck of cards. All in all, not a lot to go on. There was a desk with two small side drawers that had been ripped from their slots and turned upside-down under it. I sifted through the paperwork, uncovering a sheaf of letters. Looking through the correspondence, I realized the smart thing to do would be to cross-reference them against the entries in the address book I'd found earlier — and left in the basement.

I started back down the stairs again, past Shirley's door, which remained determinedly closed. Yusuf came out of his room and walked behind me down to the front hall. I turned to meet him at the bottom of the stairs, preparing to ask him a few questions.

"Excuse me, please." He tried to push by.

In the cramped vestibule, a sunbeam came through the fanlight and caught on the brown skin of his face; his thick black hair, generous mouth, and wide-set eyes worked together to make a handsome face.

Unlike Danny, who had proven too nosy, and Shirley with her quiet but determined curiosity, Yusuf appeared to not care whatsoever about the missing tenant. Rather than being reassuring, his lack of interest seemed more suspicious than otherwise.

"Excuse me, please." Even in his rudeness he remained stiffly polite. "I must leave the house. I'm running late." English wasn't his first language, so perhaps the urgency of his departure came across more bluntly than intended.

"I was hoping to have a word with you." Late or not, I had questions.

"Of course," he said. "But later. Right now I have an appointment I must attend."

"You don't have five minutes you can spare for me?"

"No, I'm sorry, I don't. I must leave now, late as I am." Unlike Shirley, he didn't seem afraid, but like her, he was determined to end our conversation.

"I won't keep you, then. But I'll need to talk to you when you get back."

"Yes." He pushed past me, escaping out the front door with more haste than seemed necessary. I stood alone in the front hall, wondering what waited at the other end of his urgency.

The only other door in the hall popped open and Danny looked out. "Slippery one," he commented.

"Were you listening in?"

"I'd ask you not to hold your conversation right outside my door." He swung it wide so I could see into his bedsit. It was a room full of clutter: an array of cards dealt into four open hands on the table, science fiction paperbacks lying face down, the spines stretched, newspapers unfolded on the bed, a 35 mm camera between two candlesticks on a faux mantelpiece, mugs with coffee dried and caked to their insides, driftwood, tin soldiers, a mess of twigs that might have been a bird's nest. Danny returned to the one chair in the room, hunched over the bridge column in the newspaper, and threw the three of diamonds into the middle of the table. He noticed my look. "I was trying to replay this game" — he held up the newspaper for me to see the strange coding of bridge notation — "when I was disturbed by you trying to pin Yusuf down. And fucking unsuccessfully, I might say. So, if you ask, yes, I did hear you. I wish I didn't, but I did. You hear everything in this house. Lots of noises, squeaks, and starts. It's a miracle I ever sleep."

"What's that supposed to mean?

"What do you think it means?"

"I don't know — that's why I'm asking you."

Danny was the only one who'd provided me with any information, but there was something about him that was both shrinking and prickly. "Sometimes there are noises in the night, people wandering around. Every time someone goes to the washroom, you can be sure I'll hear it. They're walking on my fucking ceiling. Maybe playing a little hanky-panky. What do you think? Young people a long way from home. It's easy to get lonely, but that'd just about kill your mother-in-law, eh?"

"Who?"

"This is getting a little gossipy for me. I don't know who and I don't care. I'm down here listening to the patter of footsteps in the darkness, wishing I were asleep. You go up there and dust for fingerprints if you're so inclined."

"No names, huh?"

"Good luck." He shook his head and pulled the door shut again. No one wanted to talk to me. Thank God I had Rosie at home.

In the basement I picked up the address book and my journal and headed back up the stairs one more time.

I stopped at Danny's door and knocked: "What is it?" he called through the panel.

"If you can hear everything," I asked, "then how did someone get in here and up to the third floor? And the mess they made up there, that wasn't done in the quiet."

The door swung open. He had a maroon windbreaker on his back and Chelsea boots on his feet. "Day shift is fast approaching, so I'm out of here. I don't get paid to talk to you." The cards still lay on the low table, but his manner was the same, and he pushed past me and started down the hall to the back of the house. "You've got a lazy mind," he said. "Stop asking so many questions and think for a minute. Maybe the room got trashed when I was out on shift; or maybe they were professionals who knew what they were doing and did it quiet. Either are possible — even both."

I followed behind him, into the kitchen, but he'd already yanked the back door open and stepped down the steps into the messy scrap of concrete, gravel, and scrub, where the house's single parking spot merged into the alley.

Or, I thought as he pulled the door shut behind himself, maybe it was done by somebody already in the house.

V

I RETURNED TO the top floor and pulled the curtains of the bedroom to let the light in. A yellow police cruiser was parked across the street outside the boxing gym. Without a chair to sit on, I leant over the desk and started copying the address for Jack's parents from an envelope into my notebook. They lived up north of the city in a small town, unimaginatively called Midhurst; in the middle of nowhere, or the middle of somewhere. There was a number on a rural route, and when I cross-referenced names against those in the address book, I had the phone number, too. The world wasn't catching fire with my detective work, but this was a starting place; I might find my mother-in-law's missing tenant yet, and even if I didn't, between the two of us, holding his personal effects for ransom in this cold, grasping life, we might be able to squeeze the back rent out of his family.

The girl in the art-smut photo was still on my mind, and I was just starting to search in the address book, under *M*, on the off chance that models were listed by profession, rather than name, when the doorbell rang. It wasn't my house, so I let it ride, and kept on with my work. There was no heading for models, so I started on an alternate route, looking up all the names I could. On the first page, there was an Alice, an Andrew, and an Amy with their seven-digit numbers following. *B* gave me Betty, Bobbi, Blinken, and Barb. Lots of women. I was copying the names and numbers into my book when a commotion from the front hall percolated up the stairwell. It was my mother-in-law's voice competing against a duet of baritones. She was holding her own, but I'd heard enough; I scooped my notebook off Jack's desk and headed back down the stairs.

Approaching the front hall, I could hear the patient professional voices of the men becoming strained as my mother-in-law's determined words rose over them: "You don't come to my house and bring these police in here like this is a bad place. What do you do that for? Why are you all here with your cars parked out front and then so many police in my house like there's something wrong?"

As I descended the final run of stairs, the group came into view, their feet first and then their bodies and heads, crowded into the hallway at the base of the stairs, and spilling out the door onto the stoop, fighting for space with the tenants' boots stacked against the wall, and spring jackets still hanging on hooks.

"What do the neighbours think? I have a nice house. With nice tenants. The neighbours, they see so many police cars parked all around the house. They talk. Are you —"

"I'm going to ask you again, Mrs. Gentilini, does Jonathan Turner live here?"

"And I tell you one more time I don't know no Jonathan. Now go. Leave me and my house alone. No Jonathan here."

Two uniforms stood with their feet on the sill, holding the door, without room to step into the vestibule; the two plainclothes cops inside were not doing a good job of controlling the situation. Their eyes shifted to me in unison, as if their training was so complete that their feet, minds, and eyes moved in lockstep.

"Shut the door!" shouted my mother-in-law. "Shut the door. Everyone is seeing."

"Is this one of your tenants?" asked the older of the two detectives, his thin grey hair slicked back over the tapered dome of his skull.

Another insult to Flavia — that her son-in-law had been mistaken for one of the renters. "He's not a tenant. Family. The husband of my daughter. What do you think —"

"I don't know." He maintained his patience. "That's why I'm asking questions. Sir, I'm going to ask you: Does Jonathan Turner live in this house? We have sufficient reason to believe that he does. We have a driver's licence on record that lists this as his home address." He referred to a piece of paper in his palm. "102 Ossington Avenue. That's correct?"

I'd made some mistakes with the police in the past, cut corners, and ended up out of the PI business because of them. It had made sense at the time, but right now there wasn't any reason to mess around. "There's a Jack Turner who lives on the top floor. I think maybe my mother-in-law didn't recognize the name Jonathan. He's been missing for ..." I looked at Flavia, "for a week or more now. I came by today to help my mother-in-law look around to see what we could see and find out where he's got to. Trying to get some of the back rent he's owing." A geometric indent appeared in the centre of Flavia's brow, and while it reminded me that she was related to Rose, it didn't portend good weather.

"And what did you find?" said the older detective, picking at the loose knot of the striped tie that held his unbuttoned collar in place.

"Not here!" shouted Flavia.

The plainclothes officer lifted his palm on the end of a straight arm, to create the universal stop sign to try and slow Flavia; his shoulder holster showed beneath his jacket.

She ignored his caution. "Shut the door."

"We need somewhere to talk," said his partner, younger, bigger, and broader with a shaved head the colour of copper. He looked like someone I'd seen before, but I couldn't place him. He said to Flavia, "You find us a space out of this hall, and we'll shut the door for you."

She shot him a look that might have blanched his tan, but he held steady and returned her gaze. She blinked first. "In my apartment." She turned and started down the hallway toward the back of the house.

"You boys stay here," said the senior officer to the two uniforms who'd just crossed the sill and stood in the small space at the bottom of the stairs as the rest of us snaked behind Flavia to her basement apartment.

We sat at the kitchen table, and the older officer found a card in his jacket pocket, passed it to my mother-in-law, and said, "I'm Detective Cull and this is Detective Rice. We work out of Fourteenth Division. You can see the address on the card here. We've come calling today with news. Jonathan Turner, the man you called Jack Turner, was found dead on the Exhibition grounds, underneath the Flyer earlier this morning." He saw that this didn't mean anything to Flavia. "Under one of the roller coasters. The coroner is currently performing an autopsy, so I won't speculate on the cause of death at this stage, but suffice to say, given the circumstances, the positioning of the body, and where it was found, we have to treat this as a suspicious death."

I could see Flavia, across the table, trying to understand what this might mean about the rent money.

"We'd like to take a look at his room, and to interview the tenants and ask you some questions."

"Let's start with you, Mrs. Gentilini," Rice, the younger detective broke in. "How long has Jonathan, or we can call him Jack, to keep it simple — how long has he lived here?"

"Two and a half years. He was the first tenant when we started to rent rooms. Always a good tenant. Such a good boy." A transformation had taken place; Flavia's voice was softer, as the news of the death filled the basement. Jack's life had been cut short, but for Flavia, there were also the not unreal challenges of the lost rent money and the damage the investigation, with its potential to get unsavoury, might do to her rooming house's reputation. I could understand. Her emotion was real: the bluster of anger was her default, but beneath it lay fear. And there was truth in the worry that renting the room of a dead man would be more difficult than usual; certainly having two rooms — and one of those a double — to rent on short notice was a hassle she didn't need. Thank God the body hadn't been discovered upstairs in the room itself.

"He was a good tenant?" asked Rice.

"Always a good boy. Just this last month he got behind in the rent and then he disappeared. He was so busy; I don't think he wanted to not pay the rent. And now he's gone."

"Which room did he have?"

"He was on the top floor," I said. Rice shot me a look that implied he'd rather have it from Flavia, but I wasn't to be deterred. "He had two spaces: a room and a small darkroom. He was a photographer."

Cull raised his eyebrows at the mention of photography, and I remembered Danny's thoughts on cameramen; the detective's eyes returned to his pad and he made rough scratches with his pen. But now I'd opened my mouth, his next question wasn't about Jack. "And what's your role in this situation?"

"Like my mother-in-law said, I'm family. She was having some trouble with a tenant — Jack was behind in the rent and hadn't been seen in some time — so she asked me to come and take a look."

"And your name is?" Cull pursued.

"Patrick Bird." I don't know if I was being paranoid or not, but I felt the two exchange a look.

"He's a private detective," announced Flavia.

I shook my head to make my disagreement known.

"Great," said Rice. "We need all the help we can get." The sarcasm scraped up against me.

There was a moment of quiet, with the only sound being the scratching of Cull's pen and then Rice came back with another question: "Licence?"

"Not anymore," I said. "My mother-in-law likes to boost my credentials a little."

"An amateur, eh?" said Cull. "Perfect. So, what have you found for us so far in the case of the missing lodger?"

I brought the detectives up to speed on my activities on the third floor. I downplayed the interactions with the tenants and focused on the mess we'd sifted through in Jack's rooms.

Rice's dislike for me seemed to be growing: "You mean you went into his rooms and went through his stuff without —"

"I'm not sure they're his rooms if he hasn't paid his rent in —"

"He owed me money." Flavia jumped to my defence.

"— and disturbed a crime scene before the officers could arrive."

"No one knew it was a crime scene until you arrived. There was no alternative —"

"He owed me money!" The loudness of the outburst was followed by silence, and we sat around the table at an impasse.

Cull, the senior of the two, lifted his head from his notepad. "Of course, Mrs. Gentilini, I understand. It isn't easy to be a landlord — or, I should say, a landlady — in this city. You took a reasonable approach. It's an unfortunate situation to have the space disturbed before we were able to secure the investigation scene, but I appreciate that neither you nor your son-in-law was aware of Turner's death earlier this morning. I'm going to need the names of the rest of your tenants, where their rooms are in the house, and if you can tell us, an idea of their schedules if we aren't to find them at home right now. Let's start on the first floor. Who has the front room?"

Flavia held a finger up and said, "*Momento*, I get my book."

She disappeared into the second room and Rice looked over at me. "Patrick Bird." I felt it coming before he turned to his partner. "You know the name, Cull? Our boy here has a habit of helping widows out all over the city. Do you remember the last one? Maybe she wasn't a widow when it started but she sure as hell was when it ended." He shook his head.

It was calculated to get me going, but before I could react Cull snapped, "Stow it, Lieutenant. We've got a job to do here."

Rice and I held each other's gaze for a minute and when it got too silly, I looked away.

The young cop looked over at Cull, smirked, opened his mouth to say something, thought better of it, and looked away at something over my right shoulder.

Cull threw a smile of conciliation at his partner, but his face looked old and tired; the splotches of red on his nose and cheeks stood out under the basement's fluorescent lighting. He looked back at Rice and when their eyes met, I felt the struggle and tension across the table. Cull's eyes were soft and wet, they almost looked like they could tear up, but somehow he held Rice's glare, and it was the young detective who looked away first. Flavia bustled back, a spiral-bound notebook in her hand; she licked a thumb and turned the pages as she sat.

"I have all the information here for each room," she said. Cull reached for the book, but she shook her head and held it in her hands. "First floor, Danny Blinken. He drives a taxi. Sometimes he works nights. All night long and then he comes in in the morning. He smokes. Second floor, at the back, Shirley Burton, she's a nurse. From Jamaica. Next Mr. Yusuf Mohamed, he's a medical student at the university —"

"Regular United Nations you got here," commented Cull.

Flavia didn't like to be interrupted, and her look made sure to let him know. "Front room on the second floor:

empty. And now the third floor is empty, too. Two empty rooms. And Jack had the double room on the third floor, so really three."

"How long has that front room been empty, Mrs. Gentilini?" Cull said in his quiet voice.

"Already three weeks now. My tenant Paul left. A nice boy, too, but he didn't stay very long ..."

"So he left at the same time as Jonathan — as Jack?" pursued Cull.

"No, no." Flavia shook her head multiple times, surprised that Cull could get it so wrong. "Paul, he paid up. Paid everything up. He let me know and said goodbye as nice as anything. That was," she pulled a pair of half-moon glasses out of her front pocket and perched them on the end of her nose to confirm the date, "May six. He didn't give notice, but he paid for a week he wouldn't be here to make up for it. Jack, he's been gone for about two weeks now. He disappeared sometime in there. I'm not sure exactly when. The last rent he paid was for the week of May six." Her finger pointed at an illegible scrawl in the notebook. "But I saw him at least once later because I remember asking him for the week's rent after May thirteen."

Rice was impatient and broke in: "We're not talking about when he last paid his rent. When was he last seen?" The detectives had a point: it was a trifle suspicious if Paul had checked out at about the same time that Turner disappeared. Now one was dead underneath an old wooden roller coaster and the other gone. But there were always plenty of comings and goings in the transient world of a rooming house.

"But Flavia," I said, self-conscious about using her first name in front of the detectives, "you told me that you last saw Jack on the eighteenth. You saw him as he was rushing to catch a bus."

"He told me he would get the rent to me and then I never saw him again."

Cull, more conciliatory than his partner, said, "Okay. You haven't seen him for most of the month. But all the same, he was alive on the eighteenth. Almost ten days ago now. Still, give us the name and information about this nice boy Paul. What's his last name?"

"Paul Edward Bridgman." She read the name from her notebook.

"This one sounds Canadian," said Cull.

"Paul Edward Bridgman. How do you spell Bridgman? Does it have an *E*?"

Flavia, tracked under the letters with her finger as she read them off: "*B-R-I-D-G-M-A-N.* I wish he could have stayed longer. He was a good boy. Quiet. Paid upfront. He paid the whole month. And then he paid a week in advance and was gone."

"No *E*? And you're saying he was just here a month?"

"Yes. Short time. It's not easy being a landlord."

"And what was his profession, Mrs. Gentilini? Where did his money come from?"

"He told me he worked in real estate." Flavia didn't look so convinced about this.

"Did he say which company?"

"I ..." Her head was down as her eyes scanned up and down Paul's page in the notebook. "I ask. But I don't see here." She raised her head, smiling. "I know," she announced. "I remember. He told me he was looking for work as a real estate agent. He said that he knew I didn't want to take someone without a job, so he would pay the whole first month up front." She smiled at the memory. "And he was working. He must've been working. He was out every day. Like he was going to a job."

Rice raised his eyebrows and looked at Cull's impassive face which was focused on my mother-in-law.

"All right, Mrs. Gentilini," said Cull, "maybe you can take us upstairs and show us around. Bird: your services will no longer be needed. We'll take it from here."

There it was: the big brush-off. It appeared that my second go-round as a PI was coming to an end. But I'd been wrong before — so often that I worried it was becoming a habit.

VI

A FEW DAYS later, I had *Rubber Soul* spinning on the turntable in the little living room off the hall; when the volume was turned up, you could hear it good enough in the kitchen. I was stirring the grey slush of oats simmering on the stovetop, John was singing all about a real nowhere man, and Rose came into the kitchen and said, "I forgot to tell you that I got an appointment this morning with the doctor. I want you to come, for us to be together when we get the news."

The oatmeal was thickening and seething, the bubbles less frequent, coming now as eerie exhalations that peaked and steamed. I stirred it, scraping the bottom of the pot, with a short wooden spoon that had a few dents.

Rosie and I were still waiting and hoping, and every day our confidence in the pregnancy grew. I snapped off the flame and stirred the porridge once more; it gave two last exclamations out of air holes that appeared in the sludge without warning, like wounds in the grey skin, and then subsided. The baby wasn't in my mind all day every day, but when it crawled into my head, my thoughts ricocheted from unjustified pride to outright terror. We didn't know what we were doing. Did Rosie have the same doubts? So often she seemed older, at least more mature, and balanced in her outlook on the world. Her face, slightly jaundiced in the yellow kitchen, looked fuller and fleshier. Were the effects of her pregnancy already visible?

And then I remembered: "I can't make it. I forgot something, too, your mother called yesterday and asked me to go down and help her again this morning. I'm sorry."

"Well, arrange that around the doctor's appointment. You can go there anytime. It doesn't have to be at ten."

"But it does. She wants me there then because Jack's parents are coming to get his stuff today — at least what the police left behind. And it's at ten."

Rosie turned from the cupboard where she was pulling a bowl out and looked at me. "But I want you there with me today. At the doctor's. I want us to get the news together."

"Can they tell at the doctor's, the same day and all, if you're pregnant? I thought …" I didn't think much, not having a clear idea of what was involved in a pregnancy test — only vague concepts that didn't add up: like peeing in a bottle, tropical frogs, blood tests, and rabbits pausing in the middle of a meadow, their ears perked up into the air, their little noses twitching as they sensed danger nearby. It all felt a little pagan and witchy.

My mind flopped again, and although I didn't say anything, I also had the impulse to be there to protect my Rosie from whatever the doctor might subject her to. I carried our bowls of oatmeal over to the table.

"But it doesn't change how I feel. I want you there. Can't you rearrange with Mama? I don't want to be on my own." She grabbed my hand and held it to her shoulder. "I wish you could come with me. I'm feeling all up and down."

I pulled my chair closer to hers and put my arm around her. "Your condition," I said, hoping the euphemism was broad enough to cover all contingencies. I'd taken a break from job-searching yesterday, after a couple of depressing and discouraging experiences of "not hiring right now," and dropped into the library at Gladstone to read up on this new journey we were about to embark upon; and now I was flashing my newfound knowledge. "Feeling emotional is a good sign. As good as anything. Let's take it to mean that you're pregnant. Let this be our moment when we know. Together. And the doctor can just confirm."

"We're having a baby. You're responsible, too."

She was putting it baldly, and the idea of responsibility again tangled up my pride and fear. I shovelled a quick spoonful of porridge into the hatchway but only succeeded in burning my tongue. A gulp of cold milk eased the pain.

"Maybe we can walk down together and I can drop you at the doctor's door, and keep on going to your mother's place."

Rose sniffled and nodded her head. She peeled a mildly green banana, sliced it into wheels, and dropped it on top of her oats. "And after this time helping my mother, you'll find something steady?"

I knew what she was saying and on top of everything else, it was the end of the month: June rent was due tomorrow. That's where this was coming from and where it was going. Flavia collected her rent by the week, but money was on her mind, too. "Your mother wants to ask the Turner family for the back rent. Or really, I think she wants me to ask. That's what this is about. The missing money and once it's collected, I'll be finished helping her."

"And after, you can find a job. Maybe that's something you could do — collecting rent. Like a property manager in a big building, or maybe a collection agency." It didn't sound like much fun to me.

The walk to the doctor's office let us know that summer had arrived. Even before the sun was cresting, there was a warm breeze, and the world was a riot of green, green, and more green. We walked through the alley behind our house, passing our neighbours' backyards; our street was home to Italians — like Rose — Greeks, and Portuguese who loved their gardens and had their tomatoes, peppers, and eggplants in the ground now, just seedlings, little plant babies, waiting for summer to explode overhead. I took Rosie's arm: "Boy or girl?"

"Shush. Let's not get ahead of ourselves. We can think about that when we know for sure."

"You feeling better about going to the doctor?"

"I'll be okay. I wish you were going to be with me. But you're right. Today, probably all they're going to do is have me pee into a bottle."

"Not much I can do to help there."

I dropped her at the office on Bloor and watched her climb the narrow stairs to the waiting room on the second floor through the plate-glass doorway: the swish of her skirt, her ankle joint beneath her socks, and her sensible white flats. And she was gone and my reflection was staring back at me and I felt a little foolish.

The sun shone. I walked. My tongue still had the numb ache from where I'd burned it on the porridge at breakfast. These were strange times: since we'd gotten this news — which technically we still hadn't — every emotion was new; or if not new, felt and seen at a distance, and I could stand back, and feel it, and see it at the same time and know that it was all different now that I was going to be a father. So strange and unique, but something that happened every day, all over the world: it was just that it was happening to me right now. Before I knew it, I'd arrived at my mother-in-law's house on Ossington. The door opened as I came up the front steps to the stoop and Flavia appeared in one of her famous flowered housecoats. She'd been waiting at the door as the welcoming party.

"How come you can come here whenever I call?" she asked. "When are you getting a job? Rose works."

And I was doing her the favour. I was saved from having to respond by the arrival of Yusuf, behind her with his over-size textbooks tucked under his arm. Flavia stood in the door-way, blocking the way, and he perched awkwardly behind her, looking contemporary in an open shirt with pointed collars beneath a suede waistcoat. It wasn't what I would choose to wear, but he managed to pull it off — even to cross cultural borders and look Yorkville groovy. He paused awkwardly, in-capable of saying anything, of alerting Flavia of his presence, of asking to get by, deferring perhaps to her age, gender, or position in the household — or a combination of the three.

I said, "Yusuf's trying to get by."

Flavia turned, startled, and stepped out of the house onto the stoop. Yusuf bowed his head the slightest amount and slid past and down the steps. He gave me a cursory nod and was on his way.

Flavia recovered, nodded, and said, "Good boy. Hard worker. Always studies. He's going to be a doctor." I'd heard it before, and that only added to my feeling that the comment wasn't about Yusuf, who was now out of earshot, but about me and my failings. Thankfully, she didn't know about the baby on the way.

She put her hands on the rusting ironwork of the railing, looked out onto the roadway, and through her sheer force of will managed to make a passing car stop and park. Two passengers exited the vehicle, checked an address on the back of an envelope, and started toward the house.

Mr. Turner, who had been behind the wheel, was tall with a high dome of a forehead; his jacket and tie looked out of place as he approached the stoop. The most notable thing about his wife, walking at his side, was how similar she looked to him: the same high forehead, the same wire-rimmed glasses, and the same clean, smooth face. Had they initially been attracted to each other through the mirror of seeing themselves in their partner, or had the days and weeks, the months and years somehow moulded them as they grew together into twin manifestations of the same ideal?

There was an awkward silence as they approached the house; we stood and stared at them, unsure they were who we thought them to be — they didn't look anything like the photo of Jack with his dark locks and facial hair. From the sidewalk they sized us up as they matched the address on the envelope to the house where their son had lived.

I was determined to break the tension. "Mr. Turner? Mrs. Turner?"

"Yes," she responded. Her husband stood silent by her side as they reached the bottom of the three concrete steps leading to the stoop.

"I'm Patrick Bird." I hated saying my full name out loud, feeling foolish like I was shouting it to the world, even though I understood this was how people introduced themselves. And there was the fear, no matter how unlikely, that as had happened with Danny Blinken, the cabbie, and the cop, Rice, that they might know my past. "And this is my mother-in-law, Mrs. Gentilini. She runs the boarding house."

"Thank you for agreeing to meet us. I'm Constance Turner. Please call me Connie. And this is my husband, Gregory." He inclined his head slightly to one side to acknowledge that he was part of the conversation. The weight of the introductions, the father's silence, and being face-to-face with the family's grief made me understand that asking for the rent money would be tougher than anticipated. Flavia and I hadn't game-planned, so I wasn't sure if she would be the one doing the asking, or if she'd toss me the grenade at the last second.

"Come inside. Come inside!" shouted Flavia to the whole neighbourhood.

The door shut behind us, closing out the brightness of the day, and we stood in the close vestibule at the bottom of the stairs, under the fanlight cut in the front door. "Patrick, take the family upstairs to get Jack's things."

I turned back to the man and woman crowded in the hallway, "Let me just say, from my mother-in-law and myself, how sorry we are for your loss. It must be ..." It was a bad day for the world when it needed to depend on my inarticulateness for its empathy. I stumbled on: "It must be so difficult for you."

"Terrible," said Mrs. Turner.

"Terrible," I echoed and turned. "We'll go up to the third floor and get Jack's belongings." It was a long climb in a silence that grew more oppressive with each step. The rooming house was quiet today. All the doors were closed as if the tenants had shut their doors to keep out the sadness in the stairwell.

After the police had finished their work, Flavia and I completed a second cleaning to improve the rooms from what we had found on that first Tuesday morning. A new mattress had been bought; the shattered and broken equipment from the darkroom had been bagged up and disposed of; the floor had been swept and mopped. The rooms now looked barren and empty, not much of a life lived. The shirts that had hung in the closet were in the steamer chest, the paperbacks whose spines had held were stacked square in a box, and the small china Buddha that had sat atop the bookshelf smiling now lay on its back beside them. And although the parents had been spared the initial chaos and disaster, it was unclear if this was any easier for them. Mr. Turner removed his glasses from his face and dabbed at his eyes with a handkerchief that wasn't too clean. I spoke from a need to fill the empty air. "The police may have taken some things, such as his address book, for their investigation, but everything else is here. You may need to check with them about the other stuff."

I was about to continue showing them, as if they couldn't see themselves, where the clothes lay in the trunk, the camera, with its cracked lens, the box of books and knick-knacks when Constance spoke, "We don't have much faith in the police right now. They seem to be taking a very cursory approach to this whole ..." she allowed herself a sniff of the stale air of the room before finishing, "affair."

Her husband blinked silently and tilted his gaze to the ground. When he raised his head to look at his wife, the torture of their shared pain brought a chill into the room as if we stood at the edge of a great polar ocean and its frigid waters lapped at our feet.

"We're not happy with the way they're approaching the whole investigation," said Connie. She was the verbal one of the two, voicing the bitterness they felt; Gregory was just brooding silence. They maintained an intense unity, so when her voice sounded, it felt like it came out of both of their mouths, as if their minds, like their appearance, had melded into one. "Their coroner did the autopsy. He ruled the death a drug overdose."

This was news. But my mind was stuck on their twin-like appearance: as Rose and I grew old, would our roots, twisted and gnarled, weave together to the point where we, too, thought, felt, and even looked as one?

"Heroin," said Connie. "It wasn't heroin. That might have been the cause of death, but Jack was no drug user. If there was heroin in his body, then that's proof of murder not the other way around. Gregory is a doctor," she explained. "They can't lie to us."

Now the conversation had started, there was no denying it. The dam holding the frigid northern waters had been breached, and it flowed across the tundra, threatening to flood everything in its path.

But again, her conversation turned — this time away from the police — to me: "Did you, or your mother-in-law, find any hypodermics — or as the police call it — 'gear,'" she spat the word, "or paraphernalia that would suggest drug use? You don't do heroin without needles and burned spoons, little plastic baggies, and matches and lighters." She'd done her homework.

"Nothing." I rattled the cardboard box and Buddha rolled over onto his bulging stomach to stare at the bottom of the container. "Not even an ashtray."

"People don't tidy up and hide their stuff before they overdose," said Connie. "We've hired a private investigator. I'm telling you because he'll want to come here and see where our son lived. It's likely he'll want to talk to you since you were the first to see the room."

There weren't a whole bunch of private detectives in Toronto.

"His name is Sidney Cowan," she said.

It was a name I knew.

VII

I KNEW SID: I'd worked for him. And that hadn't gone so well. It was three years since we'd last spoken outside the police station downtown when I'd turned in my star and turned on my heel. He wasn't a bad guy, but I couldn't stand the friendly paternalism that came with his oversight, and the yoke of authority had rubbed my neck raw; viewed through the lens of time, it was a relationship doomed to fail. I wondered if he'd call me with questions on this one, or if he'd give it a pass. He had plenty of other connections, especially inside the force, and he might just look the other way if his police sources came through; but he was conscientious in his work and wouldn't let a grudge keep him from doing what was best for the case and the client. Maybe we'd talk. "I know Sid Cowan," I said. "I used to work for him."

"You were a private detective?" asked the father, looking more alive than he had yet. I wasn't sure whether his tone indicated suspicion that investigators were falling out of the trees or interest that there was another person who could help in the search for answers.

"I worked for Sid for a short time." I spared them the details.

He fell quiet again. Thankfully, Connie rescued us from the vacuum of silence: "So our man, this Sidney Cowan, will need to come by and see the rooming house. Should I arrange that with you — or Mrs. Gentilini?"

"My mother-in-law."

"I guess that's everything, then." She lifted the lid of the steamer chest on its hinges and lowered it shut. "Gregory and I will take one last look around. And then we'll settle up with Mrs. Gentilini on the rent. Or is it you we should be doing that with? I brought my chequebook."

Bring on the Protestants: here were the people who understood debt and personal responsibility. The need to chase down the bereaved parents had solved itself. Maybe property management was my calling. I named a number that covered the three weeks of rent and something for my time as a cleaner; it seemed like a lot to me in my unemployed state, but in the context of a life lost it didn't add up to much. Connie moved to the desk, where, still standing, she leaned forward and wrote out the payment, stopping to ask me the spelling of Gentilini. She tore along the perforated line and passed me the slip. Gregory opened the closet door and looked at the lonely coat hangers, lifeless windchimes, hooked on the rail.

I stood awkwardly with the cheque in my hand. "I'll give this to Flavia and then come back up and see how you're faring. You might want to look in the other room — Jack's darkroom — the door's open — just to double-check that nothing has been left behind. Most of the material there was destroyed or moved back into this space for you, but take a look to make sure you have everything."

"Thank you," said Connie in a voice that conveyed no gratitude. I didn't blame her. "Junkies don't have their rooms searched," she said bitterly to no one in particular.

Her words were still in my head as I descended through the house, past the closed doors of the second floor, and then down again, by Danny's room and the empty kitchen, and into my mother-in-law's subterranean apartment. Was it possible Jack's mother was wrong in this case: would an unpaid dealer, or an addict looking to score, wreak the destruction with anger and vengeance? Could the spectre of addiction, the need for more, more, more, and the cold calculating economics of supply and demand, explain the carnage of the two rooms? She didn't think so, and I was inclined to side with her.

Flavia studied the cheque carefully and then beamed at me. "Good boy."

I'd delivered.

"They are still upstairs?"

"Taking a last look around. And then they'll be off."

"Good. I have a couple coming at noon, to look at the apartment. They want a bedroom and a little sitting room. For two." She was learning her trade, upselling Jack's rooms to something more; soon she'd be calling them a suite. The timing was cut close, but dollar signs drove the world, all the way around the horizon and back again.

"You want me to stay until Jack's parents leave?"

"No. I'll wait in the kitchen and see them when they come down."

"All right. I'll say my goodbyes now, then."

I did and came out of the house and crossed the street. Already, early that morning, the quick, slick sounds of the skipping rope scuffing the floor, the dull thuds of padded gloves hitting a punching bag, and grunts of exertion spilled out of Sully's Gym where Muhammad Ali had trained just a year earlier when he came north to take on our very own great white hope. George Chuvalo hadn't beat the champ, but he'd hung tough and made Ali work for every punch he threw. And Ali, in his famous interview, right there in Sully's Gym, loved our little world north of the forty-ninth, saying we were as nice as could be, that everyone treated him great, and how different it was than where he came from. It was clear what he was saying, and as was typical in our small world, we had that glow of smugness that we weren't like them: we were better than our neighbours to the south. As if that was all that mattered to us.

Through the open door, a pair of feet danced on a mat, and the blur of a skipping rope slapped against the matting. I turned away from the gym and headed up Ossington. Above Dundas there was another stretch of rooming houses, cracked steps, peeling roof tiles, fading paint, and little square patches of grass, the same size and colour as a billiard table, out front of each one. A car horn honked. I kept walking, but it was persistent, and then the taxi pulled up in front of me, the driver leaned over to the passenger side, rolled down the window, and said, "Hey Patrick, you ignoring me?" The points of Danny's wide collar stuck out over his sweater.

"I didn't know it was you."

"Get in." I made to pull the door open, and he snapped. "Not the front. This is a fucking taxi, not your mother's car."

"I'm not a fare."

"It'd look better if you were," he said. "Then the top light goes off and that way if anyone's watching, nothing looks out of place. I'm going to put the meter on, but don't worry. No charge."

"If anyone's watching? What the hell are you talking about?" We were rolling north now, passing College. "Take a left on Bloor," I said.

"Not doing that. And whatever you do, don't tell me your address. I don't want to know."

"What's going on? If you're not giving me a ride home, where are we going? And what's all this 'people are watching' stuff? No one's watching me."

"I didn't say anything the first day you were at the house," said Danny, "because I didn't know Jack was dead. And then when the police arrived with the news, well, I don't like them too much either — some history there we don't need to go into — so I thought I'd just step out of the picture a bit and make myself scarce. Being a cabbie doesn't help your opinion of the cops. They're so fucking tribal and grasping — it's a bad combination. So, like I said, I made myself scarce. But here's the thing: before Jack disappeared, he gave me something to hold on to."

I had a sinking feeling. Was Danny about to produce a baggie of powder to incriminate Jack, the drugs and gear Connie had referred to with such confident disdain, and make the overdose make sense? Then it'd be my job to tell the parents and take their memory of their boy and twist it until he was no longer recognizable in the distortions of his secret life.

We stopped at the light at Dupont where warehouses and old factories backing onto the train tracks poked up into the sky, signalling the end of the residential neighbourhoods to the south. We were already north of my house; Danny met my eyes in the rear-view, leaned forward, popped the glove compartment, stuck his hand into its open mouth, and pulled out a manila envelope big enough to hold the Eaton's catalogue. It was big enough, but flat, holding only a few sheets of paper — no drug baggie here. In the middle of the envelope, he'd written PB in a thick pencil and put a circle around it. My initials on the evidence. Perfect.

"Here it is. He asked me to hold it. I put it at the bottom of the glove compartment and let it sit for the last ten days. Jack was smart. He saw it coming — that someone would search his room. But now he's dead, so I'm giving it to you."

"He's your friend, not mine. Why don't you open it?"

"Because I'm not stupid." I wasn't sure what that made me. "You came into our house and asked all these questions. You can do what you want with it. If it suits you, turn it over to the police; if you prefer, tell the family you found it hidden in the kitchen and thought it must have belonged to their son; if you want, burn it in a barrel. It doesn't matter to me. It's yours now."

The taxi was back in motion ducking under the train tracks between Dupont and Davenport, the envelope was in my lap, and Danny had two hands on the wheel. It sure seemed like the envelope was mine.

"You didn't open it?"

"No, thank you."

"And Jack asked you to take care of it, and your solution is to pass it on to someone else who didn't even know him and get the hell out of town. Doesn't seem like you're much of a friend."

"Jack's dead: nothing I do is going to change that. Driving a cab, you learn to keep your nose out of other people's business." I felt like Danny had already told me the opposite on the first day I'd met him. But plenty of people, especially those who liked to talk, said all sorts of things backward and forward. Ossington ended and he took a lazy left, palming the wheel with one hand, and making a circular motion, and we were on Davenport and the envelope was still on my lap. "There are people like you who want to know everything, who want to solve problems, who want to make the world a better place," it seemed a generous assessment, but maybe he was just stroking my ego, "and then there are those like me who just who want to keep our heads down and get to the end of the day, sleep in our beds, and wake up tomorrow without any more grief than needed."

"But why did Jack give you the envelope?"

"No idea. But he got himself killed for what's in it. That's a good enough reason why I'm not opening it up. It's enough that I'm passing it on to you. If I had any sense, I'd just put a match to it. No, thanks."

"You don't think he overdosed?"

"Is that what the police are saying? It's horseshit. Jack wasn't a user. Anyone who knew him could tell you that. It's a convenient way to die if you need him out of the way, but anyone can tell you that Jack wasn't shooting."

"Then it's murder."

"Are you sure you aren't a private detective?" He shook his head at me in the mirror.

"But what am I doing with the envelope?"

"That's your problem, not mine."

"I could just leave it in the back of the car now and walk home."

"You could, but you won't."

The challenge tempted me; I could walk out on him and his stupid smirk. But there were still the parents, numb with grief, and Sid coming onto the case any second. Without much effort I could take the envelope, hold it, and pass it on. I didn't have to do anything more than Danny — could just be the conduit that transferred the envelope from point A to point B without a second thought: the path of least resistance. Maybe marriage had mellowed me. "All right then, get me a little closer to my house. And I'll take this off your hands and we'll leave it at that."

"I knew you'd see it that way." The skin around his eyes creased into a delta of fine lines as he smiled in the mirror. "You're a good man, Patrick Bird." I shook my head, and he said, "Don't sell yourself short. You might be a hero yet."

I wanted to be done with him, to leave the cab, to go home, and put the envelope somewhere safe until Sid came and picked it up when my thoughts jumped back to Cull and Rice's visit to the rooming house. I said, "The police were interested in the missing lodger, Paul Bridgman, the one who had the front room on the second floor. They think it's a little suspicious that he disappeared at more or less the same time as Jack."

"Is that what they think?"

"That's the way I was hearing it when you took a powder out the back door."

"Good for them."

"C'mon, Danny, you lived in the same house as the guy, you must know something about him. Give me something. Anything."

"You want something on Paul?" He turned left onto Bartlett and started south, back toward my house. "All right. I'll tell you: he wasn't what he said he was. He told me he was a draft dodger. That fit with his accent. He was American, from the Midwest, or maybe the South. I don't know, I'm not good with accents. But he was too old to be a draft dodger, and he didn't have the politics. If the army came knocking on his door offering him a gun and a chance to shoot people in Indochina, he'd have been over there blazing away in a second."

"You're sure he was American?"

"He said he was a duck and he quacked like one. What more do you want?"

"How old was he?"

"Around the same age as me, about forty. Old enough to know better and too old for the draft."

"What was he like?"

"Look. I didn't know him. Maybe saw him at the breakfast table once or twice. Went out for a beer with him to the Drake once. Just small talk. But he wasn't draft dodger material; he was right out in right field the way only an American can be."

"Doesn't it make you wonder? Bridgman disappears right before Jack does. And then three weeks later, Jack's dead. I'm telling you, when we find Bridgman, we've found the murderer."

"Think so? You're making is sound so simple, solving the case on day one."

"You in?"

"Not me, my friend. You're on your own with this one. Here's Bloor. You live around here, eh? You got a nice ride free of charge. Now I got work to do."

WALKING ALONG BLOOR Street in the warm weather, my curiosity was burning about the big envelope in my right hand. As soon as I got home, I'd be fighting the dangerous impulse to just rip it open and look inside. Danny had warned me of the risks and had shown the way, not opening but letting the contents rest easy, unseen. The gummed flap was sealed, which seemed to speak to the truth of his story, but it was possible that he'd been handed the envelope open, looked inside, and sealed it after. It would have taken a mountain of disinterest, even for him, not to take a peek. Or maybe he knew more of the backstory — from Jack himself, or through something he'd seen in the rooming house — than he was letting on. I pressed the envelope flat against my chest; that action seemed to call more attention than otherwise, so I switched to carrying it loose and casual at the end of my fingertips, but waving it for the world to see seemed horribly conspicuous. Delaware Avenue, where Rosie and I lived, came and I turned the corner, happy to escape the busy commercial thoroughfare and be two steps closer to home. The back end of the Ossington subway entrance came up on my right; just a couple of years ago they'd opened the line running east–west, and if you lived close enough, you could feel the vibrations of the underground trains in your basement.

Crossing Northumberland, I checked over my shoulder, but there was no car crawling behind me, no suspicious pedestrian dogging my steps, no furtive eyes peering from behind a window, other than the *duenna* across the street who was always staring out with her unblinking gaze — her presence more reassuring than not.

Through the door and the envelope was in the house and all the time I hadn't even considered where to hide it. I passed down the hall, even narrower and darker than the one at Flavia's, and into the tiny living room where we had a card table, a couple of easy chairs, and the hi-fi. I pulled the first record my fingers touched from the long row of spines filed vertically along the floor, Blood, Sweat & Tears' *Child Is Father to the Man.* The cover showed the band, eight guys, six sitting on stools, arranged in a loose semicircle, two standing behind, and each one had a ventriloquist's doll sitting on their lap, or held at their chest, with a replica of their own head on the dummy. I slid Danny's envelope into the open sleeve. The peculiar cover photo: grown men with their alter egos sitting in their laps. Shouldn't it have been the other way around, with the children, the dolls themselves, holding the grown men on the wooden joints of their knees, their stiff little fingers poking into the flesh of the band members' backs to control them? Isn't that what the title meant?

"Pat," the call came from upstairs. It was Rosie's voice. I filed the album back into the upright row, alphabetically, just between *Sergeant Pepper's* and Johnny Cash, and started up the stairs.

"What were you doing?" She lay on the bed on top of the covers, wan in the light filtering through thin curtains.

"I just had to take care of something when I got through the door."

There was an awkward moment, made worse because of the rush of love I felt for her small frame laid out on the bed and the sudden realization that I'd brought something with the neon danger sign on it into the house. "Are you all right?"

"Aren't you going to ask about the doctor?"

I sat down on the edge of the bed and took her hand in mine. It was hot and clammy. "Are you all right?"

"You already asked me that." She rolled to face the wall. "This isn't how I imagined it when you came home. I thought you'd rush up to see me and want to know what happened."

"What did the doctor say? Is everything okay? Is the baby okay?"

"We're having a baby. You need to start paying attention."

"I am." It was the wrong answer.

She shifted onto her back and looked at the ceiling. "The doctor didn't say anything. He just took a urine sample, like you thought would happen. We should know next week. The appointment's on Monday. Add that to your busy schedule. And then I came home." Her eyes came off the ceiling to meet mine. "And I didn't feel so good and kept not feeling good. And wondering where you were." She smiled a lazy smile lying on the bed. "I feel nauseous."

"That's not great. But it is great. Isn't it?"

"Yes," she said. "We don't need a stupid doctor, do we?"

"Not yet."

"But it's no fun feeling sick. I'm not sure I'm going to be very good at it."

"You're going to be the best mother in the world."

And she reached her arms up and pulled me down to her and we lay on the bed together in the darkened bedroom as the afternoon sun climbed in the sky, reached the top of the stairs, turned the corner, and began coming back down. And for a time, I didn't think about all the jobs I didn't have or Danny's strange behaviour or Jack's dead body, riddled with heroin, crumpled under the Flyer; or his sad parents, so alike in appearance, so different in approach; or the odd couple cops, Cull and Rice, who'd been interested at one point, but weren't anymore; or the envelope I'd just hidden inside the Blood, Sweat & Tears record. I didn't think about anything but Rosie. Rosie and me.

That evening after we'd eaten dinner — or mostly after I'd eaten dinner and Rosie had pushed the food around her plate with a fork held limply in her hand — we sat outside in the warmth, marvelling at the length of the day and how bright it was. Rose asked me about my day and I told her about Jack's parents and their discontent — Connie's determination, the mama bear in human flesh, and Gregory's morose silence, deep in mourning, already giving up on life — their dissatisfaction with the police investigation, and their unprompted offer to pay the rent. I didn't divulge my long and circuitous ride home and the hot-potato envelope Danny had passed to me. There was no need; it had a temporary resting place in the record sleeve, and then it, too, would be off and elsewhere, and Rosie never need know. She had enough to worry about already — making a baby and trying to keep her food down — without taking on anything more. She latched on to the news that Sid, my old boss, had been called and might need help in this new case.

I stared at a whip of a peach tree in the yard that was beginning to blossom. All the backyards along this stretch of the street had them, courtesy of an enterprising neighbour with a green thumb. I shook my head. "It's not going to happen. When I left that job the first time, it was a forever goodbye. Sid isn't going to hire me back."

"You never know." She took my hand and worried it in her own, small, busy, and warm.

"But I do. I was there the first time around. He'll call me to get some background; I'll talk to him, but it's not going to lead to work."

"You never know," she said again, and her hope for my employment, rather than boosting my mood, tamped it down.

Sid didn't call that evening, or the next day, Saturday. The calendar turned from May to June and another month's rent hightailed it from our bank to the landlord, and the stress of my unemployment lifted its ugly head out of the swamp and caught me in its beady-eyed gaze. All weekend long, I was distracted, waiting for the phone to ring so I could unload the envelope and get it out of our house, where I felt its presence in the living room, radiating an unseen evil, nibbling at my thoughts and causing a nagging anxiety.

On Monday morning we were back to the doctor, and this time I joined Rosie and heard him confirm the news: she was having our baby. The medical profession put its gold seal on the matter, and we knew on a different level. And there was more happiness and joy, and nausea and worry. I could almost hear the brakes in Rose's mind squeak as she pumped them to hold herself back from asking me what I was doing to find something to bring money into our household; I could feel her counting the days on the calendar and calculating the dates when she would need to stop her job, hefting heavy trays and fighting off the leers and stares — and worse — of the paying customers. And as she had these thoughts, I had my own about Sid's unexplained silence. Was the bridge burned so badly that he wouldn't even call for information that would help his client?

That afternoon, with Rose off at her waitressing shift, conscious of Jack's sealed envelope, still safe in the stack of records, I took matters into my own hands and called him. Sid couldn't know about the photographer's envelope, nor understand how important it might be. It was a little after four, the same time I used to phone in with my daily roundups when I worked for him; his number was still in my memory like the forgotten chewing gum under a classroom desk, calcified, brittle, but still there. There was a hint of nostalgia in the air as the phone threw my coffee-stained breath back at me; a bell rang somewhere across the city, and I waited for him to pick up.

"Sidney Cowan."

His voice was exactly as I remembered it. My eye twitched, and the dead air on the line went on too long before I recovered and said: "Sidney, this is Patrick. How are you?"

There was a pause on the other end of the phone, the grim crackle of the line, and I jumped in again before he could say anything: "I'm phoning about the Turner case. I have something I think —"

"I'm off the Turner case."

And now it was my turn for a moment of speechlessness in this slow and stilted conversation. "Off the case?"

"That's what I said."

"So you aren't …?"

"Nothing."

"But I have," I said slowly, conscious that somehow the conversation had become about me, and not the case, "something the dead man left in the event anything happened to him."

"You should give it to the police."

"The family told me the police had closed the case and they didn't sound too happy about it. They said they'd hired you."

"Yes. Your name came up plenty when I spoke to the family and nosed around the rooming house. I met your mother-in-law; she seems like a very nice lady. You do her proud. She told me you're looking for work; time to find a steady job and settle down." Thirty seconds in and Sid was already pissing me off.

"My understanding was the police closed the case: death by misadventure," I said.

"That's what I was getting from them, too. Still, if you have new information, they might reconsider reopening it. It's worth a try. There's nowhere else to go with what you've got."

"And if you saw it …"

"I told you, I'm off the case."

Something didn't make sense. "You were fired?"

Our talk was grinding down, and I could hear Sid reaching for words and squirming on the other end of the line, like a worm on a hook, not quite able to close out the conversation. "No." He made a mirthless guffaw. "I wouldn't put it that way. Let's just say that we reached a mutual agreement. Both parties. But I should be going now. Rachel's calling me."

Maybe his wife really was calling him, but I felt the brush-off: "Bye, then. Say hi to Rachel for me."

"I'll do that. And hi to your happy bride. What's her name? Rosemary? It's been a long time since we talked. It's good to hear your voice. Take care of yourself."

And then the dial tone. I stood in the kitchen, alone, and the yellow paint on the walls sang the same song as the buzzing in my ear. I dropped the receiver back on the cradle, trying to understand what had happened, when the phone, hanging on the wall right beside my head, startled me with its ring.

"Patrick Bird here." Was it the construction company in Etobicoke, the one I'd applied to so long ago now that I'd pretty much given up on them, calling to offer me the job as a drywaller's apprentice?

"Hello, Patrick. This is Constance Turner." She started right in. "We met last week at the rooming house where my son lived before his death. You helped us pack up his belongings."

"Hello, Mrs. Turner. Yes, I remember. How can I help you?"

"We've hit a snag. Our private investigator quit on us." That wasn't the way Sid had explained it. "And we were pretty upset when that happened." It was hard to imagine their stoic faces bending much one way or the other; they had that dogged determination in their grief, refusing to accept the official police word, pushing on regardless.

"We knew that you'd previously worked for Mr. Cowan, not that that comes as a recommendation to us at this stage. He let us down. Badly. So, rather than rolling the dice in the Yellow Pages, we thought, at least we'd met you, and you seemed like a serious young man. We'd like to ask you to take on the job."

There was a pause that I didn't immediately fill, but she picked up the silence and continued in her flat voice. "We'll pay you the same amount we were paying Mr. Cowan. Too much time has passed already; at least you're up to speed on the details, having been there from the beginning. Are you interested?"

Caught off guard, still catching up, I missed the cue to respond as I stared across the empty kitchen and tried to make sense of the strange dance this case was so far.

"I don't mean to press you," she continued, "but we need to have an answer immediately. If you're not interested, I'm going to the next number."

Things were moving fast, and the idea that I could tell Rose I had work and was bringing money into the house would be welcome news, but the one thing I didn't want to do to this poor couple was to provide false hope. "Listen, Mrs. Turner, I just want to be up front with you and play it straight. Unlike Mr. Cowan's agency, I don't have a licence. I'd be strictly freelance. And that could prove to be a little tricky with the police. They likely won't take too kindly to my involvement in a case they consider —"

"The police," she said with as much contempt as the line could hold. "We're through with them."

And I thought of the mystery envelope still hidden in my record collection and the jump I had on everyone else. This was what I'd always wanted to do; I'd flamed out on my first go-round. Not everyone got a second chance. Maybe, with a child on the way, this was the time for me to finally grow up and get something right. "I'm in, Mrs. Turner. Count me in. I'm on the case. Starting right now."

"That's great," she said. I could almost feel her husband's grief over her shoulder as he listened in behind her.

IX

WE ARRANGED THAT the Turners would come to the city and see me the next day, but I assured them I'd start right away. Ever since Danny had passed me the envelope, my curiosity burned to know what was inside, but between some new-found restraint, the busyness of home life, and Danny's example as a warning, I'd managed not to give in. But now that I was officially on the case — or at least semiofficially for the non-licensed PI — I was damned if I was going to wait a second more before breaking the seal. I pulled *Child Is Father to the Man* from its resting place, reached into the cavity of the puckered cardboard, and grabbed the hidden envelope. Placing it face up on the kitchen table, I saw again the lettering on the outside. Not words, but stray block capitals written in a thick pencil: PB. I didn't like that Danny had tied my initials in with this mess. Below the letters in the same heavy lead was a near-perfect circle with an *X* inscribed inside, like an election day marker that gave an ominous vibe to the package. But I was too close to the prize to futz with the exterior when the real mystery was inside. Taking a serrated knife from the kitchen drawer, I worked under the gummed flap and cut through the paper. Putting my hand into the interior, there was an irrational fear, as if a small animal lurked in the darkness waiting to snap its sharp teeth on my prying fingers.

Sounds from the front door: the reverberations of the aluminum screen, the tumblers turning in the lock, the creaking of the hinges, and the footsteps in the hall, and Rose was home from work, interrupting the tension of my big reveal. Zooming out from the moment, I saw our little family's vulnerability as Danny's warnings echoed in my mind. A tremor scurried down my hand; I startled, jerked it out, and stuffed the envelope into the junk drawer to the left of the sink.

In the dim light of the hallway, Rose sat on the bench using the toes of one foot against the opposite heel to pop her shoes off; she bent and tossed them into the pile of footwear that littered the hall's tiles.

She looked up and gave a tired smile at my greeting.

"You okay?"

"A restaurant's probably not the best place to work when you feel like puking."

"Ugh."

"Ugh, and worse."

"Oh dear."

"I'm not sure how much longer I can keep it up. Or maybe — well, not maybe —but right now, it's not good."

The unspoken meaning floated in the air between us, and I took the pause to share my news. "I got some work today."

"You did?" Her face brightened, or maybe it just reflected the walls as she passed into the yellow kitchen with the afternoon light streaming through the back window making it all the yellower.

"Yes." I described the conversation I'd had with the Turner family. "I know it's not a forever job, but it's something. Any money will help, and they're paying Sid's rates. Maybe you want to take a little time off — phone in sick — I mean you're legitimately sick — if you're not feeling great."

"It's no advertisement for the food when you're green at the gills." With her first step into the kitchen, I could see that her face lacked the enthusiasm I'd anticipated; the sparkle didn't jump to her eyes, and her smile had no oomph behind it.

"My gig with the Turners will help, and as soon as it's finished, I'll get something long-term. Something good. Steady. I promise."

"I know." She turned on the tap, ran the water until it was cold, and angled a glass beneath the stream. "I'm wiped right out. I'm going to go lie down. You'll come up and see me?"

"For sure. I'll be there in a minute." Rose was home, but the mystery envelope was still on my mind.

She drank the water in gulps, rinsed the glass under the tap, turned it upside down on the dish rack, attempted a smile, failed, and passed out of the kitchen.

"See you soon," I called after her, crossing the room to the junk drawer: batteries and Band-Aids, birthday candles, a roll of tape, a family of clothes pegs, dusty coasters we never used, and the envelope Danny'd given me. I put my hand back into its open slit, grabbed what I could, and dumped the rest onto the table. It wasn't much: a single picture and two strips of negatives. Photographs from the photographer. It was what made sense. And now to see what they were.

The print showed three men in an outdoor setting that looked like a café patio. And although there were three men in the photograph, and they were all in the same place at the same time, they seemed to all be in their own space, each disconnected from the other. The first man, in the foreground, took up almost the entire right third of the image. His face was so close to the camera, turned away in an unfocused blur so it was impossible to see his features or identify him. He was looking down, in one-quarter profile, the blur of his glasses' arm visible as it rode above the cheekbone and hooked under the smear of an ear. Thin hair straggled loosely down the back of the neck; higher up it looked like it might capitulate altogether.

In the middle ground was the second subject, looking down in three-quarter profile. His dark hair, parted in the middle, moustache, and a thick patch of hair beneath his lower lip, all suggested he was from another era, perhaps some renegade squire off on his own, or a peasant with aspirations, one that might find himself inexplicably leading the crowd, a pitchfork raised above his head, agitating against the enclosure of land or the rate of taxation, calling for blood.

Behind him, in the middle of the photograph, between the others, was the third figure, sitting on the patio. Multiple tables, each with a checkered cloth, which, even in the black-and-white photo, one identified as red and white, ranged across the brick plaza; a sugar canister, a rectangular box holding paper napkins, and a single carnation in a thin vase completed the setting. The man at the table was the only customer visible: he wore a tired suit jacket, the collar of his light shirt open over the checked lapels. His small eyes looked into the distance, at an oblique angle, seemingly unaware of the camera. In contrast to the figure in the midground, he wore his hair short, in an approximation of a marine flat-top. In these modern times, he had the buttoned-down look of a square: conservative and old-fashioned. But despite his jacket and monochrome shirt, despite looking slightly younger than the blur of the first man, he did not give off the air of health or stability. He had the aura of the estranged loner: solitary, alert, furtive, almost feral in the coiled tension of his awareness.

I didn't recognize any of the three, and try as I might, I couldn't force my understanding to evolve. The café umbrella's distorted advertising did not add up to any word I knew; the letters INZA were readable before disappearing beyond the curve of the canopy.

The phone rang.

I left the photo on the table and moved to where the receiver hung on the wall.

"Hello."

"Patrick, it's Sidney." Twice in a day after three years of not talking.

"Hi, Sid. Long time, no talk."

He laughed. A pause stretched between us. "Rachel asked me to call you. She ..." He stumbled again, having trouble figuring out how to say what he wanted. "She thought I should call you to warn you off this case. I don't know if you're still interested in detective work, and I didn't know if … well, she thought the Turners might offer you the job when I pulled out. And I wanted to let you know, if that should happen, under no circumstances should you agree. I …" Again, the awkward pause.

"What is this, Sid? What are you talking about?"

He ignored me: "This isn't a case you want to be messing with. The police pulled out; told me to pull out and now I'm trying to do you the favour, to help you out. To warn you off. The message is coming from up high. Very high."

"I'm already in," I said.

"That's what worried Rachel." I could hear his breathing coming across the line. "I know you've got that streak of stubbornness in you, but —"

"You phoned me up to compliment me?" I was picking up the vibe: Danny's approach to the envelope; the police's quick decision to call it death by misadventure and close the case; and now Sid turning down a client and good money on someone else's say-so. No one wanted this case. It was more hand grenade than hot potato. But no one else had a pregnant wife ready to give up her job; and I'd just told her I was bringing in a little money for the first time in two months. And Sid was right: I had some some stubbornness. And some curiosity, too.

"That stubborn streak. Yeah, it's stubbornness if you look at it from the one side, but you could call it perseverance or dedication. Stick-to-it-iveness. Whatever you like. Are you fishing for compliments?"

I remembered why I couldn't work with him. "I gave them my word." I wasn't about to quit — and if everyone thought I would because they were all telling me to, they sure as hell didn't know me.

I could hear Rachel talking to Sid on the other end of the line and then Sid said, "But honestly, Patrick, we go way back. Your mother is all alone in this world, with only you. Think of her and just give that poor Turner family a call and your apologies. Nothing'll be lost. I know there's a part of you, that when you hear me saying you need to throw in the towel, then nothing makes you want to work it harder, but just make the smart decision."

"It's not like that, Sid." I felt the strange stirring of emotion that had proved so dangerous in the past, simultaneously appreciating and resenting that he was coming on like a father. Every compliment, no matter how well-intentioned, was still a judgment.

"You've got a family now. You can't be thinking just of yourself. You need to consider everyone. Your wife, Rosemary."

"Just Rose."

"Rose."

More silence.

"At least tell me you'll think about the warning and consider it. And talk to Rose about it," he said.

"It's not like that." I wasn't going up and telling Rose I was about to quit the job before I'd even started. And I wasn't going to scare her about the danger, all the warnings I'd been given. I was in, and that was all there was to it.

"Think about it. It's easier and safer to get out now, before you start. You just don't know what you're going to turn up. And once you trip over something, once you see it, you can't unsee it. And once you know and you have that knowledge — or even if someone thinks you do — you can't close your eyes and magically unknow it."

"What the hell's going on? If you know what's happening, say it." There were the three men in the photograph: the blurred head in the front row, long-hair in the mid-range, half-turned away from the camera, looking like the medieval parvenu, and the square at the café table all by his lonesome. I'd already seen. These three didn't look so tough. I felt, for the first time since I'd hung up the phone with Gregory and Connie Turner, the clear feeling that I could do this; the unexpected bounce of confidence that I was going to show the world a fucking thing or two. To show Rosie, and Danny, and Sid and Rachel, and my mother-in-law, and Gregory, and Connie. Sid could warn me till he was blue in the face, but I was going to show the whole fucking world.

"I'm not quitting."

There was a pause; he said, "Listen, Patrick. Listen to the warning. You might not want to quit right now when you're talking to me. You don't even need to tell me. I'm all right with that. But remember: it's never too late to change your mind." I didn't know if he was waiting for me to respond, but after a pause, he added, "It's never too late to change your mind until it is too late, you know what I mean?"

We said our goodbyes. It was more final than the last time if that was possible. Everything was feeling final right now, like on the Flyer when you felt the chain pulling you up to the top of that first mountain, and from the crest you could look over on the whole exhibition, the bandstand, and the Bulova clock tower, and all the rides and games, but mostly the track running down the hill in front of you, and then you started down the decline, feeling the drag of the cars behind you, still on their upward climb, holding you back, but once they crested the peak, the rush was on, and you were speeding down and screaming and laughing and flying toward that impossible first turn.

I hooked the phone back on its cradle and returned to the photo and the envelope. In the flurry of calls and warnings, I hadn't even looked at the two short strips of negatives; within their perforated borders, both ribbons held four images, each about an inch square. Holding them up to the light, I could make out the interior of a tavern, and two men at a pool table, but the reverse of dark and light in the sepia squares was hard to decipher. Another mystery for me. Tomorrow's to-do list was growing.

X

ROSE WAS UP and at it early the next morning to get to work in time for the breakfast shift. I could have been more focused on her, but my thoughts were still running on the events of yesterday. She didn't seem to mind, and, with a stray clump of strawberry jam on her lower lip, said, "It's good to see you back at work. You're happier when you've got something to do."

"Jesus, Rosie. You're trying to make a Protestant of me."

She laughed and stopped, her mood jumping. "We're going to baptize the baby, aren't we?"

"Affirmative."

She laughed again. "Maybe we need to start going to church now we have a child coming."

I groaned.

"We can't just show up when the baby pops out, can we?"

"That's how we got married."

She shook her head, and I leaned forward and wiped the jam off her face with a finger, cleaned it in my mouth, and kissed her.

She pushed the chair back and stood. "Time for work."

I saw her to the door, kissed her again, and was ready to start my new job, all in line with the perfect marital dream we were living. The Turners were arriving at ten, which was still a couple of hours away, but would come up fast, so I went in to check the state of our front room. It was the best room on the first floor, and Rose jokingly called it the parlour, but we didn't use it much because of its gaping window onto the street. And, although I didn't like sitting on display for the whole neighbourhood to see, it was too dark with the curtains drawn. I pulled them clear and let the light in: children on the way to school, shouting and running; a tennis ball bouncing across the street, and a dog chasing it to the curb. A car cruised slowly down the street, honked at the mutt, and pulled into a parking spot just a few houses up.

The light didn't help the room much; there wasn't enough furniture, just an old plaid chesterfield and an overstuffed recliner pinning a Persian carpet to the hardwood. The seating had been inherited from the in-laws, and I'd picked the rug up off the street in my bachelor days and it had stuck for now. Three seats would be enough: the fake parlour would have to work.

I still had a little time, so I pulled the secret envelope from its hiding place in the record rack, found the notebook I'd taken to Jack's rooms lying abandoned on a shelf, and set up at the kitchen table.

The book fell open to where the photo of the naked model was folded in the binding: here she was, Turner's mystery girl looking up at me. On the notebook page itself were the six names I'd hurriedly copied out of Jack's address book in the moments before the police arrived. I flipped the photo over, and there on the back, in the faintest pencil, visible now in the bright light of the kitchen, was the name AMY BERNHARDT. Amy was one of the numbers I had in my notebook. I turned the picture back over, wondering whether it might not be too early to call and see what she knew when the front door banged open. Rose ran in. The bathroom was on the second floor; she made it to the kitchen sink and threw up. I left my studies to rub her back as it heaved and shuddered with the spasms of retching. There was something awful and intimate in standing at her side and feeling her body convulse beneath my hand under the alien force that bent her insides to its will.

I moved my hands up her shoulders to comfort her. She brushed them away. "Not now."

"You're going to need to phone in sick."

"It's too late for that."

"But you can't go to work like this."

"I'll be better now it's out of my system." She stood up straight and moved from the sink while I ran the water to sluice out the mess. Just looking at it made me feel queasy. The acid of the stomach bile had taken all the fibres and solids, the flesh and chaff, and reduced it to an unholy sludge; the liquid ran through the drain into the pipes below. I was digging the residual solids out of the basket strainer with my fingernails when she spoke: "What's this?"

The optics weren't good, but her tone made me bristle. "It's a photograph."

"I can see it's a photograph: a photograph of a naked woman. I'm out the door a minute and you've already got your dirty pictures out?"

"Rosie. It's part of the job. The guy who was found dead under the Flyer, this is one of his photographs."

"The one you decided to put in your pocket. For fuck's sake." And then in one of those abrupt U-turns, I found so difficult to follow, she said, "I need to brush my teeth." Her footfalls sounded, first stomping out of the kitchen, and then clumping up the stairs to the bathroom. I stood alone, rinsing the sink out and felt the afterburn of her anger smoulder and smoke in the yellow kitchen. When I turned the water off, the house was silent. Amy still lay on the kitchen table, her expression a challenge, a dare, drawing me on, but perhaps I should have read it as a warning as stark and clear as what Sid had given me on the phone the night before.

Upstairs in the bedroom, Rose was curled on her side, facing the wall, silent; she didn't turn to look at me when I entered the darkness. I sat on the bed beside her and took her limp hand in mine. It came to life and pulled away.

"It's nothing. It's just part of the job. I need to follow up on all the leads, the contacts this photographer Jack had."

"Can you phone in sick for me? I need to tell them now," she said.

"Yeah, I can do that."

When I hesitated she changed her mind and said, "No. I'll call them in a minute. Don't bother. I don't need you to do it for me."

I reached for her hand and again she resisted. "If you fuck up now, I'm going to kill you."

"I'm not going to —"

"Shut up and listen, would you? Why can't you ever listen to what I have to say? Don't screw this up. Not now."

I shut up and listened and let the words sink in. The warnings were coming fast and frequent. "I love you. We're having a baby." When she didn't respond, I started to feel antsy, like I had to get moving on this job — my first work in ages — but felt like I couldn't leave her while we were locked in the cold war of marriage.

"Go. Go do your job," she said. And even though her words mirrored my thoughts, somehow her expressing them made it impossible for me to follow through. This was the test where she asked me to choose between her and the girl in the photograph, and if I took a step in the wrong direction in the carefully laid minefield, I'd find out, and quick. I sat on the bed, beside Rose, both of us immobile, in the darkness, and time passed. Or maybe it stood still. Or it lengthened and stretched and slowed and warped and ceased to exist in the isolation of our discomfort. She said, "Go," again in a toneless voice that held no love, and I felt the terrible cowardice of inaction, frozen on the bed beside her.

Something shifted, and I stood. "I need to work. The Turner family is coming this morning."

"I know," she said.

"I didn't do anything wrong."

"So you keep telling me."

"I love you." There was the silence of her pointed refusal to say she loved me, but the spell had been broken and my feet were moving; I closed the door to the bedroom and went back downstairs where Amy was waiting, lying on the kitchen table, staring up at me with that look in her eye and I could almost hear her asking me what was I going to do about it. Right beside her was the book with the number. Somehow it had come to eight thirty, a whole hour and a half before my guests were due to arrive; it seemed a reasonable time to call. I dialled the number and listened to the ringing on the other end of the line. It went on and on and then a click and a slow mumble came across the wire: "Amy here."

A lot had happened that morning, and I wasn't as prepared as I should be when she picked up. "This is Patrick Bird, and I'm an investigator looking into the death of Jack Turner. I found your name in his address book." I didn't mention the photograph. "And I'm going through and following up with his contacts. Would you have a minute to talk?"

"Right now? It's still early. I'm just getting up. Or are you thinking in person?"

"I'm not sure." That was the truth, wasn't it? "I'm going through Jack's address book and trying to get a gauge on how well you knew him. My preference is always in person, and I have some photos I wouldn't mind you looking at. But if you tell me you only ever met him once and that was three years ago, then over the phone would be fine."

"No," Amy said. "I knew Jack pretty well." Her voice was waking up now, throwing off the low tones of sleep. "We're both photographers — well, I am — he was — trying to make it; figuring it out. We were coming up at the same time. Poor Jack. What the hell happened? The newspaper said an overdose, but … no, that isn't him."

"You're a photographer?"

"That's right. Does that surprise you?"

"I thought …" I caught myself before my toes were any further down my throat and managed to play it better than

I could have hoped. "It's just that I have some negatives I need made into prints — and also a photograph — could you enlarge that?"

"Work?"

"I can pay. I'm not asking for charity in memory of Jack. Just charge your regular rates. But I need it as fast as possible."

"For Jack, I can probably speed it up. I could do that."

"Where are you in the city?"

"My studio's at 888 Dupont, right at Ossington." I knew the building, it was an old broom factory, some sort of a workshop for the blind that was still industrial, but now an unlikely mixture of factory space and studios. Danny had driven me by it just a couple of days earlier on our grand tour.

"Can I bring the negatives by?"

"It's early."

"I can be there in half an hour. If I drop the negatives now, could I pick them up later in the afternoon and we could talk then?"

"Right now? It's got to be this morning?"

"I'm in a rush. I have a ten o'clock appointment with Jack's parents."

"I'm barely up."

"I know. I just want to get started as fast as I can. I've already lost a couple of days."

She consented, gave me the number of her studio, and signed off. I looked at the picture of the model on the table, wondering whether the name on the back meant Amy was the photographer or the model, folded it back in half, dropped it into the notebook, and tidied that to the shelf above the records. The briefcase was upstairs. I thought about running up to get it to hide the envelope of negatives inside, but was just too lazy. "I'm heading out," I shouted up the dark patch the stairs made in the ceiling, and rushed out into the morning without waiting for a response.

The warehouse wasn't far, but I missed the company car Sid had provided in my last go-round as a PI. There was a certain lack of dignity showing up everywhere on foot, although it was infinitely better than stepping out of the streetcar or — shame of all shames — riding a bike. Amy's directions took me through a parking lot behind a filling station to a fire door someone had propped open using the newspaper's classified section rolled as a stop. To the right, Plexiglas windows were cut into a pair of doors that swung into a factory's shop floor. Machines and people working as one in the relentless din of the industrial dream: each worker dancing a lugubrious dance with their mechanical partner in the name of production. A dusty letter board on the outer wall listed all the building's businesses: TRIPLE EIGHT PHOTOGRAPHY was on the third floor. A man in coveralls pushed through the door from the factory floor and the industrial noise rose in volume.

"Stairs?" I asked him.

"There's a freight elevator," he said and pointed down a hall lit by a single bare bulb.

As I walked under the light, my shadow raced from behind, caught up, overtook, and then stretched in front. The freight elevator had a grating that slid open with a groan. I dragged it shut and tried the buttons mounted on the interior. Something must have worked because the big platform creaked and rose up the shaft. At the third floor, I stepped from the cage onto a worn hardwood corridor, looking for 307. A marker scrawl of numbers and arrows on the unfinished plywood directed me to the left; I found the door I was looking for and knocked on it, my fist echoing in the tunnel of the hallway. I waited for too long and then the door cracked open an inch or two, held by a chain, and a thin face with a blunt bob and a man's shirt done up all the way, the collar loose on a slender neck, peered through the crack. Was it the girl from the photograph? I couldn't be sure, looking at two inches of her face framed in the opening. Her hair was done different, that much was sure.

"You're the detective, then?" she demanded.

"That's right. Patrick Bird."

She frowned. "And you want me to rush this work? Negatives you got from Jack?" Her hand made a motion in the crack of the door to receive the envelope. It wasn't how I'd imagined it. These were important photos — Jack had died for them — they were potentially going to break the case for me, and I was just going to pass them through a crack in the door to someone I'd never met, and who wasn't showing me any trust?

"When can I come back for them?" I hedged.

"Maybe two. Phone me first. If I don't answer, it means I'm in the darkroom and you'll need to wait. It'll be twenty dollars for same-day service."

It fit my schedule, but still I stalled. My hand hesitated as it held the envelope; her long pale finger and thumb closed on the package and drew it from me through the crack in the door. She slid a business card back at me.

"Two o'clock," she said. The door shut and a bolt slid on the inside before I could repeat the warnings that had been given to me.

XI

I WAS HOME with a few minutes to spare before the Turners were due. A faint tang of throw-up hung in the hallway waiting to greet my guests. I called a loud and friendly hello up the stairwell and passed back into the kitchen. There was a note from Rose on the table saying she was feeling better and had gone to work after all. I propped the front and back doors open to get some air through the house, feeling a level of relief that she was off and at work; I wouldn't be listening for her footfalls, worried for her health and happiness, my head in two places while the clients were over. I rinsed the sink with a shot of bleach and moved the garbage bag from under the counter into a bin with a lid in the shed tacked onto the back of the house. Things didn't smell as bad as they had on my immediate return, or maybe my nose had just become acclimatized to it. I grabbed my book from the shelf above the records and slid the snap of the glamour girl — maybe not Amy — out of the book and into the *Child Is the Father of Man* record sleeve. The Turners didn't need to see her.

I peeked into the parlour to make sure it was ready. But looking in there, I saw, perhaps for the first time, how the house might appear to guests, what their discerning eyes might detect: the dust motes dancing in the sunlight, the paucity of decor in the square room, the tired furniture. The only thing I liked at that moment was the plaster design on the ceiling; a broad putty knife had made half circles from one end of the room to the other, giving the impression of waves lapping overhead, and when I tipped back in the recliner it almost felt like I was swimming in the ocean. The Turners could have the couch; I'd sit in the La-Z-Boy. It was the worst chair in the world in trying to upsell myself to professionalism — but it was what I had. I sat, cracked my notebook, looked at a blank page, creased my brow, pretended I was a real detective, and was immediately distracted by movement outside.

It was the clients, just as at Flavia's house, punctual to a fault. In the darkness of the fake parlour, through the front window, I could see the expressions on their faces as they looked at our semidetached home with its short metal fence, the rust fighting through the cracked green paint as it drew the perimeter around the scrappy crabapple tree growing in the middle of a tiny patch of grass. The concrete steps up to the porch weren't quite even; the salmon paint on the front door wasn't conventional. I'd painted it Rose's favourite colour, somewhere between pink and orange, for her as a birthday present that year. Gregory's face was pinched in the sunlight, Connie's face unsure — or maybe it was judgment being passed on our home.

Getting out of the recliner took an effort, and I made it. The door stood ajar. "Good morning. Come in." I pushed the screen open to welcome them.

"Good morning," said Connie, leading the way. Again, I was struck by the similarity in their appearance; more like brother and sister, with their pale skin, curly colourless hair, high foreheads, and glasses. And so different from the photograph of their son that I'd found lying smashed and crumpled in the broken frame on the floor of his room.

"We can meet in here." I ushered them into the first doorway off the hall and they sat side by side on the couch, looking old, countrified, a little overwhelmed in the big city.

I sat in the recliner, conscious I didn't look professional, spread my notebook across my knees, and was about to ask about their drive down when Connie spoke: "We want you to know that we're not happy with how the investigation has gone so far. The police let us down. Completely. They view Jonathan as an addict. A drug user. They think that … I don't even know what they think. They're doing their best not to think. Because if they did, they'd come to a different conclusion awfully quickly."

Gregory nodded his head in short, sharp jabs to punctuate her words.

"Of course," she continued, "we're not blaming you for their behaviour, nor of that man, Sidney, who told us he could help us and then right away said he couldn't. It's hard for us to think about Jonathan's death without feeling we've been let down. Stood up. Stalled and put off. It's a terrible feeling. Our son is dead."

Gregory Turner's gaze came up from the floor to meet mine; the light from the window glanced off his glasses, giving him an eyeless mask of grief.

"He's dead," said Connie. "Nothing you do will bring him back. We understand that. But that doesn't deny our right to an answer. We need to know what happened to him and why. We need a real answer. Not the runaround we've got so far."

She took her glasses off and dabbed her eyes, which appeared much smaller without the lenses to magnify them, like currants in a hard-baked biscuit. "This isn't how I meant to begin, but what I'm trying to say is you need to treat this job with respect. We've been through a lot, and for someone else to drop Jonathan's case, at this stage, after what's come before, would be too much. We can't have that. We won't accept it. If you are with us, you need to be all in."

"Think." Gregory roused himself beside his wife.

"Think before you say yes." She took up his sentence. "If you agree to take this case, we need to know you won't let us down. It's a lot to ask, and with all due respect to you, Mr. Bird, you are still a young man. You are not, as you expressed on the phone, a licensed private investigator, you don't have an organization behind you, you don't have a proven track record. If this is too big, now is the time to say so."

It was an impossible situation: I couldn't say no, not with them sitting in my front room spilling their grief onto the rug with its faded hunting scene, the pale horses giving chase, the frightened stag on the run.

But Connie didn't give me the chance to respond. "We liked you when we met you," she said. "We had a good feeling. It was just ten minutes. When Sid at the agency quit on us, we had nowhere to turn. We didn't know anyone else, but I remembered that you'd done some of this kind of work. Your mother-in-law, the Italian lady, mentioned it, and Mr. Cowan said something also. So we grabbed the phone, almost without thinking, and called you. And since that time, we've realized we don't really know you. We have no references. Nothing."

"You're just someone we met who has a bit of experience in the field," said her husband, breaking his silence without betraying any confidence in their decision.

By this stage I was almost dizzy from trying to determine whether they were begging me to take the job or convincing me I didn't have the chops to handle it. The herky-jerk dance of opening the door for me to escape and slamming it shut to demand my commitment had me discombobulated. A peek at my bank book would convince them how desperate I was for work.

"I'm in," I said. "You're right, I have shortcomings. I'm young, inexperienced, not a full-fledged organization. True. But what you'll get from me when I work the case is my full commitment. I won't rest until I've found the answers or you call me off. If you hire me, I promise, if nothing else, you'll get all I have to give." I heard my voice bounce off the bare walls of the room, my pitch sounding ragged and weak in my ears.

Connie took her husband's hand in hers and closed it between her two. Without looking at him, she said: "That's what we wanted to hear. That's what we needed to have said. We've had our hopes burned to the ground already; nothing's going to change that, but we can't cope with people dickering in the ashes."

"Do you have a contract for us to sign?" said Gregory.

"No, I —" I should have seen that coming.

"I thought that's why we came to town today," he said, his head coming up, his glasses catching the light again.

"No, I —"

"It was that man Sidney who was insistent that we sign a contract," said Connie.

"Let Patrick speak." A tension stretched between the two.

"I am not an agency; I don't have a licence. If you are fine with it, a handshake works for me."

"All the paperwork in the world wouldn't hold Mr. Cowan to anything," said Connie.

"I asked you to come to see me today because I had questions that need to be asked so I can better understand Jack —"

"Jonathan," said Connie. "We call him Jonathan. Jack is his city name." Two names — maybe there were two lives, one in the fields and meadows of his rural upbringing, and a different one, tucked away in the alleys of the concrete jungle.

"Jonathan. Of course, we could have talked on the phone, but in truth, I prefer to meet in person so we can see each other, and I can get a feel for what you're saying and really get my teeth into it." I was playing loose with the truth: what was needed was cash and I needed it upfront. My first bill, paying for the photographs at two, was coming due soon. And I didn't have a car to drive out to the small town they called home.

They sat, for the first time, silent as stones on the couch. I was prepared to give up the facade and admit I needed them to come to me because I didn't have a car when Gregory spoke: "Understood. The phone has its uses, but it is no substitute for good old-fashioned conversation."

"Agreed." I was thankful he'd roused himself from his silence and bailed me out. "I have some questions to ask, so please bear with me. And some of them might be difficult for you, but the fuller a picture I can get of Jonathan, the more I know about him, the more it will help my investigation."

Connie nodded her head in understanding without a word. I didn't have the list of questions I threatened but threw out the first thing that came to mind: "When did you last see your son?"

That brought her to life. "His body was found on the morning of May twenty-seventh. He was home with us for most of the week before that. Gregory took him to the Barrie bus station that Sunday, the twenty-sixth, to go back to the city."

"Home in ...?"

"Midhurst," said Gregory. "It's north of Barrie."

"We don't live in the village," said Connie. "We have a farmhouse about a mile or two outside."

"Not to farm," said Gregory. "We live there and rent the land to a farmer."

"Gregory's a doctor." Connie seemed to do a lot of the explaining for her husband.

"And Jonathan came up for a visit?" I said.

"He came up," agreed Gregory.

"I don't know that I'd call it a visit," said Connie. "It was unannounced. On the afternoon of —"

"The nineteenth. It was a Sunday. Sunday the nineteenth."

"He just walked into the kitchen without a word of warning. He told us he'd taken the bus to Barrie and hitched up from there."

"Was that strange? That he would show up without any warning?"

"He didn't have a phone," said Connie. "There was one in the kitchen at the rooming house, but it was locked for long-distance calls —"

"And not particularly reliable for us calling in, either," said her husband. "Often it goes unanswered, and sometimes when it is answered, you're not sure that the person at the other end speaks English. At least not that you can understand." He seemed to realize what he might be saying and clarified, "I'm not talking about your mother-in-law, Mrs. Gentilini."

"When Jonathan first moved to the city, we used to have a system and call him every Sunday evening at six," said Connie, "and he would make sure he was in the kitchen at that time. And that worked well enough. But things got busy and the routine didn't stick and it was more irregular after a while. But he wrote once a week, and of course we wrote to him."

Connie could talk: she filled the void before I even needed my unwritten questions. Lacking originality, I returned to the first one: "So, his arriving home was a surprise. Usually, it'd be fair to say, you had some warning when he was coming?"

"That's right." When Gregory failed to pick up the thread of her thoughts, Connie kept going. "Perhaps in the happiness and excitement of seeing him, we didn't consider why he had come unannounced as much as we should have. But as the week wore on, there were warning signs. Maybe we're only seeing them in retrospect, now that we know something was wrong, but they were there."

"Warning signs?"

"The surprise arrival," she said. "He had almost no luggage. Just an overnight bag. Didn't bring his camera. He didn't like to go anywhere without his camera. He didn't call from the station for a ride but hitchhiked from town. I don't like that. It seems like begging to me, but young people see the world differently than I do."

"And then his demeanour. It was as if he didn't really come home for any reason," her husband said.

"He wasn't coming to see us — he was just coming home. I understand that children get older, they grow up and go out and become independent — we weren't the centre of his life. But family is family: that bond should never be broken. And if we weren't the magnet pulling him in — then what was the force pushing him toward us? Something must have chased him out of Toronto. I think he was afraid. He was running from something."

"He never said that," countered Gregory.

"But he was. And what happened just confirms it."

"How long did he stay with you?" I asked.

"The full week," said Gregory, as grimly as it could be said, and I suddenly saw his prototype as the sour-faced farmer holding the pitchfork in that painting. Maybe he had a little more hair, but he had the same dour expression, the same resigned air of anger and grief mixed in equal parts and shaken together into a cocktail of misery.

"And that's what made us so sure that what went wrong was no accident," said Connie. "He was up with us for a week, barely said anything, and when he returned to the city, the same day, or the next morning, he was dead."

"I know you've told me this already, but I need to ask again," I said, knowing my question would likely cause pain and anger. "Jack — Jonathan — died of an overdose. In the week that he was with you, were there any indications that he was using drugs — hard drugs —"

"None," Connie was quick to answer.

But I wasn't finished with the question: "— or conversely, any indication he was suffering from withdrawal? I know this is difficult, but his behaviour isn't completely inconsistent with someone who is trying to kick a habit. He comes north, suddenly and unplanned, away from the temptations of the city. He holes up in his bedroom where he can't get what he needs and sweats it out until he's through the worst of it at least. And then he emerges, thinking he's kicked it. But he doesn't understand it isn't about quitting — it's about staying quit. And when he gets back to the city …" I let my voice trail off. I felt their sorrow as I said it: they'd lost their son.

They sat silent. Connie took off her glasses and her eyes were very small in the pale clay of her face.

"I need to ask every —"

"We understand," said Connie. Her voice didn't sound like she did. "And I'll tell you what I told you last time we met. Jonathan was not using. Gregory is a doctor. A country doctor and thank God we don't have any of that kind of problem up where we live. But he understands these things and Jonathan didn't act like an addict when he was with us. That line of thought isn't realistic. It's the line the police took, but only as an unthinking shortcut to get to a quick conclusion, and not as anything serious."

There was a silence. Through the window a powder-blue car crawled up the street looking for parking. I refocused and forced myself to continue, "And what did Jack do when he was home with you?"

"Jonathan," said Connie through the frost. "And that's another problem. He didn't do much of anything," I heard her anger in her tone, and for all my new-found maturity,

I felt a peevish dislike of her; she wanted no stone left unturned except for the ones she didn't want turned. "He was up in his room a lot. Told us he was sleeping. Sometimes he was with us downstairs in the kitchen. Of course, he ate his meals with us. He was polite when spoken to, but withdrawn."

Here we were again: young Jack — Jonathan if they wanted it that way — upstairs sweating in his room and his parents sticking their heads in the sand. "And his rooms at the rooming house were searched; someone wanted something of his. It's not an overdose," she said.

But it was just as possible that whoever trashed his rooms was looking for drugs as much as for anything else. Were the pictures Amy was developing going to show me a deal gone wrong; the guilty partners who were owed money; the pusher who had hooked him? I held my tongue; those were questions for another day. There was no value in causing more misery here than necessary.

"It's that rooming house," said Mrs. Turner. She didn't appear too worried about stepping on my family feelings. "He said as much when he was home. He pretty much told us."

"It wasn't quite as direct as all that," said Gregory.

"But the one time we did try to ask him what had brought him home, he said he was having a problem with one of the lodgers in his house."

"What sort of problem?"

"He didn't say." It was Gregory who spoke.

"Like he was waiting for things to blow over?"

"It's the little Jamaican girl," said Connie. "That's where heroin comes from. Those people have a problem with it. Not us here in Canada. I never liked the idea of him living in that house. It was bound to cause problems."

"You mean Shirley?" I said.

Gregory's mouth formed a straight line.

"Is that her name?" said Connie. "Or maybe that sinister Pakistani fellow is involved in this as well. Isn't that where they grow opium? On that side of the planet? In their poppy fields." That the focus was back on the drugs after they'd been so easily dismissed was an unlikely shift. "When we were there, he was lurking silently in the hallway. Very suspicious. Carrying around those big textbooks as if that provided an excuse for anything. And that wooden face. The both of them seem somehow …" She trailed off and glared at Gregory, who looked down.

"I'll look into it," I said, hating the clients and hating myself. Here were my problems with work back again: half an hour in and I was ready to quit. There were more questions in the back of my mind, but I didn't want to talk to the Turners anymore. "I'll get down there right away and start at the rooming house."

I PRIED SOME money out of their pockets, wrote a receipt on a piece of paper ripped from my notebook, and got them out the door, ushering the ugly underbelly of grief onto the porch, down the steps, and away, away, out of the city, back to their home in the middle of nowhere. The problem was at the rooming house: that wasn't news. Anyone who'd seen the carnage of those two upstairs rooms knew there was good reason for Jack not to go back there. Better his rooms turned upside down than his head. But it had been both.

It could be Shirley; it could be Yusuf. It was possible it was Danny: he had a certain shiftiness about him that Rose had sensed before this mess had even started, and he was already in the middle of the situation; he presented himself as the friend and helper, but bigger deceptions had been pulled. And there was still the mystery man, the roomer who'd paid in full and disappeared into the night: Paul Edward Bridgman. If Yusuf had a face that was hard to read, Bridgman had a name so bland and innocuous as to make it suspicious. And the timing of his disappearance didn't help, either. I stood in the silence of the kitchen, glad the clients were gone. I hadn't disliked them immediately, the way I sometimes had when working for Sid, but it'd crept up on me slowly and got me to the same place in the end.

I ate a ham sandwich, checked the clock, washed the dishes, looked at the clock again, saw it wasn't two yet, and phoned Amy anyway. She picked up on the second ring. I asked about the photos; she told me they were on the line drying, and I started the trek back to the warehouse to see what I could see. The facts spun around and around in my head like in the big drum dryer at the laundromat: there was a photograph and two strips of negatives — one of these things wasn't like the other. The negatives belonged to the photographer — that was the obvious conclusion. But why had Jack included a photograph with the negatives? From what I'd seen when I'd held the celluloid strips up to the light, the print wasn't a child of the negatives. The photograph was of three men: foreground, middle, and background, outside at a café. Toronto wasn't much for patios; Yorkville, yes, but the background architecture didn't look like that neighbourhood — these three looked like they were off on a European vacation.

The reversed light and darkness of the negatives showed two figures indoors — the inch-square thumbnails too small to read much further. If Jack had the negative of the café shot, the logical step would be just to make the whole package negatives. Why add a photo? And if Jack didn't have the negative, why didn't he? He was the photographer after all. The only answer that made sense was the photograph wasn't one he'd taken. But if he hadn't taken it, how did it come into his possession? Was he even the one who'd included it in the package? There were too many questions.

At the warehouse the rolled newspaper still propped the door open and the repeating loop of the factory looked and sounded just the same as it had that morning. The concrete floor of the hallway was still dark and stained with a motor oil birthmark, and my shadow again raced backward against my movement, caught me as I passed under the bulb, and darted ahead, stretching longer and thinner with each step. The freight elevator wasn't waiting, and when I pushed the button to summon it, its groans and machinations sounded over the factory's tattoo as it descended, grumbling down the open shaft. It was a summer day outside, sunshine, peonies, and white cotton-ball clouds drifting through the sky, but as I waited in the darkness, far from the hallway's lone bulb and listened to the elevator's chains clanking, the cold creep of fear passed down the back of my neck. The mesh cage descended to my level, feet appearing first, shiny black shoes, and then the black slacks, stovepipe-straight, creases ironed sharp, the white shirt split in two by the narrow tie, and to top it all off, the clean-shaven face hiding behind mirrored glasses. He slid the grating and stepped from the elevator into the hallway. I don't know if his unseen eyes glanced in my direction, and if they did, what they made of me; but his tight figure, tucked-in and buttoned-down, was incongruous in the low-rent warehouse, home to the sock factory and artists' studios. He fit neither extreme and didn't even fall into a happy medium; he was in a different movie. I took his place in the elevator, clipped the sliding door shut, and pushed the button to take me up and away. He didn't turn to look, but the back of his head, with every hair in place, didn't ease my fears. He passed down the long hall, as the elevator began its rise, and this time I watched as his retreating shadow grew smaller and disappeared under him. In the churn of my mind, where the shifting slides on the carousel were flickering fast, I wondered if I recognized his face. The half-open platform of the freight elevator rose through the building, and I tried to make sense of his person — the line of his jaw, the angle of his head, the freshly shaved chin.

On the third floor, I knocked on Amy's door.

"Who is it?"

"Bird."

"Slide some ID under the door, so I know it's you."

"I just called you twenty minutes ago."

"That was twenty minutes ago. This is now."

The blood was running cold up here, too, closer to the sun. The frost had dropped on the unfinished walls and dusty floor. I wouldn't have been surprised to see a cloud of breath puff from my mouth as I pulled my driver's licence out of my wallet, slid it under the door, and stood waiting in the hallway. Sounds came from inside the unit: footsteps coming and going, the click of a camera and the winding of film, the flare of a match, a discreet cough. The door popped open on its chain, and Amy stood in its two-inch vertical frame with a cigarette in her hand and her eyes on me. Her face was thin and austere, her black fringe only making it paler; she was trying hard to look tough, but the effort undermined the effect.

I had my ideas, but asked anyway, "What's with all the security?"

"You try living here as a single woman and you'd know quick enough. They call it free love, but someone always ends up paying and I'd just as soon it wasn't me."

I nodded my head. Fair enough. Yorkville had proved to be pretty much the same thing. "I gave my ID at the door. Am I good to come in?"

She passed the card back to me through the crack without answering.

"You have trouble just now?" I asked. "The guy who came down on the freight elevator when I was coming up seemed a little out of place."

She drew back from the doorway, and her eyes flicked down.

"Was he bothering you?"

She maintained a silence, but I could see my questions were hitting the mark. Then we heard it: the whirr and the clank of the elevator dropping down the shaft to the first floor, away from us, and the fear swirled in the air like swells in the ocean, and the undertow was pulling at me as it came in and out. "Is there a stairwell?" I asked, conscious that last time I'd asked I'd been directed to the elevator.

"No. The fire escape's on the outside." The old broom factory would never be zoned residential; Amy lived here just the same.

And then we heard it again, the elevator coming back up, the clicking and clanking, the squeals of the gears, and the rattle of chains. The man in the hallway; Amy's locked door; the warnings from Sid and Danny; the mystery surrounding this case: panic surged as I stood exposed in the hallway. I looked through the space between the frame and the door at the sliver of face visible and caught her eyes. "You need to let me in."

Without a word she shut the door, and I thought for a second I might be the sacrificial victim; thrown on the pyre to stave off the spectre of evil for another year. I heard the security chain drop through the closed door, and it swung open. I jumped inside. She shut it quick, set the chain and bolt, placed her index finger to her closed lips, and pantomimed that we should move farther back into the open space of her studio. I followed. Leading me to a work table, she pointed to a tall stool, and I sat, as she found my original envelope and placed it in front of me. Next to the letters *PB* she'd written $20 — Rush and I realized I wasn't the only PB in this world — the blandly named Paul Bridgman would do just as well.

The big windows over the parking lot and gas station let daylight stream into the warehouse, chasing out the claustrophobia of the hallway. But even as the light cheered the world, we heard the elevator stop at Amy's floor, the sliding of the grate, and the echo of footsteps on the dusty hardwood, coming up the hall and passing our door. I didn't want to breathe in the big space of the studio with just a wooden door between me and that spectre dressed in a suit and tie who'd already given me the chills once. The steps came back. A knock on the door. I was glad the wood was solid, and the bolt and chain were set. Amy blew a puff of smoke across the space between us. It hung in the air, grey in the sunlight, and dissipated. She balanced the cigarette on the lip of a tin ashtray and leaned her arms on the table. The knocks ended, and we sat silent like children hiding in a game of hide-and-seek, but there wasn't any of the thrill of deception with horror lurking on the other side of the door. The tall stool had become uncomfortable; I wanted to move, to shift to standing like Amy, but dared not for fear its feet would scrape on the floor and give away our presence. But give away what? It was obvious we were here. If he had enough information to be in the building and knocking on this door, he surely knew we were cowering behind it. It was a charade we were all playing, and as long as we didn't make a sound, he had to make the next move. Amy and I exhaled in unison when the sharp clicks of his shoes on the hardwood retreated down the passageway. Our ears caught the sliding of the grating and the slow trundle of the elevator as it descended.

Amy was about to move when I whispered, "We don't know that he's on the elevator — he could have sent it down empty."

She nodded and moved to the bank of windows over the parking lot, using the elevator's noise as cover. Each window was about three feet square and divided into quadrants by a grille. The fire escape she'd told me about was just outside, a rusty appendage, zigzagging down the north end of the building. Her pauper's balcony was cluttered: a tired-looking spider plant shooting off runners to all the compass points, a cracked milk crate, and an ashtray full of rainwater, the butts swimming in the birdbath.

I wasn't ready to step outside yet. Sourface in a suit would need to show, find his car, and drive away before I'd be willing to risk exposing myself. I crossed back to the apartment's door, stood with my ear pressed to the wood, and listened. The elevator had stopped its grumbling; if I strained hard enough, I'd hear something — my senses were so supercharged that I could talk myself into believing shallow breaths were coming from the hallway. I closed my eyes to focus and when I opened them, Amy was waving me to the window. I joined her at her perch over the scene below, and there he was, walking through the gas station to the grocery store parking lot. He popped a door open on a light blue car that might have been a Ford Falcon and got inside. It pulled through the lot and headed east, across Dupont, into the city.

Amy lit another cigarette. "What the hell have you gotten me into?"

"I don't know. Was that guy in the suit up here before I arrived?"

"He tried. I don't know where he got my address." She glared at me.

"Not on this end. I only found out this morning, when I called you."

"There are enough creeps out there without having to deal with professional ones." We stood at the window; there was the possibility the blue car would just circle the block and come back for a return engagement.

"How else can you explain that he had my address? It had to be you." Her eyes gave it to me again. I looked back out the window. "This is my home." There was no despair, only anger.

"What did he want?"

"He wanted to get into the apartment. That's all I can tell you. When I cracked the door, he tried to put his shoulder into it and pop the chain right off the wall. I'm damn lucky I had my foot against it."

"Jesus. Did he say anything?"

"Nothing. Just knocked, and then tried to barge his way in."

"And when you got it locked back up …"

"Not a word. But I could hear him on the other side of the door."

"Did you call the police?"

"What for? To have them tell me I can't live here and sic the housing inspector on me. There'd need to be more blood on the wall before I call them."

Looking into her face to assert my innocence, I shook my head, refusing to accept responsibility. It wasn't my fault no matter what she thought. And I saw it: she was the model in the picture. She'd changed: chopped her locks off, gone for a straight bob, and put clothes on — straight, loose garments that hid her figure.

"How did you get into this business?" I asked.

"I used to work on the other side of the camera, if that's what you're asking. I was a model, but Jack helped me get started taking photos. It's a better world from this side — a little warmer when you get to keep your clothes on."

I wasn't winning any popularity contests.

"So you knew Jack well …" I let it hang in the air between us.

"Once," she said. "Once we were close. But no more. He has — had — other interests."

"Drugs?"

She moved away from the window, back into the apartment with its white walls, images, framed and unframed, the open kitchen, a single mattress propped off the floor by two rough skids, a navy-blue comforter spread neatly over it, a standing screen hiding something behind it, exposed pipes running across the ceiling.

"They ruled his death an overdose," I said when she didn't answer.

She shook her head. "No, not Jack."

The studio was crowded with the tools of her trade: thin sheets hanging from the ceiling, drywall baffles on runners, umbrellas with light bulbs fixed inside them, and snaking electrical cords.

"How did the photos turn out?" I asked.

She pushed her dimpled chin toward a butcher's block where the envelope still lay. "Take a look for yourself. I printed them all, even though they mostly look the same. The photograph — I'm not sure what you wanted me to do with that. Nothing I can do without the negative. So I'm returning it just as you brought it."

I dug a bill from the Turners out of my wallet, gave it to her, and shook the envelope; the pictures and negatives spilled out onto the wooden block. She was right. They all looked pretty much the same. The prints showed a pool table at the back of a tavern. Every photo showed the same two men: hovering over the felt, drinking their beer, lining up a shot, chalking a cue, or reaching for the bridge. And I knew both of them: they were the same two from the earlier photo. It was the medieval squire and the square who'd been sitting at the café table. Now I just had to figure out who they were and why they were so important.

"They're not his best work," said Amy. "If you hadn't told me, I'd say that Jack didn't take these photos. The lighting's terrible here. No definition. No contrast. And the composition … you can see from the negative strip that he was firing fast — just one after another — and from the angle of the shot he was probably sitting down."

"Like he was —"

"Sometimes he went for that. A kind of cinéma-vérité look. But he did it better. Even when you want it to look rough and gritty it takes some craft to get there."

"Do you think these guys knew they were being photographed? Maybe this was some kind of stakeout."

She picked up one of the pictures of the two men playing pool and studied it for a moment and I scanned out over the parking lot, looking for the blue car. "No. Maybe. This one looks a little stiff. She pointed to the man with short hair. He looks like he might be in on the shoot. The other one: I agree, he's not posing, he doesn't have any idea his photo is being taken. And then she brought the picture right up to her face. "Wait." She crossed the room, found a magnifying glass, brought it back, and held it over the black-and-white face, and I circled behind to peer over her shoulder; we both stared through the circular frame and she placed her finger on the face of the long-haired man with his moustache and patch of hair under his lip, and said what I was thinking: "That's him. The man who was here earlier. He's cleaned himself up. Suit and tie and haircut. Shave and shower. But it's him. I'd swear to it."

I nodded in agreement and reached for the original photograph, the one of the three men. We stared at it together: no magnifying lens needed.

"I don't like this one bit," she said.

I didn't like it either. I didn't like it when I was packing the photographs in my briefcase; I didn't like it when I was staring at the helter-skelter of the fire escape that finished on the short roof of the neighbouring building, the whole rusty zigzag being exposed to every eye at the gas station, in the parking lot, and on the sidewalk; and I didn't like it when I'd made my decision, passed through the door, out into the hallway, and was waiting for the lumbering elevator to climb up the shaft to meet me. The cage was empty, and I still didn't like it.

Not sun, nor warmth, nor the spring air, clear and clean, nor returning home could make me like it. But here I was in the middle of it. I needed to get back to the rooming house and talk to the tenants and Flavia, to show them the photos, to force Danny to participate, to yank his head, with a moustache more like a walrus than an ostrich, out of the sand and make him look and see if he knew one of the three faces. I needed to get the nurse, Shirley, to stop hiding behind silence and fear, to look at the pictures and tell me what she knew. I needed to push past Yusuf's obsequious mask, playing his part as the Westernized gentleman, and find out the truth. It wasn't a good feeling, knowing one of the figures from the photo was already ahead of me and had changed his appearance, as easily as a chameleon shifted its colour, and was now something sleek, moneyed, and dangerous, that knew me, knew I had the photos, and maybe even knew where I lived.

I put the key in the lock of the front door, but the bolt wasn't set. Rose must be home from work. I exhaled a slow breath and let the frenzy of my thoughts dissipate. "Rose," I called, and in the silence that followed, I felt the creep on the back of my neck again, that strange tingling when the internal radar sounds and the early warning sirens howl into the night sky. I looked at my watch to calculate her usual return time: was there anything happening today? A doctor's appointment, groceries needed, a visit to her sister's? I hadn't left the door unlocked.

"Rose," I called again. This morning — it seemed like another life — hadn't gone well; it, too, had been loud with this same tense silence. She hadn't said she loved me, and now I loved her more than anything in the world. I stuck my head in the first room, the fake parlour, and saw the innocent couch, the hardened recliner, and the hunting scene on the rug. Mrs. Turner's half-empty glass was where she'd left it on the small side table, dust motes on the skin of the water. I ran up the stairs, two at a time, and into the small bedroom, dark with the curtain drawn, but nothing hid under the ocean swells of the unmade bed; the front room on the second floor, where the loveseat faced the black-and-white TV — empty. The bathroom door was ajar; the tiles and porcelain stared back in unhelpful silence at my questioning look. I pulled the shower curtain, relieved to find nothing behind it. The back room would be the nursery when the time came but was mostly used for storage now. Empty again. I pulled the curtain to let the light in; and through the window I saw the deck chair unfolded on the grass, and Rosie lounging with a drink by her side and a magazine open in her hands. And looking down on her from the second-floor window, seeing her safe in her seat in our yard in the sunshine of spring, I loved her so much it caught my breath.

"Hey there!" I called through the screen, and she sat up and looked around, not seeing me. "Hey there!" I shouted again and tapped on the glass; this time she swivelled, found me, and waved awkwardly over her shoulder. I came down the stairs, through the kitchen and the chaos of the mudroom, and into the garden, and there she was in the light, and there I was beside her and things seemed good for a moment, but the intangibles that make a house a home had been fractured, the innocence had been shaken, its safety questioned.

"What were you doing upstairs?"

"Looking for you." I grinned and squinted. "The door was open when I came home, so I knew you were here, but I couldn't find you. I called, but you didn't answer." But not a word about my panic. There was enough going on in Rosie's life without me spilling my fear onto her lap.

"You've found me now." She sipped at her lemonade, an inch of liquid and a couple of ice cubes losing their fight with the heat. "Let me finish my article. I'm so happy to put my feet up." She lay back on the recliner and rolled the hem of her shirt up a little to expose her midsection to the sunshine. I went back in the house, locked the front door, hid the photos back in the record sleeve, dug another lawn chair out of the mudroom, set up beside Rosie in the sunshine, and decided I wouldn't do any more sleuthing today. I'd stay home and make sure my Rosie was safe. All the questions would still be here tomorrow.

THE NEXT DAY came and, sure enough, the questions were still there. Oatmeal and coffee, toast and jam, and Rose and me leaving home at the same time. We kissed goodbye at the back entrance to the subway station on Delaware and I made a beeline for Flavia's rooming house. I'd show up first thing and catch the tenants before they'd got the sleep out of their eyes.

It was too early for the chime of the doorbell, so I used my key to let myself in. The in-swinging door stopped four inches in, bumping against Shirley getting a jacket off a hook behind the door. We were both startled.

"Good morning," I tried.

She nodded, not reassured by my words.

"I'm Patrick, Mrs. Gentilini's son-in-law."

"I know you." She fumbled through the mass of shoes on the tiles at the foot of the stairs and dug out a pair of white sneakers.

"I was hoping I could ask you a few questions before you go to work. I'm helping Jack's family and I want to talk to everyone in the house."

The whites of her eyes showed, and I remembered Mrs. Turner's interpretation of events at the rooming house. "I don't know anything. I have to go to work." She slid the second foot into the shoe, laced it quickly, pulling the loops tight and doubling the knots.

She rose to her feet and we stood awkwardly in the narrow hallway.

"I have to get by."

"I just need you to look at a photograph to tell me if you know anyone in the picture. I fumbled with the quarter-open briefcase, the unstable hinge in my hands, and wished we were in the kitchen, where I could place it flat on the table; wishing also that I could have met Shirley there, sitting and calm, allaying her fears. Hemming her in and scaring her wasn't a good conversation starter — after the events of yesterday, I knew that as well as anyone. But her panic seemed overblown: was it the surprise of my early arrival in the front hall, her worries about being late for work, Danny's paper-thin door and sharp ears right behind her, or something she knew about Jack and his death? The first photo was in my hand; I pushed it at her.

Her brows went up, but her mouth stayed still. After a long pause, she said, "I don't know them." I don't think she'd ever played cards, but if she had, she wouldn't have done well.

"Look again," I wasn't moving. "Which one?"

"I have work. The clock not stop for —"

"Is that what's bothering you?"

"I can't be late." Her eyes met mine with determination. Whatever the problem was, it was real.

"I'll walk with you — go your way, and you can tell me about the person you know in the photograph." She'd given up telling me she didn't know anyone.

She nodded.

I opened the door and sunlight streamed into the hallway. I wanted to put the photo away. "Last question and then we go: which of the men do you know?"

She pointed a cracked finger at the figure seated at the table.

"The guy sitting down?"

She nodded again.

I dropped the photo into the briefcase, stepped outside, and held the aluminum screen open for her. "How do you know him?"

She followed me through the door, turned, looked up to the second-floor window, the way Rose had the day before when I tapped on the glass, and said, "It's Paul. Paul who live here last month."

Things were coming together. "Paul Bridgman?" Two out of three: I was making progress before the sun even got high in the sky.

She shrugged. "If that what he call himself." I waited for her at the end of the walk and she turned north up Ossington.

"Where are we heading?"

"The streetcar up the corner." She was calmer now, out of the house, on her way to work, after crossing the point of no return and identifying the figure in the photo.

"You knew Paul?"

She nodded.

"Tell me about him."

"He was" — she searched for the right word and ended unhelpfully with — "a man."

"But what kind of — did you ever talk to him?"

"He was a dirty man," she said, and I heard the force of her emotion. "I didn't like him. He talk foul. And he act foul. I didn't like being in the house with him, and I glad when he leave. He didn't respect … he not respect anyone and I won't be disrespected."

She sounded like she meant it. Approaching Dundas, coming up the gentle slope to the intersection, she lifted her head from where it had been staring at the pavement, and turned to me, her eyes coming at mine with a challenge. I couldn't meet it, and this time it was my gaze that fell to the ground. The long shadows of morning were still stretched out on the ground, and already I had the second of the three figures in the photographs identified and now character analysis to go with it. I really was the early Bird.

"Did he know Jack? Was he friends with Jack?"

"I don't know. I work. The men at the house do what they want, but I'm out on my job. I work. I don't know what they do when I'm out."

We crested the hill, Dundas crossing Ossington at an unlikely angle. She turned to me, a memory surfacing, or a seed of trust emerging, and said, "One time, I see Paul go into that house." She pointed down the street. "Another house that rent rooms. I have a friend who live there, a Filipina girl I work with. One time when I call on her, I see Paul going in the house."

The streetcar was coming along Dundas toward us, and I felt the pressure of the clock. "He was looking for a new place to stay? You think he's living there now?"

She shrugged. "He had a key, like he live there. He open the door with it. He not looking for a room when I see him."

"But he lived at your house. He already had a room. Why would he need two rooms?"

"You the detective."

"It doesn't make sense."

"I tell you what I see with these two eyes."

The grating screech of the vehicle's brakes announced the streetcar's arrival and she turned away from me to board it.

"Which house?"

She was already on the stairs climbing into the tram and said over her shoulder, "It has a blue door. There's a Jamaica flag over the second-floor window. You'll see it." Someone rushing for their commute pushed by me and took their space on the stairs, and Shirley disappeared, swallowed by the streetcar. The doors sighed, as they folded into each other like cards being shuffled, and the vehicle pulled forward along the tracks. I crossed the street and started down the incline to look for the house with the blue door.

It was on the first block, across the street; in the second-floor window a green-and-black flag with a yellow *X* pretended to be a curtain. I rang the bell even though it was early. I didn't have long to wait. A man with a greying afro and a colourful shirt opened the door and looked out at me. "You don't see the sign in the window?" he said. "'No Rooms.'"

I pulled the café photo from the briefcase and held it up to him. "I'm not looking for a room. I want to know if you recognize any of the people in this picture."

He took it from me as we stood on the stoop and his eyes ranged over it a few times. "You're a police officer? It's hard for me to say if I ever see these boys before. They all look the same to me."

"I'm not a cop. I'm helping a family out. Their son was killed. Private investigator."

"That true? I never knew they exist."

He stepped back into the house and motioned with a chin that was sprouting a few loose curls that I should follow. "This one." His index finger picked out the same one as Shirley; the short-haired square sitting at the table. "He here for a short time. Just passing through."

"Does he still live here?"

"No more." He shook his head.

"Who's ringing the bell so early?" came a harsh voice from the depths of the house.

"Avon calling," said my new friend. And to me, "You best talk to the landlady if you got plenty of question. She can give you times and dates and all that. All I know, George is gone — and good riddance. He was a foul-tempered bastard. Took a room but was never here. Said he worked nights and needed a place to sleep during the day, and maybe he did once or twice, but not regular. And there was no job, that for sure."

He stepped aside and slid out of sight to a back room; a Chinese woman with short hair and a short manner pushed past him. "No rooms," she said. "No rooms." She made as if she was trying to sweep me out of the house.

I flashed the photo at her: "You know anyone here?"

She pulled the photo from my hand and looked at the picture. "This one. He stay here."

"What's his name?"

She looked suspiciously at me, but I must have passed the eye test because she came back with "Ramon George Sneyd." Everyone knew the same guy, but every time a different name.

"He might have been George" — came the man's deep voice from the back of the rooming house — "and he was snide, through and through, but you can't tell me he was no Ramon."

"Does he still live here?"

"No more. No more. He gone a month." The same time he left Flavia's.

"Was he a good tenant?"

She gave a big shrug. "He paid the rent. He leave the room tidy. He not bother people."

"He bother me," came the voice from the kitchen, happy to contradict. "Everything about him bother me. But he's gone and now everybody happy."

"And his room?"

"Rented. Too late. You can't have it."

"Did he leave anything behind?"

"No." Emphatic. "Newspapers. Newspapers everywhere. All he do was read the newspaper. And now, time for you to go. Leave me and my house alone. We don't do anything wrong. Goodbye, goodbye."

"Goodbye," came the chorus from the kitchen.

I got her to spell Ramon George Sneyd's full name, and then it was goodbye at the second rooming house.

XIV

THE FACES IN the photos had been identified; the man at the café table was Paul Edward Bridgman, alias Ramon George Sneyd; the other man, in the middle ground, who in the photo sported a pageboy haircut, had shown up in person at Amy's studio, sharp, clean, and dangerous, a knife right off the whetstone. And I had a photo shoot of the two of them playing pool, like rejected publicity shots from *The Hustler*. But what did it mean? Why had the photos jumped from Turner to Danny Blinken? And had there been one earlier jump: from Bridgman to Turner before they got to Blinken? But why? I kept banging my head against the same wall without putting the least dent in the plaster.

Shirley and I hadn't bothered to lock the door when we'd left three-quarters of an hour earlier. I pushed it open. What a difference forty-five minutes made: the house was alive with the sounds of breakfast. Yusuf and Danny were in the kitchen, one getting ready for his day, the other, winding down after the night shift. The student had an array of fruit, melon cubes, orange slices, and his famous pomegranate seeds splayed on a plate beside a thimble of coffee that looked like darkness itself; the cabbie sat hunched over a half-eaten hamburger, a stubby bottle of beer in his fist. They looked up on seeing me enter their kitchen.

"Nice of you to knock," said Danny, lifting the bottle to turn a page of the newspaper in front of him.

Yusuf looked at me and looked away; a reluctant "good morning" escaped from his broad mouth.

I dropped my briefcase on the table and popped the snaps. The lid opened on a spring mechanism. "Morning. I need your help."

Yusuf met my eyes but his expression didn't commit one way or the other.

Danny was more direct: "Not now. I just had a long day's night; not in the mood." When I pulled out the envelope he'd so unceremoniously dropped in my lap like a grenade with the pin pulled, he raised the volume. "I told you, I'm not interested."

"But —"

He stood and his chair screeched against the tiles. Again, I was in the position of being the roadblock — this time between him and the hallway back to his first-floor room. And he was a whole bunch bigger than Shirley. There was a pause while we glowered at one another. Yusuf popped a piece of melon in his mouth, doing his best to ignore us.

Danny reached for my forearm and I braced myself against the door frame and held my ground.

The basement door opened, and Flavia came through it, demanding, "What's happening here? I keep a nice house. No fighting, boys." I was facing Danny, so I couldn't tell if Yusuf was included in this blanket admonishment.

The cabbie had a mind of his own and wasn't about to be told by anyone, including his landlady, how he should behave. He took advantage of my divided attention and shoved my shoulder. I tottered, stretched for support, and grabbed at the table. It wobbled. The briefcase fell from its perch and bounced on the floor. The loose photos slid out the mouth of the envelope and onto the kitchen tiles.

"Look what you've done," Danny said.

"Boys. Stop."

Yusuf lifted another pastel cube to his mouth.

"You can't unsee them now," I said, for there they were, spread across the floor. "Sit down and tell me what you know."

"Goddamn you, Bird. I told you I didn't want any part of this." But Danny sat. "But no, you have to drag me into it. I help you, on the one condition that I don't have to see what's in the envelope, but that's not enough for you. You really are a fucking piece of work."

I took my eyes off the cabbie for a second, stooped to recover the photos, and spread them on the table.

"That's Mr. Paul," said Flavia, sticking a thick finger on the figure sitting at the café in the sunshine.

"But that's Montreal," said Yusuf, dabbing at his lips with a white handkerchief.

"But what's Mr. Paul doing in Montreal? He never left a forwarding address," said Flavia, still focused on the responsibilities of being a landlady.

"What the hell do you know about Montreal?" asked Danny, glaring at the student.

"My cousin lives there. This is Prince Arthur Street, just around the corner from his apartment."

"Cousin?" said Danny, looking like he didn't believe a word of what Yusuf said; he picked up the photo to look closer. "It doesn't look like Yorkville. I'll give you that."

"But why did he go to Montreal?" said Flavia. "Didn't he like it here?" I hadn't thought about the sequence of events, about when the photo of the three men had been taken in relation to the set of prints from the pool hall. I'd assumed that it'd happened before Bridgman, alias Sneyd, had flown the coop, but there was the possibility it was taken after and sent back in the mail.

Danny, brash as ever, put my thoughts into words: "The photo is from before he was here. It's from last summer. Patio season hasn't started yet. Look at the leaves on the trees. That's midsummer and ..." He looked up at me, and then Yusuf, and the words died on his lips.

"He told me he was a draft dodger," said Yusuf.

"He's no draft dodger," said Danny. "He's too old for that. And likely too stupid for the army. And that's saying something."

"What about these?" I pressed my advantage, shoving the second set of pictures, the eight Amy had just printed, into the centre of the table.

Danny looked with disgust: "That's the Columbia House. Just down the street."

"On the corner of Queen." I recognized it now.

"That's the one. It's the kind of place your friend Bridgman liked to spend his time at."

Just two blocks away. "You ever go there with him?"

"What's this, the third degree? I'm the guy who's helping you."

"Everyone's helping. Yusuf identified Montreal."

Yusuf shook his head; he wasn't getting dragged into this.

"But why Paul?" said Flavia. "Jack is the one who owed me money."

"I'm investigating his death now. And I'm getting closer," I said. "We know what some of his friends look like."

"Detective Bird rides again," said Danny.

"Are you going to find his friends?" Flavia said.

"You got your money," said Danny. "What do you care?"

Yusuf broke the silence, rising from his chair into the space between them. "I must leave now to get to the lab."

Danny took the break as an opportunity to stuff the last bite of his hamburger into his mouth.

Flavia also moved on to more practical matters. "Light bulbs. I bought new light bulbs. We need to replace the one in the hallway upstairs. And one in the bathroom, and here." She gestured to the fixture in the kitchen. "You can help."

"Just keep it down," said Danny. "I need to get some sleep." He pushed back the table, folded the newspaper under his arm, and brushed past me.

Flavia muttered something under her breath and Danny chose to ignore it. The party was breaking up: the front door banged behind Yusuf, Flavia disappeared down the stairs in search of her light bulbs, and Danny into his room. Alone in the kitchen, I packed the photos back into the envelope and then the briefcase.

I completed my mother-in-law's chores, standing on a chair, rather than dragging the wooden stepladder from where it lay dirty and rotting against the back of the house.

She made me a coffee and sandwich in her basement apartment with the television playing on half volume in the background. She was full of the news of Rosie's pregnancy, so the conversation focused on the need for her daughter to stop waitressing and the necessity of my getting a job. I was grunting my agreement now and then to keep the conversation going when the images on the television caught my eye and I was up and out of my chair to crank the volume. "Thank you, John. And again, regularly scheduled programming has been interrupted to discuss last night's shocking shooting of Senator Robert Kennedy. Senator Kennedy had earlier that night been declared the winner of the California primary. When leaving the hotel through the service area, he was shot multiple times at close range and is currently in critical condition at Good Samaritan Hospital. A suspect is in custody. We're going to go now to Mary-Lou Snelling live on the scene for an update on this breaking story."

"What is it?" asked Flavia.

I shushed her as the scene shifted to Los Angeles. But all they could show was a reporter standing outside a downtown hotel that might have been anywhere in the world if not for the palm trees swaying in the background. The tele-journalist repeated the same thin facts and the shot switched back to the news desk. I pushed the power button and the screen imploded to a white dot of light that glowed for a second, popped, and disappeared.

"Another assassination in America."

"America? New York?" Flavia was focused on where she had family.

I shook my head, and she poured more coffee into my mug. I didn't want to hear about murder and assassination, death and gunshots. The silence of the basement was as harsh as the words coming through the airwaves. Bobby Kennedy wasn't anything to me; nor his brother John; not Martin Luther King Jr., nor Malcolm X. But still, the news had its effect. It was a different world south of the border: guns and violence and the scars of a civil war that had never healed. Another country, so different from our little mosaic north of the forty-ninth where the whole world lived in peace and harmony, even right above my head in this very rooming house.

The news had soured my mood: I wanted to be free of Flavia and her plans for my future, out of the basement with its electric lighting and low ceilings, far from the television with its messages of death and violence. I stuffed what remained of the sandwich into my mouth, chewed hard, and gulped; it scraped down my throat and into the pit of my stomach. I said a hasty goodbye to Flavia, verging on rudeness, and climbed the stairs out of the basement.

I had a hand on the front doorknob when Danny's door popped open and he stood on the threshold, a fevered glow lighting his face. "Did you hear the news?"

"Bobby Kennedy?"

The assassination had revived his energies. "Yes." He was almost smirking in his twist of tension. "Bobby Kennedy. Another one. What the fuck is wrong with them down there?"

No response seemed required. He stepped closer to me.

"It's just a couple of months since Martin Luther King was killed." His eyes met mine as if there was something unsaid he wanted to communicate; I thought he might reveal it, but his mouth clamped shut.

He shuffled his feet and looked to me to carry the conversation, but I wasn't in the mood to talk politics, particularly with someone so erratic and unpredictable. "I've got to get home." I reached for the door.

"Yes. You take care of that wife of yours."

I stepped outside, but there was no silence waiting for me on the street. The wail of sirens with their oscillation of despair cut the air. The volume increased as I climbed the rise to the corner of Dundas and saw, eastward, milled outside of Bridgman's second house, the one Shirley had just shown me that morning, a massing of police cars blocking the roadway. A streetcar stood immobile, locked in its tracks, as cruisers, parked sideways, blocked traffic in both directions. Passengers spilled out of the tram's doors onto the street.

The warnings I'd gotten from everyone and anyone had me worried. I wanted the pictures of the three men returned to their hiding place inside the album cover before I got myself investigating the cause of this police raid. But things were changing: the same police who'd lost interest in Jack Turner's death and swept it under the rug were here now, investigating Bridgman-Sneyd's second home and closing down the street before lunchtime. The missing tenant had to be the missing link between these two investigations.

There were two sets of photographs, two men showed up in both, two dates, and two locations. What did it mean? Both men had been at the Columbia House Tavern and, given the proximity to the rooming house, I made the assumption it had been while Bridgman lived on Ossington: April or May 1968. And then that other photo: at a café table that Yusuf had identified as being in Montreal. The two men connected again: this time, assuming it was recent, was the summer of 1967. Same pair, different city. And then there was this house on Dundas, the other house, the one where Bridgman went under another name, calling himself

Ramon George Sneyd. He had a couple of personas, if not more. And his friend, whatever names he might use, had a couple of different looks: the medieval squire and the terrifying buttoned-down stalker that Amy and I had had the distinct pleasure of not meeting in the warehouse on Dupont. Who was this shape-shifting stalker who gave off an aura of latent violence and somehow knew Amy's address before I did? And what was the connection between the two men? There was a lot to investigate, and now here were the police back, returning with even more interest.

XV

THE BUZZ OF police activity slowed as the perimeter was sealed; drivers leaned on their horns and their angry bleats echoed up and down the street. A cop took control of the intersection at Ossington, diverting the traffic north or south, away from the closed-down street. Most of the rubberneckers began to disperse now the screams of sirens no longer demanded their attention. Two cruisers were parked perpendicular to the street at either end of the block, and inside the zone, a further cluster of unmarked cars sat idle. I stood on the crest of the hill and looked down at the activity, trying to make sense of the chaos. This police presence was far larger than when they'd first shown up at Flavia's rooming house to share the news of Turner's death. It had to be more than just another body. I'd been there, talking to the landlady and the friendly tenant, just a couple of hours earlier, and there had been no signs of crisis then. The grunts in uniform were roping off the area and closing down the sidewalk running on the north side of the street.

I knew the photographs, hidden within the walls of the briefcase, would be safer stored back in their hiding place in the record sleeve at home. And it wasn't that I didn't care, but this looked too big to pass up on. As I came closer, I saw Rice and Cull, the two officers from the first day, resting their backsides on the hood of their car, Cull smoking a cigarette and looking out past the perimeter. I waved. Rice looked away and Cull made a short nod with his head in acknowledgement.

"What's going on?"

"It's the fancy PI. You tell us," said Cull, standing from the car that formed part of the barrier and flicking his butt onto the roadway where it smouldered next to the cruiser's whitewall.

"Looks like a big operation you got going here."

"We got going?" Rice said. "We got nothing. The Mounties, you mean?" He jerked his head toward the house.

"Where?" Although he'd said Mounties, I didn't see their trademark red serge, Stetson hats, or regal horses. It wasn't the way they showed at the Royal Winter Fair.

"What he means," said Cull, "is we're just crowd control: secure the perimeter, keep out the riff-raff — people like you — while they do their work."

"Their case now?" I said. "Squeezed out by the big boys?" I knew how it felt.

Rice spat. Cull looked at the plainclothes figures passing through the blue door. I waited but nothing more was coming.

"Why all the sudden interest in the city's rooming houses? You two told me the people who live in these dumps weren't worth the hassle."

"That's not what I said," said Rice. Something about him looked familiar.

"Don't tell me you found something to care about after turning your back on Turner's death."

Rice got up off the hood of the car and took a step toward me. He was big and broad and with his bald dome and dull eyes, I realized why I thought I'd seen him before.

"Do you get Yul Brynner much?" I'd seen *The Magnificent Seven* a few times, including just a week back on TV.

Cull reached out a lazy hand to restrain his partner, but his words were for me: "Don't poke the bear. You might not like what you stir up."

Rice stopped at the touch of the senior officer's hand. He met my eyes. "Are you trying to ask me where I'm from?"

I didn't think I was, but I was curious now. "You could put it that way."

He squinted. "Well, here. Born in Canada. Just down the road, out toward Windsor."

Cull laughed. "Here we go."

Rice shook his head. "Shut up, Cull. My family's been here for over a hundred years, came up through the States. Not that you would care."

"He thinks you're taking a shot 'cus he's black," said Cull.

"I can pass; some of the time I do."

"Best of both worlds." Cull had a lot to say this afternoon.

"What would you know about it, old man? Sometimes passing almost makes it worse. Can see it and hear it from both sides but don't seem to belong to either." He paused, self-conscious of what he'd said. Cull failed to hold his gaze and looked away. Rice turned to me. "You asked, so you got it."

"More than you wanted, probably," said Cull.

"I hear you." My response to Rice didn't seem adequate; I couldn't tell whether I'd burned the bridge or if it was just being built.

"And you're still on the case," Rice said, "and I'm not. It wasn't my choice that we dropped that one. And now Cull and I are just playing backup for the horse patrol. Move along, Bird. There's no reason for you to be here."

"Don't you fret. I've got an interest, too. And as long as I stay on this side of the barricade, I'm not a problem. It's a free country."

Cull smirked. "Think so? I don't know. Bird, you're the kind of guy who can conjure a problem out of thin air. Best for you to move along. Nothing to be gained by getting involved in this mess."

Rice clenched his fists and opened them. He looked at me and then away. The heat from the sun brought a flush to his face.

"But what the hell's going on?" I wasn't about to let it go. "There's nothing happening in the house, I was just here." I stopped too suddenly.

Cull smiled. "You were just here? This is pretty, isn't it, Freddie?"

Rice shook his head.

"He was just here." Cull began to laugh. "D'you hear that, Freddie? He was in the house. This house?" he asked me. "You know your mother-in-law lives down the street, not here, don't you?"

"In this house?" Rice repeated the question.

"This one here."

"Before the Mounties?"

"About two and a half hours ago," I said, checking my watch. I hadn't planned on telling them I was a step ahead, but given their attitude to the Mounties, maybe we could figure a way to all be friends.

"Look at that." Cull was enjoying himself. "Our amateur gumshoe, all by his lonesome, tracks down the most important house in the city a full hour before the RCMP. Those cowboys, the whole fucking lot of them, spent the last month combing through their records to come up with this address and you just stumbled onto it. I have to imagine they'd want to talk to you."

"Are we going inside?" I asked. This is what Sid meant when he talked about my need for restraint.

Rice couldn't take it anymore. "Can you believe these fucking idiots? They bring a whole army down here and close off the street and still get beaten to the punch." That wasn't enough. "And by you."

I couldn't tell if it was a compliment or an insult.

Cull smiled: "The *Federales.* Our national force. They should have brought their horses with them, the better to chase you down."

Rice wasn't seeing the humour. "The useless fuckers."

Cull popped another cigarette into his mouth and looked at me. "Oh, to be young and give a shit. Don't sweat it, Freddie. It's a beautiful day in the neighbourhood. Sunshine and cigarettes, and fine conversation with Mr. Bird. What more could we want?"

Rice stood, seething, the dormant volcano perched above the coastal town. He wasn't opening all the way up yet, but the tectonic plates were shifting. He said, "Are you going to tell us what brought you up to this house this morning of all days?"

My photos weren't safe and sound, hidden in the stack of records — no: just the thin leather wall of the briefcase hid them from the same pair who'd shut the investigation down the first time. But maybe if I made some gesture of goodwill and played one of the cards I had, while still keeping the best ones in my hand, we could reach an agreement of sorts.

I was just about to commit when Cull said, "You're young, too, Bird. You can appreciate that kind of attitude. Freddie thinks the Mounties pulled rank and left him to run crowd control out on the sidewalk — 'Please use the other side of the street, Granny,' — while they do all the fun stuff. He's got ambition." He tried to laugh, but it ended up sounding like a couple of coughs from his tired lungs. He flicked his lighter and cupped his hand. "Wants to change the world. Doesn't like being at the bottom of the ladder. He'll learn. There's time. You do what you're told and life is so simple."

Rice turned on his partner. It was like he'd forgotten I was still there. "That's right, Cull. Keep counting the days down to retirement. Don't think we haven't heard this song before. You know, I wouldn't care if those cowboys in there showed any sign of competence. But …" he trailed off, unable to come up with words to describe his disdain for the boys in red.

We stood in silence and I thought I'd try once more: "So, what's all the interest?" And interest from the Mounties: in Canadian cities, it was rare for the federal force to pull rank and jump into the fray.

Cull smiled his mirthless smile and shook his head back and forth — I was the younger brother who didn't understand the rules of the game and was there on sufferance only.

But Rice had had enough. "This is the interest," he lifted himself off the hood of the car and pulled a folded sheet from his back pocket.

As his big hands began to unfold the paper, Cull sprang to life, "Freddie, don't —"

"Shut up, Cull. I'm tired of doing what you tell me." He stuck an arm out and stopped the older detective in his tracks. "We've had enough of doing things your way and look where it's got us: standing on the sidewalk and doing nothing while the RCMP rummage through an empty house. At least Bird has an interest in solving the case, not just counting the days till his pension comes."

"This is a mistake, Freddie."

But Rice, having successfully fended off the first rush from Cull, wasn't to be denied. He unfolded the paper, once, twice, three times; through the back of the standard white page there were blocks of type and the dark black squares of photographs, but the final reveal was still in process.

Cull made a last plea: "Don't do it, Freddie. I'll have to write you up. Think about your future."

Rice stopped and sneered at Cull: "Give it up. You wouldn't write anyone up. Never. Don't tell me you'd take on more paperwork than necessary. And you think you'd risk your retirement by saying what this partnership did on the biggest case of the decade? No. Just sit down and go back to counting the days, Cull."

He turned to me and handed me the paper. I flipped it over and there it was:

WANTED BY THE FBI

CIVIL RIGHTS—CONSPIRACY

INTERSTATE FLIGHT—ROBBERY

JAMES EARL RAY

Below the type were three photos in a row: the first two were mug shots dated 1960, one in profile, and the other straight on; the third looked like a natural photo, the face was looking into the camera, the subject wore a bow tie and black jacket. In all three the face was familiar: Paul Edward Bridgman, Ramon George Sneyd, James Earl Ray. Call him what you'd like: here he was, Dr. Martin Luther King Jr.'s assassin.

I'd seen the face before on the television news and the covers of the newspapers. We'd all seen the face of Dr. King's killer. But I'd never thought to look for it here in our city, across the border, away from the crime scene. Only now, seeing it fresh, after staring at the photos in the briefcase until my eyes hurt, after hearing that he'd been living under an alias in the second rooming house, did it appear obvious; and in making the jump, I cursed my failure that I hadn't made it earlier.

I folded the paper up and passed it back to Rice, careful to be as ignorant as I could as I tried to assimilate this new information. "What's this? I don't get it." They could spill their cards all over the floor, but I'd keep mine face down on the table for now.

Cull shook his head mutely, turned away, and took two steps toward the house as if he didn't want to know Rice's answer. "That's your man who was living here. In this house." The detective flashed his eyes at the second-floor window. "Went under the alias of Ramon George Sneyd."

"James Earl Ray is here in Toronto?"

"Was," said Rice.

"Jesus Christ," said Cull. "Quit while you're ahead."

"Why don't you make a coffee run, old man? You want a coffee, Bird? It's on Cull."

The senior detective's eyes flashed, before reverting to their habitual dull sheen. "Yeah, sure. What do you say, Bird? How do you like your coffee?" Whatever Cull's thoughts, wherever his moral compass lay lost in the weeds, he still had survival instincts; get the hell away from Rice and his loose talk.

"Milk, no sugar. I'll have a large."

"Fuck off." He turned and pushed past the barrier with a few friendly words for the boys in uniform on the exterior and started up the hill to the Lakeview Diner.

"Was?" I asked.

"That's what it looks like," said Rice. "Of course, those bastards," — his eyes indicated the house — "don't tell us anything. But the story is, he came to Canada, took an alias, got an address, and got himself a fake passport. Seems we give them out to whoever asks. The passport was issued and sent in the mail right here. That's about a month ago now. So the assumption is he's flown the coop and is travelling using false papers. We'll see. The Mounties have spent the last three weeks going through every passport application in Canada looking to pair faces to that," he waved the paper he'd taken back, "and they finally made their match. They pulled the address and here we are. And now the word is out all over the world to look out for Ramon George Sneyd."

"I got something for you." It was only fair. It seemed safer now Cull was gone. Without mentioning the pictures, I let him know what I had: that Sneyd was the same man as Flavia's favourite tenant, Paul Bridgman, and our simple little death by misadventure was suddenly back on centre stage now that James Earl Ray was in the picture.

"Shit. And these idiots haven't figured it out."

"I think it's tied up with Turner's death." I was curious to see what Rice thought of that.

"And I won't be telling them. Still stuck on Turner's death." He shook his head. "It's old news now, Bird."

"The dates line up. Or at least pretty close."

"Not close enough," said Rice. "Bridgman, Sneyd, Ray, whatever you want to call him, was long gone before the body was found."

"None of this makes sense," I said. "What does he need two rooms a couple of blocks apart for?"

"The one house to live in," said Rice, "the other is the mail drop."

"You going to tell ...?" I should've asked him before sharing what I knew.

"I'm not giving anything to these assholes," he said, looking up at the house. "They screwed up and let him across the border and gave him a passport, and they let him leave. It's their job to put it back together. Look at them cleaning out the stable after the horse has left. Just shovelling shit. What are they going to find at this stage?"

"Are they making an announcement or anything?"

"Not sure. I don't think so. Not right away. They'll be taking pictures today so they can share them when they make it. But for now, they want to keep it quiet and not alert Ray that they're on to him. You can be sure they'll get their share of publicity once the opportunity presents itself. And keep your mouth shut. Don't be running to the press on this one — and not just on my say-so. It's the right thing to do if we're going to bring this piece of shit in."

"I'm telling you, this ties in with Turner."

"Turner? No." He made it sound pretty final.

Maybe it was coincidence and Dr. King's killer was just passing through; except I knew the dead man was holding and hiding photos of this same James Earl Ray. And not just holding them, but scared out of his mind and passing them on. His room had been ransacked for them, and his life taken. And then, the pressure had come from on high to shut the investigation down. Seeing that trashed room again in my mind's eye, remembering the violence and hatred that had torn it apart, thinking about the bereaved parents, recalling yesterday's encounter with the photo's second man in Amy's warehouse, feeling the enormity of events closing in on me, I understood that, just as Danny and Sid had warned me, this was bigger than me. It was scary: scary for me, and for Rosie, and for Amy, and for Flavia and all her tenants. But it was too late to stop it now and too early to throw in with Rice. I'd tried, but he wasn't interested in the Turner killing. I stared at the Dundas rooming house, no longer wanting to enter it, not wanting to rub shoulders with the Mounties and their FBI friends, not wanting to expose myself as someone in the middle of this mess, not wanting to prove the conspiracy behind Dr. King's assassination, not wanting to solve all the world's problems. I wasn't giving up: I wouldn't leave the Turners with no answers, alone and grieving in their house in the middle of nowhere. But I wasn't ready for the next step.

Rice had sparred with Cull — maybe he was someone I could work with; someone who cared and wasn't too frightened to follow the trail of blood and cartilage no matter how high up the command chain it took him. I looked up to make an overture — and if he'd met my eyes, I might have done it. But he was looking at the approaching coffee, as Cull arrived with three Styrofoam cups in a little cardboard box, steaming in the sunshine. And the moment passed.

XVI

BACK HOME, THAT afternoon, as was all too familiar in my shiftless life, I spent the time moving from couch to chair to bed and back again, trying to get comfortable in an uncomfortable world. There was no relaxing, now I knew the case was bigger than me; the fears and nightmare scenarios ping-ponged around my head without respite. The photos in the battered briefcase wouldn't leave me alone; more than once I went downstairs, pulled them out, spread them on the kitchen table, and looked at them this way and that, trying to understand what there was to see. Ideas sprouted in my mind, the shoots stretching toward an unseen sun.

Other than the people, there wasn't a whole lot, but I was beginning to organize them in my mind. The middle figure was someone who'd met Ray in Montreal in the summer past and now again this spring in Toronto; he was the sharp and dangerous shape-shifter who, now all tidied up with a short haircut and a nice new suit, was on my trail. He'd showed up at Amy's warehouse and I'd felt his shadow, close behind me, for a couple of days now. He was the danger I'd been warned about. If there was only one photo of him and Ray, it wouldn't prove much, but there was one from before Dr. King was killed, and a second after; this was the compelling evidence of the depth of the relationship: before and after. And then there was the blur of that third man in the Montreal picture: was he here in Toronto helping Ray or just a passerby caught by the snap of the camera? His quarter-face was a smudge, too close to read.

It was a relief when I heard the key in the lock and Rosie's steps in the hallway; I'd been waiting all afternoon for her return. We kissed in the kitchen and she sat on one of the wooden chairs and put her feet up on another.

"Long day?" I asked, trying to wait for the moment when I could tell her my news.

"Yes, long. That's why it's called work. It's a lot to be on my feet all day and the smells. Ugh. Getting a whiff of bacon — which happens about every twenty seconds in the rush — is enough to make me gag."

"Yeah." I reached from my chair to her shoes, undid the laces, slid them from her feet, and placed them side by side on the floor. I peeled her ankle socks off, rolled them into a ball, tucked them into the right shoe, and worked her hot feet with my fingers.

"You're home early," she said. It might have been a neutral statement. Or not. "Oh, that feels good. I thought you were going down to Mama's."

"I was there." My voice sounded defensive, and I hated it. There was a part of me that knew I shouldn't tell Rosie — she was busy growing a baby and working full-time, and didn't need any extra worry right now — but there was another part that needed to say something. I was worried: she needed to know the danger so she could take precautions until we got through this together. I wavered; the phone rang its shrill squawk. "It's probably your mother," I said.

"For you?" She smiled.

"Maybe. But let's let it be for now. I'll call her after we talk."

Rose managed a shrug without seeming to move her shoulders. The phone kept ringing. I wanted to tell her what I'd found but the constant interruption made conversation impossible. After about the twentieth ring, the bell felt like it was imprinting itself in my head and I'd changed my mind about answering it. I stepped across the kitchen and pulled the receiver from the wall. "Hello." The irritation sounded in my voice.

There was silence on the other end of the line.

"Hello," I said again, but it didn't produce a different result. "Hello." For the third time, but still nothing. I hung the phone back in the cradle, trying to master the fear climbing through my body, trying to tell myself that the terror wasn't rational; there had been no one on the other end of the line, it was a wrong number, it wasn't a big deal. But I couldn't convince myself; the patience of the caller, the eternal ringing, the calculated silence, all seemed a deliberate message: I know who you are and I know where you live. And I know you have the photos.

"That was weird," said Rose.

"Yeah." I held my voice steady, forcing myself to talk through the fear, even though I'd lost my appetite for conversation. Suit-And-Tie knew where we lived: that was what the phone call said to me. It shouldn't have been a surprise: we weren't hiding. Any third-grader with a telephone directory could find us. But it was the way he did it, calling to let me know he knew. Was he watching the door, waiting for Rosie to come home before dropping his dime in the slot? If I ran down to the subway at the end of the street, could I catch him still lounging next to the payphone? Did he want to talk to her and not me? Did that explain the timing? To put the fear of God into her? The creep of terror I'd felt yesterday in the warehouse crawled back onto my neck and set its tiny leech teeth into my flesh — here in my home.

Rosie stretched and yawned. "But you were going to tell me about your day."

"Yeah," I took a gulp of air and rushed in. "A lot's happening. The case is opening up. It's moving." And I told her about the negatives Danny had given me, the photos, the first half of my morning and how I'd managed to ID two of the figures in the pictures with the help of the tenants in the rooming house.

"Let me take a look at the photos," she said. "This is exciting. You always used to have funny stories about the clients before we were married, when you worked for Sid. Do you remember?"

"All those sleazy divorce cases?" I got up, went into the living room, got the record sleeve, brought it back, and put it on the table. "I was just trying to impress you with my worldliness."

She slid the photos out of the envelope and spread them on the table. "That's the way to a girl's heart, talking about cheap motels and divorce." I picked up her foot again, and she smiled. "Maybe you should be a detective, after all. But I don't like the danger. Not now." She looked down at her stomach. "But I think you're happier when you're not moping around the house all day. And after Mama's you just came home?"

"Sort of. But on my way home, in the two hours I'd been at your mother's house, there'd suddenly been a huge police raid on the house on Dundas that Shirley had shown me. There's more happening in the case. You'll hear it all soon enough, but I can tell you now."

"Hear it? From where?" She caught my tone and straightened up, adjusting the foot in my hands.

"Things are happening." Now wasn't the time to waver. "I ran into the two officers from the first day, Cull and Rice. The young one, Rice, told me the man who was living at Flavia's, and at this other rooming house, is James Earl Ray, the guy who assassinated Martin Luther King." Ray's face stared up at us from where he sat at the café table in Montreal. "This one." I put my finger on his forehead.

"He was living at Mama's house?"

"Yes."

"But ...?"

"He's gone now."

"But what about the dead man? Did James Earl Ray kill him as well?"

"Ray was gone two weeks before Turner was killed. So that seems impossible."

"But what's the connection, then?"

"Yeah," I said. "The connection is that it appears that the dead man, Turner, had these photos of James Earl Ray."

"So Turner knew who Ray was?"

"I don't know. Maybe. I'm not sure." My theories were shifting and settling over the course of the afternoon, and now I spoke them aloud for the first time. "I think maybe Ray commissioned him to take photos of the meeting with the second man so there'd be a record of the two of them in conversation."

"But why would Ray do that?"

"To have some backup." Maybe I shouldn't have been sharing this all with Rosie; maybe she was the wrong person to tell at the wrong time, but I needed a sounding board as I tried to figure it all out, and I just kept plowing forward as the pieces rearranged themselves before me. "So he could prove he wasn't in this alone, and maybe use that information for leverage and protection. If he's arrested, everyone's going to say they don't know him, they never met him, and just throw him to the wolves. But if Ray has a photo of the meeting — or two meetings over time, then it's harder for people to deny they know him."

"But it doesn't make much sense. Why would Ray want to take his friends down? Isn't the story always that people protect their associates? That they'd rather die than be a snitch?"

Her questions were pushing me to articulate my worst fears about Ray and the photos, ideas that had been swirling around my restless head all day long. I didn't want to give it a name, to say it out loud, but here we were. "But what if the second man wasn't his friend? What if the second man was ..." I searched for the word. There didn't seem to be anything that would convey what I meant. "What if Ray had a handler," — that was the word I was looking for — "someone who put him on his way, who set him up, who egged him on, who helped him across the border and got him settled here in Toronto, who provided him with money for rent and a plane ticket? What if Ray was the puppet and it was the handler who pulled all the strings?"

"But what does that have to do with Jack?"

"The pictures are Ray's guarantee. His proof that he wasn't in this alone."

"But who is this handler? What kind of a person wants another to assassinate someone?"

"Maybe a rogue agent? Some part of the machinery of the U.S. government — let's say FBI, and Ray decided his insurance policy was to have the photos taken, and that way if he ever gets caught and pulled in, he has some bargaining chips?"

"That's what you think?"

"That's what I'm coming to. I'm still trying to piece it together."

"And so why was Turner killed?" We were getting there now.

"Because he had the photos." I paused as the idea was still forming in my head. "Because he had the photos and wouldn't give them up. Because he'd seen the photos. I'm not exactly all the way there. From the handler's point of view: Ray lets him know he needs more help. He makes demands. He drops a hint he's got photos — proof — of the two of them together and he'll use them if he needs to. As soon as the handler starts to investigate, he finds out there's a photographer living in the same house. It doesn't take too much to add up that he's your man. The handler catches up with Turner, who denies he has the photos. But something about the situation spooks Turner. He's starting to see it's too hot. So he asks Danny to hold the evidence outside of the house. Danny hides the photos and Jack disappears; he goes up north to where his parents live and just hangs out for a week or so, away from the danger. His mistake was coming back. That's when this one" — I put my finger on the figure in the middle ground of the photograph — "caught up with him."

"But why didn't he just give this handler the photos?"

"Because he didn't have them."

"But he could have gotten them back from Danny."

"I suppose so. But maybe he was trying to protect Danny."

"I've met Jack. I don't think he'd work with James Earl Ray. That part doesn't make sense to me."

"Maybe he didn't know who he was."

"I hope not. We don't know that Jack took the photos. You only have Danny's word for it, and I wouldn't trust him an inch."

"But Jack was the photographer."

"Anyone can take a picture," Rose insisted.

"But you need a darkroom to develop them."

"I think you want to ask Danny a few more questions before you believe everything he says."

"And," I said, feeling argumentative as she tried to shift my perspective, "Jack's the one who got killed, not Danny."

"I'm not arguing that." She frowned, looking as though she didn't like the thought emerging in her mind. "It's just … couldn't Jack just give the photos back to handler? Why is he holding them? What does he gain keeping them?"

"It might have just been too late. The handler might have wanted to kill him simply for seeing what was in the photos, quite apart from having the prints — let alone the negatives. They want to destroy the prints, as concrete evidence, but it's also a danger when there are witnesses who can put these two faces together in the same place, at the same …"

I felt Rose's foot freeze under my hand, realized what I was saying, and looked up at her, feeling her fear and anger growing to produce a blast of heat. "And you have the photos? And you showed them to me?"

"I …"

"You want to put me and the baby in the same danger as you? Is that it? A man's already dead? And you put a target on our backs? Patrick, you're so stupid. Use your head."

"That's what I'm trying to tell you," I said. "Things are dangerous. I'm telling you, so you know, not to scare you, but so you can be safe."

"I can't believe this."

"We're in danger. We need to be careful and look out for each other."

"Oh, Patrick."

"This is my work. You keep telling me to get a job and this just fell into my lap. I had to take it."

"Of course, it isn't your fault. Nothing ever is. But trying to make it mine! Go ahead and quit again, and it'll all be on me. I know how you think. How stupid am I? I've known it all along. You can't —" she stopped and we stared at each other in silence. I looked away and she jerked her feet to the floor and stood.

"We can't fight now," I said. "We have to —"

"I'm pregnant," she said. "I'm carrying our baby. I don't have the energy to fear for my life. I don't have it in me to worry that someone's coming to the house to kill you — and me, too — and the baby — now that you've gone and spread these photos all over the table. Why do you have to be so stupid?"

I stood.

"No." Her eyes were wild. She put a hand out to move me from her path to the arch that led to the hallway. "Get out of my way. Leave me alone."

"I didn't set out to get us in the middle of an assassination."

"I know, Patrick. It's never your fault. Blame someone else."

She was past me now and in the darkness of the hallway, just a silhouette against the light coming through the transom over the front door at the bottom of the stairs. Her hand was on the bannister and one foot was on the bottom step when the doorbell chimed.

It froze us both. Her face backlit in darkness, her fury rushing like a hot wind to where I stood in the bottleneck of the hall beside the stairwell. And then on the second note of the doorbell, the temperature dropped and the beads of sweat on my hot face went cold. We stood still and silent after the shouting and banging; whoever had come calling would have heard us in the second before the bell was pushed. Pretending we weren't home wasn't an option.

"Go upstairs," I whispered. "Go into the bedroom, shut the door, and lock it." The household lock wouldn't withstand a hairpin. "Go."

In the moment of fear, Rose did what I said and disappeared up the stairs, and I heard the squeak of the hinges, the wood bump against the stop, and the click of the lock's button being depressed. I scooped the photos on the table back into their envelope and back into Blood, Sweat & Tears' *Child Is the Father to the Man* sleeve and shoved it into the standing stack beside Johnny Cash's *At Folsom Prison*. Alphabetical order even in the chaos of the moment. The chime chimed again, sweet and saccharine, a two-note sing-song hello just like the Avon lady was at the door.

XVII

IN THE FRONT room, I sidled up to the window, peered through the fading light, and exhaled a whistle of relief. It was Danny Blinken, stooped and impatient, standing on the front step.

I opened the door.

"What the hell took you so long? I've been waiting out here forever."

"It was just the second ring. Hold on to your shorts."

"I don't like waiting." This from a guy who drove a cab for a living. "Sounds like you and the little missus were really getting into it."

"Come on in. Don't stand on the porch." I opened the door wider. "I'm a little spooked here at home with some of the stuff going on in the case." I stepped back from the door frame, but he didn't make a move to enter.

"I don't like the idea of being in your house, either. I'm trying to minimize our contact." What the hell was he doing standing on the doorstep and ringing the bell if that was how he felt? "Come for a drive and we'll talk in the car."

"It's not a good time for me to go out."

"You don't make it easy to help, Bird."

"Fuck you." His erratic behaviour was beginning to piss me off, showing up at my house unannounced and with nothing to say.

"You want to solve your case, but whenever I try to help you out, you act like I'm a pain in the ass."

"I told you, I can't leave the house, that's all. And you standing at the door isn't smart, so I invited you in. That seems fairly hospitable to me. You keep talking like you've got something big to tell me, but I haven't heard it yet." The chamber of my heart where generosity lived grew taut and tight; I decided to hold what Cull and Rice had told me about the mystery man, Paul Edward Bridgman. Danny had helped me out and gotten me started, but it all had the stench of self-interest, the focus on saving his skin at the expense of mine.

"I agree," he said, his sudden friendliness enough to cause whiplash. "This porch isn't the place to talk. I like the cab. You're in the back and it just looks like a fare taking a ride. Nothing suspicious about that."

"I'm telling you. I need to stay here."

His glassy eyes probed my face. "Don't want to leave the little missus? Now the baby's on the way?"

His knowledge caught me off guard. "How the hell'd you know that?" We'd only told family about Rosie's pregnancy so far, and she wasn't showing.

"Your mother-in-law. Mrs. Gentilini. She's a proud woman. Telling everyone. Pretty much handing out cigars.

You think I can live in that boarding house and not know? C'mon Bird. Get real."

"Well, show some respect." I sounded weak.

"As I'm doing. Congratulations, to you and the little lady."

We stood on either side of the door frame, the aluminum screen propped against his shoulder, and me inside in the shadow. A car passed up the street. It was respecting the speed limit, taking care not to drive too fast in a residential neighbourhood with young children, and it wasn't the powder blue of Ray's mystery friend's vehicle, but still, I couldn't suppress a shudder as it rolled by. I was in that space between heightened perception and paranoia. Or maybe it was just reality.

Danny shifted and stood straighter, his arm holding the screen. "I can't stay here forever. I have news. Big news. That's why I'm here."

I was the one with the big news — we would all know it soon enough when it splashed on the front page of the paper — and I was pretty sure he couldn't top it. But maybe he had something else, something I didn't know. And if I blew him off, he'd hold a grudge, and I'd lose my best source. For all his personality defects, and there were plenty, he was the one who'd given me my start on the case, and was still helping. I looked down the one-way street and didn't see any traffic. It was all quiet: trees sprouting leaves, old men with straight backs sitting on their porches, husbands and wives landscaping their postage-stamp-size front yards, a squirrel running on the power line, girls skipping rope. That seemed to decide the moment. It was safe. I lived in Toronto: a long way from the mayhem and violence, the assassinations and riots, happening south of the border. "Give me a minute." I turned to the stairs.

"I'll wait in the car." Danny let go of the screen; the pneumatic gizmo that slowed its progress was broken and the door slammed. And its sudden noise made me jump as I started up the stairs to the bedroom. It was going to be a tough sell to get Rosie to see that I needed to go out right now. I was struggling to find my bearings in the uncharted territory of our relationship, but I felt it — Danny had something big. At the top of the stairs, I came face to face with the closed door; the terror of the wrong number and the chime of the doorbell were fading in the rear-view, but they still felt more like the real thing and less pure panic and imagination.

I stood outside the door for a second, figuring how I could explain to Rose that I needed to go out. A big exhale failed to straighten my thinking out, and before I could reach my hand out to the knob, it swung open. Rose had a small duffle in her hand and looked through me.

"What's going on?"

"Who were you talking to? That awful cabbie?"

"Danny. I don't know that he's —"

She pushed past me. "I'm going. Since you put a target on our home, I'm going somewhere I feel safe." She started down the stairs. "Safer," she amended. "I'm not sure I'll ever feel safe again. Here at least."

"Where are you going?"

"I can't live like this. Every time the doorbell rings, it feels like our lives are going to end. You think I should tell you where I'm going? That'd be smart."

It wasn't the time to tell her I was going out with Danny. I followed her down the stairs to the kitchen; she turned the light on and opened the Yellow Pages on the counter under the phone. She was mad at me. Mad as hell. But maybe she'd gone and solved the problem herself. If she got out, to some safe haven, then I could finish the investigation up, and when it was all over, we'd be together again. And happy. Luck came in the strangest ways.

"Do you want me to get you a cab?" I asked, but already her finger was turning the rotary dial.

"I need a cab immediately." Rose gave our address into the phone. "As fast as you can." I only heard one side of the conversation. "How long should I expect to wait? Fine." She hung the phone on the hook and sat at the table with the duffle at her feet. "They said five minutes. And then I'll be gone."

"I'm sorry," I said. There was no response. It was like I'd spoken into the void. My words disappeared, a stone dropped into the water, the splash of impact, the ripples fading, and then the still-flat surface the same as before, like nothing had ever happened.

The silence between us grew and five minutes, uneasy in the kitchen, together but apart, felt like a long time. When the knock finally came, I had the twinge of fear that when we opened the door, it wouldn't be her cab but the silent killer who'd stalked me at the warehouse and called just an hour before. But it was Rose's driver, old and paunchy with sharp eyes and a shiny forehead; she let him take her bag where she'd refused my help. Once the duffle was safely in the trunk, she settled into the interior of the cab, and when the door slammed, the interior light went off and she disappeared. The car pulled away, and I was left staring at its red tail lights like another warning signal as the shadows of the evening stretched their thinning tendrils to the other side of the street.

Danny sat scowling in his taxi across the street; I opened the back door and slumped into the centre seat as his cigarette smouldered in the ashtray under the two-way radio.

"Took your time."

"I had some things to sort out."

"Uh-oh. Sounds like a little marital discord. If her temper's anything like her mother's —"

"You might want to stop right there, Blinken."

"Just a little banter between brothers. Don't cut up so rough."

"Get to it, Danny. I don't have much time." Our eyes met in the rear-view mirror and held for a second.

He looked away and spat out the window. "That's rich. I spend half my evening waiting on you and you complain you don't have the time. Don't think you're the only one who's busy." He put the car in gear and started north on Delaware. The sun was dipping and the light was clean and clear and pure the way it is when the beams run horizontal and the sky above is fading; patches of darkness in long stripes ran across the road and through the car. I slumped back in my seat, waiting for him to stop with the sparring and tell me whatever the hell he'd come out for. I felt like Rose: not sure I ever wanted to talk again.

The cab's two-way radio squawked, static bursting between the dispatcher's words. Danny's voice cut over the steady flow, "I got something juicy for you."

"Save the mystery and tell me." The cab made a turn at the top of the street and headed into the single eye of the sun. I didn't trust him, but I'd trusted him enough to have my pregnant wife jump into a strange cab and head out alone when I knew a professional killer was circling closer. Was this some sort of setup on his part? I repositioned myself in the back seat to look at Danny's reflection in the mirror, and Rosie's suspicions about him started to steep and stew in my slow-moving mind. I only had his word for how the photos had landed in his lap, when there was another way they could have got there. My thoughts were starting to come together — it was late, but not too late.

"You call yourself a detective?" Danny flipped the visor down, and the shadow crossed his face; there was a look in his eyes at that moment that twigged a thought inside. It didn't catch, but the feeling lingered. "I get more information minding my own business and driving a cab than you get in all your running around and digging." He paused for effect. "The man who was living in our rooming house was James Earl Ray."

I didn't respond.

"The man who killed Martin Luther King in Memphis," he said.

"The police tell you that?"

"Not quite. I don't want to bore you with my life, but you pick up on plenty driving a cab."

"Who told you?"

"I have a few people who know what's happening." This was a little vague for my tastes. "You're missing the point. This isn't about me or my source. You're focused on the wrong guy. James Earl Ray, the most sought-after criminal in the world was living in the rooming house — sleeping right under Jack, who turns up dead a week later. That's the story here."

I couldn't keep my eyes on the reflection of his face with the sun bobbing in and out from behind the rear-view. "But Ray was gone before Jack ever disappeared." That was the same argument Rice had used with me. I'd rejected it when he said it, but thought I'd try it out on Danny.

"Still, it's connected. It explains the investigation — or lack thereof: how nobody wants to touch the case. The police got the word up above. Someone up above with all sorts of power put an end to it."

"But that doesn't make any sense, either. Not if no one knew it was Ray."

"I've had all day to think about that one. Come on, Detective —"

I didn't give him time to finish but lunged forward, got my arm around his neck, and pulled back hard against the seat. He tried to fight it, but his words were cut short by the pressure on his throat. The car swerved; he got it under control and eased it to the curb.

"Put it in park," I said, and he did what he was told for once in his fucking life. I thought I was the only one who'd known Bridgman was Ray, but now Danny was giving me the same news. "Okay, Blinken. I'm not going into details right now, but I need you to tell me where your information comes from. Rosie is on her own right now, and so help me God, if you are part of some plan to lure me out here and leave her unattended, I'll kill you."

XVIII

HE STRUGGLED BENEATH my arm, his breath coming in truncated wheezes, his body tensing and releasing, his hands scrabbling at my biceps. When that failed he reached higher, trying to get his hands on my face and his thumbs into my eyes.

"Sit still and I'll loosen the hold and let you have your say. But smarten up or I'll turn the air off again."

His grasping hands gave up, and I lessened the pressure.

"Jesus, Bird." His voice was raspy. "I'm helping you and this is what I get —"

"Cut the complaining and get to how you knew."

"I'm not cutting any —"

He'd got enough air for now, and I'd heard enough of his whinging: I put the clamps back on. "I'll tell you how it went," I said, as the idea of Danny's duplicity crystalized in my mind. It was Rose who'd put me on to it. "You're a smart guy, you read the paper every day, you're up on the news. You made Bridgman for Ray pretty soon after he arrived, probably the first day you met him. You have a camera in your room and consider yourself a bit of an amateur photographer — that's how you became friends with Jack. And you're the one who first brought up the idea of blackmail to me; maybe that was your conscience speaking."

"No." His croak lacked conviction.

"So, you got smart and staked out the Columbia House, where you knew Ray liked to go and drink. You're the one who snapped the shots there, but once the blackmail started, Ray and his friend must have assumed it was the photographer who lived in the house and killed the wrong guy. How do you feel being responsible for Jack's death?"

"It's not like that."

I loosened my grip on his throat, and he gulped some air. "Then tell me what it's like."

"That's not how it went. You got it all wrong. I made Ray for who he was the first time I saw him, that much is true. I confronted him; I was looking for a payout — you got that right. Call it blackmail if you want; it seemed like a good business opportunity at the time. But Ray said no: he didn't have any money and couldn't get ahold of any. He told me he had one last meeting with his guy — he called him Raul — and he wanted me to take pictures of the two of them together. He was slippery. He convinced me that was where the real money lay — that the U.S. government would pay to keep those pictures locked up. He said he was just a cog in the machine, but if I could move a little further up the food chain the payoff would happen."

"So you helped him out. Nice of you — helping out the guy who killed the civil rights movement."

"I had no love for him. It was strictly business."

"You could have turned him in."

"But I —"

I was sick of listening to him and put the pressure on his neck again and finished the sentence for him: "You were trying to turn it into money. But you needed Jack to develop the pictures you took. Look where you got him." Once I'd had my say, I eased up on his neck.

"No. Ray gave me the other photo — the one Yusuf says is in Montreal — to show me the other man — his handler, this Raul. That's how I knew who to snap at the Columbia House. I thought he was playing ball; that we were in it together."

"Together? God, you make me sick. Maybe he was just buying time until he disappeared. Maybe you got duped."

"I helped him — you're right — but there was supposed to be a payoff for me. But it never happened. He up and disappeared."

"And it got a little too hot for you to handle when Jack turned up dead."

He tried to nod, but my elbow blocked his chin from moving much one way or the other.

"So you threw it at me like a hot potato."

"I was helping you out."

"Sure, the neighbourhood philanthropist. The way you help your friends seems to end up with them getting dead."

"It's not like that. We still have the photos. We can still use them."

"We? Listen to you. Now you're planning to be the man who turns in Ray — after he's disappeared." I'd pretty much just squeezed a little truth out of him, and it wasn't pretty; it was thick and oily and noxious, puss from a wound. I released his neck and sat back on the seat. He rubbed at his throat, breathing heavily.

I was ready to get out and walk and be done with Danny Blinken once and for all, but whether I liked it or not, we were in it together, him and me. He still had more information than anyone else. He'd seen this Raul in the Columbia House. Heard his voice. Thought about it, too, which was more than I could say for some of the others who'd dropped the case as quickly as they could. So I told him about my experience with Amy in the warehouse and our close call with the newly groomed Raul.

"You see," he said, his voice still raw, "Ray was right. There are others involved. FBI. When he disappeared I thought maybe he'd been feeding me a line, buying time until he could make a midnight move and disappear from my demands, but when Jack turned up dead, then it was clear there were others in the picture. That's why I'm helping you." He seemed to have forgotten that just two minutes ago I'd had to pretty much strangle the truth out of him because he wasn't helping hard enough. "I owe it to Jack."

"Spare me."

"No really. He was my friend. This Raul, he's the dangerous one, the handler, the guy who's running Ray. You're beginning to get it."

The sun had disappeared and left a scarlet glow at the end of the world. The shadows had stopped creeping and pounced in total domination. Our ideas and theories weren't so far apart, and now we had them together in the cab's dark interior; our alliance was forged by the bond of our dangerous knowledge. But he wasn't the partner I'd choose. I stared out the window as Danny rubbed his neck. A screen door slammed across the street and an old man, sitting on his porch eyed us suspiciously. "Do you think Ray is still alive? Or maybe he's dead, and that's why we haven't seen him. That's one way these covert operations seem to solve their problems." I was thinking of Lee Harvey Oswald and how that had gone down.

"But your mother-in-law got her rent." Danny shifted his back against the door so he was halfway turned around for the conversation. "Ray settled up with her before he checked out. That doesn't sound like someone who gets surprised when they're not looking. It sounds more like his passport came through and so he jumped. That's why these U.S. criminals come north — to pick up our passports." He knew plenty even when he didn't have the details.

"Still, Raul could offer him a ride to the airport and then Ray never sees the inside of the plane."

"Maybe. I don't know. He didn't make it sound like he was going to see Raul again, but I take your point: these handlers have a way of just showing up."

Didn't I know it. "And you really think the FBI is making hits and bumping people off? In Canada? You're getting pretty deep into the conspiracy theories."

"That's how these people work. The FBI — or something worse, deeper, without a name, not acknowledged — but with FBI money. J. Edgar Hoover hated Martin Luther King; has wanted him dead for years now. I mean, who helped Ray into Canada? Who gave him money for rent? For a plane ticket? If he gets caught, you can be sure he'll take the fall; but he wasn't acting alone. Any punk can see that."

"Yeah, I —"

"The photos. You have the photos. They prove it, don't they? The photos are Ray's backup plan. He was starting to feel it, to know if things went south — ha, that's a good one — if he went back south, then he'd need an insurance policy. He needed proof of Raul's existence: that's his leverage if he ends up in court. It's the whole JFK thing all over again. Open your eyes. This is how the world spins."

"And so you're sure this rogue agent, Raul, is the one who killed Jack." It was what I thought, too. The stain of reds and oranges where the sun had disappeared under the horizon was ramping up if that was possible.

"Of course. It's obvious. Think of it this way. Ray gets to Canada. In any normal circumstance, his handler isn't going anywhere near him after the assassination. It's not a smart move. But something happens and he comes north of the border to see him. Ray held the first photo from Montreal as his safety net — he has that from the summer before and he's held it the whole time. And when Raul shows up, Ray pulls me in to get photos of their second meet, to establish their relationship over time. But this time Raul must have got wise to it."

"And when he learns about the second set of photos, he loses his cool and trashes through Jack's room. He can't find what he's looking for and decides to take it out on Jack."

"Poor bastard."

"And now I'm holding the bag." I didn't say anything more about the fate of Danny's friend and his involvement in it.

He put the car back in gear and we began our slow crawl along the residential streets into the orange glow splatted at the end of the road.

"That's right." The cab turned again, the headlights swung into the darkness and the black-and-white tail of a skunk showed for a second before skittering under a parked car. Danny's ugly smile, lit by the lights of the car behind us, appeared white and hungry in the rear-view mirror.

"Now I'm the loose end Raul wants to tidy up."

"The joys of being a detective."

"Thanks," I said. "But what about the third man?"

"Third man? You mean the blurry figure in the Montreal picture?"

"Yeah. Is he part of the conspiracy?"

"I think he's just an innocent bystander. That's what I assumed. Wrong place, wrong time. Crossing the street and getting caught in the photo. I suppose he could be your man on the ground here in Canada. The Canadian connection. You'd be surprised: there are weekend Klansmen up here, too."

And then we rode in silence as the city grew darker around us and I turned it all over again and again trying to figure it out. "But having the photos … it doesn't prove anything without the actual person. Anyone can have pictures of themselves shooting a game of pool in a tavern with someone else. It's nothing unless you can dig the other fellow up."

"True. But Ray's hand was pretty desperate. Once the deed was done, he must have been clutching at anything he could get his hands on to bail him out of the situation. It's one thing to pull the trigger; it's another to see your face on every news channel in the country and up on wanted posters on the wall. With these photos, at the very least he's building on his story and corroborating it. And you can imagine it can't be much fun to be Raul right now, knowing those photos exist. If they're splashed all over the newspapers during a trial, then the FBI will have to bury its files and cut someone loose, maybe put them under the plastic surgeon's knife like they do in witness protection; or maybe lose this Raul in six feet of sand in the Nevada desert. Like I said, it's the whole JFK mess all over again."

"That's how it is?"

"That's how it is."

"Okay. Take me home now. I better catch up with Rosie and make sure she's got to her safe place."

Danny was silent as he swung the car around. He dropped me at the house; I fumbled the key and it took me three times to get it into the lock, but it was good to know the bolt was still set. The door swung inward, I stepped into the house, and right away I sensed the emptiness and felt relief, knowing Rose was gone and safe somewhere else.

This case was big, so big it couldn't stop. It could change the world. This was newspapers, front-page exclusives, press conferences, and "we interrupt our regular programming" big. This was television reporters shoving microphones in your face, and pundits analyzing what it meant from their armchairs. And it wasn't just about the pancake makeup and bright lights — it was about real things: freedom, rights, justice, dreams, history being made, governments falling, politicians of the highest order sweating as they fought to answer the questions shouted at them, truth being made visible for citizens to see. It wasn't just a murder, one racist wing nut out on a limb doing something hateful, it was the political assassination of a leader, a conspiracy to ensure that the bank of justice remained bankrupt.

And it was on me, and only me. Danny was no real help. He'd already dodged responsibility once. I was the one with the secret photos that could swing the story and shine the bright light of truth on all the dirt these racist bastards were trying to sweep under the border between our two countries. It was on me. I'd been a fool to try and solicit Rosie's support. I needed help, but it was wrong to ask her. Wrong to put her in that position. The wrong time. I should never have pulled her into this vortex. She had her own stuff going on — our stuff.

I pulled the phone list from where it hung pinned to the fridge by a magnet and found her sister's number. My index finger spun the dial. "Tina," I said into the mouthpiece when she picked up on the third ring.

"That Patrick?"

"Yes, it's me. Listen. Is Rose with you?"

"She just arrived fifteen minutes ago. What's going on? No. Don't tell me. I'll hear it from her. Better I'm squarely on her side. No offence. She seems plenty upset."

"But she's safe with you?"

"Yes. She's just getting settled. Unpacking her bag."

"That's good. I was worried about her. I'm glad she got there."

"What's going on with you two, Patrick?" Tony, the brother-in-law, said something in the background I couldn't catch.

"I better let you go now," I said.

"What? You're not going to talk to Rose? What the hell's going on?" Tony's baritone again rumbled behind Tina's words.

"Keep her safe, Tina. And thanks for your help. Bye now." I hung the receiver on the cradle on the yellow kitchen wall, and the phone cord relaxed into its natural coil. I exhaled a long breath into the empty house, missing her but so relieved she wasn't there.

XIX

EVEN WITH HALF of my tired brain still in dreamland as I pulled up and out of slumber, it was apparent that the bed was too big. It was the first time we'd been apart since our wedding day. Our wedding night. Right or wrong, I nursed resentment about the way things had happened the evening before: Rose's unilateral decision, her refusal to talk to me, and her hightailing it to her sister's house without even telling me where she was going. She was somewhere safe, or at least safer, and that was good, but something about the way it had happened had made callouses on my heart.

But no matter how miserable I felt, there was work to be done. I'd been on the case for a couple of days now, and I still hadn't made it to the crime scene. I unchained a rusty bike from where it was locked in the dead-end space between our house and the neighbour's, dripped some three-in-one oil on the chain, and started south to the Exhibition grounds, where Jack Turner's body had been found. The Ex, as the fair was known in the local tongue, ran every year from mid-August to Labour Day, which the city counted as the unofficial end of summer; during the rest of the year the big swath of waterfront property was a wasteland of unused roads, cavernous venues, cracked parking lots, patchy grass, and empty halls. Almost all the rides came in on flatbed trucks as the summer wound down, piloted by carnies and crazies, with their yellow teeth, missing fingers, and ripe smell, but there was one roller coaster that was a permanent fixture: the Flyer. It was a replica of an older ride that used to be at the Sunnyside amusement park on the lake shore, where I'd gone as a kid. Its wooden frame ran a double oval loop; a chain system pulled the line of cars up the initial mountain and let gravity take over from there. When the train of carts rushed down that first stretch and into the initial curve, the whole structure rattled underneath; the adrenalin that pumped was half from the thrill of speed, and half from the terror produced by the shaking of the decrepit scaffolding. In the morning sunshine, the Flyer, with its peeling white paint and wooden slats, was a slumbering beast, quiet and still.

There wasn't much to see, just the dormant wooden behemoth standing, waiting for the fair to begin so it could roar again. I leaned my bike against the fence and walked the perimeter of the big wooden structure, marvelling at the maze of trelliswork supporting the track. There was a different feeling, in the ghost-town emptiness, from what you got at the end of the summer with the candy floss spinning, the barkers' cries filling the air, that huckstering spirit bursting from every corner, and the crowds jostling in line beneath the whoosh of the hurtling carriages. A seagull swooped, making a lonely screech. I'd completed my circuit and still didn't know where the body'd been found.

A couple of idle taxis waited in line outside the stadium. I approached the first.

"Hop in," said the hack, folding his newspaper and dropping it on the front seat beside him.

I shook my head. "Just trying to learn more about the body that was found down here."

"Last week. Not sure. You might try George." He jerked his head to indicate the vehicle behind him.

He sighed and reached for his paper, but before he could pick it up, I said, "You're not down here too much?"

His eyes met mine. "What? Look around. What could bring you down here, really? I had a fare that wanted the box office." He gave the trademark movement of his head, like it was a finger to point, this time in the direction of the stadium to his right. "So I stopped. Sometimes you pick someone up from one of the buildings — the streetcars barely run when the Ex isn't on. But look around. Nothing happens down here."

"But there are a few cabs here? Is there always a line, even off-season from the Exhibition?"

He shrugged. "Who can figure? Yeah, usually, it's a quiet spot. But something'll turn up. Or you get a call for a fare on Strachan or Dufferin. The Palace Arms. The Gladstone. You're not far from the city and can either pick up a fare here or be in Parkdale in five minutes. It's not a bad parking spot if it comes to that. Central."

"Thanks."

He returned to his newspaper; and I thought about a cab driver I knew and wondered if he ever parked down here.

I moved back down the line to the next car. "You George?"

George nodded without saying anything. He was younger with lank, black hair, a white shirt, and a cigarette hanging from his bottom lip.

"I wanted to know where the body was found under the Flyer. The guy up front thought you could help me."

His morose face slackened to disappointment that I wasn't a paying fare; he drew on his cigarette, put it in the car's ridged ashtray, looked somewhere south of my eyes, and said in a slow drawl, "Yeah, I can show you. I'll put the meter on."

All right, whatever: I had expense money. He dropped the flag, stepped from the car, flicked his butt, scattering a couple of gulls, and led me back to the roller coaster. We passed around the front of the ride and came out on the east side, away from the stadium and the traffic on Lake Shore, facing a big empty parking lot. He stopped.

"Here," he said, indicating a spot under the Flyer's first big incline. "The body was dragged in here and just left."

"Were you around when the police discovered it?"

"Parked up there. Where I am today." He looked out toward the lake.

"How was it found? I mean there's not much foot traffic down here."

"You're telling me. Yeah, but, strange as it seems, sometimes people come down here. Never know why, or where they come from, but there's always a few. So there was a guy down here last week, walking his dog in the early morning, and he noticed the gulls squawking over on the other side of the Flyer. The dog starts barking and drags him over there. Not surprising, with all the birds around. And when the dog barks, the birds scatter and — it's disgusting just to think about it — there's the body just lying there on the pavement."

"I thought it was under the Flyer."

"Under, beside. Close enough. There's a fence that keeps you from getting under there." He was right: the chain-link fence circled the perimeter of roller coaster, kept the mischief-makers out from under.

"It was just left out on the pavement?"

"That's what I said."

"No attempt to hide the body?"

"None. This is a quiet location. But left in plain sight. So the guy with the dog has to drag his German shepherd away from the stiff, and he comes over to the cab stand, like you did today — knows we have two-way radios. I call it in to the dispatcher, and within a few minutes there are a couple of cruisers down here, and an ambulance and they're putting the body on a stretcher, the guy's got the hypodermic still in his hand."

"The needle was there?"

"That's what I just told you."

"And the police took it?"

George took an unopened pack of du Mauriers from his shirt pocket and banged them against his open palm a few times before ripping the seal that wrapped them. He crumpled the plastic, dropped it onto the asphalt, and a breeze from the lake picked it up and took it inland, away from us. He pulled his eyes from the water to give me a look of disappointment. "I didn't see what they did. But, yeah, I'd assume they'd bag it up and take it away. Why not?"

"How long do you think the body had been there?"

"Just overnight. It was out in the open. It can't have been there for too long."

"The death was ruled an overdose."

"Is that right?"

"Does that make sense to you?"

"People overdosing on drugs? Not much."

"No. I mean, is there a drug problem down here in the fairgrounds?"

"What?" He looked across the barren asphalt and looked back at me as if I was putting him on. "Take a look around. Nothing doing down here. More up at Trinity Bellwoods, or out the other direction in Parkdale. But what would someone want to be here for? Cold wind coming off the lake at night. But maybe someone was messed up enough that they wandered down here and nodded off under the Flyer. I guess that's possible. But not likely. Maybe that's how they figure it but it doesn't sound likely to me." He squinted into the sun. "They say that kid was only twenty-four. That right?"

"Yeah. Twenty-four. What about if it was someone else that wanted to get rid of the body? Would it make sense for them to drop it down here?"

"Like if their friend overdosed and they didn't want to have to deal with it or call the cops to their shooting gallery?"

"Could be."

"I guess so. It seems cold, but I guess the body'd get found pretty quick down here. Not the worst way of doing it. Someone overdoses. They're dead, and the friends don't want to deal with the fallout if they call an ambulance. So they drop the body here — quiet place to get rid of it — but at the same time they know it'll be found: put it there to be found."

"You could drop it overnight when it's quiet and it'd be found in the day?"

"In the daylight, yeah. Whoever put it there wasn't trying to hide it. They were looking for it to get found and found fast. Or they didn't know what they were doing and just wanted to unload it quickly in a quiet spot that's pretty downtown. A body wouldn't last there unnoticed very long."

"But the needle was with him."

"Sounds like amateurs in a panic to me."

"And what about at night? Are you ever parked here during the night?"

"No, I strictly work days. But it's desolate here overnight. Nothing. Unless there's an event at the stadium, a football game, or a concert. Then it's busy. Or during the Ex, in which case you can't even get your car past the gates. But most nights I wouldn't come down here looking for business. Like I said, if you want the body to be found, this isn't the worst place in the world to drop it."

There was a pause in the conversation and on impulse I said, "You know Danny Blinken?"

"Blinken? No. Why?"

"No reason."

That seemed to end the conversation. "You want to cash out with me now? The meter's running."

"How much?"

He estimated a number and I passed him a bill and waved away the change, and he went back to his car.

I stared at the concrete that surrounded the roller coaster, the fence that ran the perimeter, and the rickety scaffolding. There wasn't much to see: strands of grass pushing through the asphalt, pieces of litter that had somehow dodged the fence and ended up in the lobster trap of the trellis, flecks of white paint that winter and wind had pried loose from the boards, all hiding in the stripes of shadow and light beneath the wooden frame. Nothing. I stared at the ground a little longer, shifting my position slightly this way and that, waiting for the clue — I didn't know what — that could tie it all together and catch my eye. But nothing did.

There was a sense of disappointment that there wasn't anything more; still, I'd scouted the scene and picked up on the mood and atmosphere. And, although it wasn't in the dark of night, like when Raul had dropped the body, I had a feeling of isolation here in the heart of the city. I'd only ever known the Flyer in the scramble of the fair, the screams of the teens as the first drop happened, the rush, and rattle of the cars, and the sticky smell of candy apples and fried grease; what I'd seen today, the windswept desolation, the concrete fields, the lonely cabs had been worth the trip. And George's words, that the corpse had been left to be found, echoed in my head, not that I could make sense of how it had served Raul to have Jack's body found. This lack of planning didn't align with his new professional look.

I retrieved my bike and pedalled off, unsure of my next move. I stopped at a greasy spoon on College for lunch, and tried to figure it out. After the empty phone call the night before and Rose's departure, there was the pervasive feeling that the danger had increased. Rose was safe at her sister's, but I worried about Amy, the photographer who'd developed the photos. And there was Rice. I'd always fought the idea of approaching him, stuck on the initial failure of the law to fully investigate Turner's death, and my residual distrust of the institution after encounters with it when I worked at the agency with Sid. But after spending yesterday morning with Rice and Cull and getting to know them a little better, I wondered if there was potential there: Rice might be someone I could work with. I didn't want to make my pitch at the station house where our conversation would be constrained by the other ears in the office. I didn't even know if I could trust him enough to call him there. I'd need to make my approach from the side.

At the diner's pay phone, I thumbed through the ragged white pages to look for Rice's home address and number but drew a blank. It wasn't too surprising: there were plenty of good reasons for an officer not to list his name and address in the public book. I'd have to go down to the cop shop after all. As I passed the Dundas rooming house, I saw the small police presence that remained, but neither of my detectives was visible when I scouted from close up. From a booth on Dundas, I made a call to the cop shop on Dovercourt, just a few blocks away.

"Fourteenth Division."

"Detective Rice, please."

"Just a second."

There was a click and a whirr, more ringing, and then his voice: "Rice here."

I hung up: he was in the building. That was all I needed. I walked my bike up to the station house, ignored the front door, and swung around to the back where I had a good view of the staff exit. There was still plenty of time before the end of the workday, and I was willing to wait.

AND WAIT I did, propped under a shade tree with my back against the trunk, my feet sticking out in front and my eyes trained lazily on the station's rear door. Some clouds moved in and there was a moment when it looked like they could pile up into a shower, but the sun rallied and chased them away. A slow trickle of people started from the building sometime after three, but still no Rice. And then he appeared, a jacket slung over his shoulder and his shirt a blazing white in the sunshine. He shifted the sports coat to his left hand, loosened his tie, and undid the top button as he crossed to one of the residential streets where the cops parked. I jumped up from under the tree and trailed behind. He was already inside his Grand Prix, painted an ugly shade of green, with the key in the ignition, when I bent down and tapped on the passenger-side window. Seeing my face, he scowled, leaned across the bench, and popped the lock. "What the hell are you doing here?" He threw his jacket onto the back seat as a way of welcome.

"I thought I'd come by for a chat." I slid into the car.

"I wish you wouldn't. It's not a good look for me. You should come in through the front door and speak to me in the squad room. This looks … it doesn't look on the up and up."

"Yeah. I was going to make a house call, but your name wasn't in the phone book. So, it was either this or walking right into the station, and I'm allergic to the inside of those buildings. I'm hoping our conversation is off the record —"

"And that's exactly why I don't like it. We should go back inside and do it the proper way." Contradicting his own words, he turned the key in the ignition and the engine coughed twice before achieving a shuddering, tubercular sort of life. The radio blared, and a song I didn't know with plenty of bass filled the interior. He snapped it off.

"But you're like me. You know something's off. And going through the official channels didn't work. You said as much yesterday. We can't talk about James Earl Ray in the squad room. Your investigation was —"

"My investigation? There was no investigation."

"That's why I wanted to talk. Maybe the two of us can work together — you behind the scenes."

He put the car in gear, and reversed slowly to angle out of the parking spot. "Uh-uh. I can't think how many things are wrong with that sentence. There is no investigation. You're jumping to a bunch of conclusions — a whole basketful. I'm not happy: that's one thing, but it doesn't follow that I'm going to risk what I've got to throw in with an amateur who doesn't even have a licence."

I let that go. "So, you'll sit on the sidelines and watch it pass by. You and Cull together."

"Fuck you, Bird. Leave Cull out of it."

"You brought him into it yesterday. Whatever. He'll retire soon enough. That leaves you. And you haven't been ground down by the system … yet."

Rice adjusted himself in the seat. His big hands dwarfed the steering wheel as they moved one over the other and the car turned onto College. The thumbnail of his left hand was bruised a solid black. He drove one short block and turned back south, circling by the station house. I thought our return to the starting point might be so he could stop the Pontiac and push me out, but it seemed this was his regular commuting pattern as he negotiated the one-way streets around the cop shop.

"Why don't I tell you what I've got?"

"Because there's nothing to talk about. The Turner case is closed and the Ray case doesn't belong to Police Services."

"Closed but not solved. Look, I'll put my cards on the table. I have photographs of the former tenant, the one the feds are now identifying as James Earl Ray; photographs of him at two different locations at two different times, and in both instances he's with another man. One was taken here in Toronto at the Columbia House, just down the street from my mother-in-law's rooming house, and the other is from Montreal, likely taken last summer. And my conclusion," — I'd take credit for what Danny and I had worked out together — "is that Ray had the photos taken for protection, to show he isn't in this alone. I have the photo of him with his handler. Turner had the photos." I wasn't going to rat Danny out — I wasn't sure I liked him — pretty sure I didn't trust him — but I'd keep him out of it, for now at least. "That's what happened at the house on Ossington, why his room got flipped, and why he was killed. Someone was looking for the photos. And that makes it a murder and not an accidental death."

Rice's Grand Prix, stuck behind a streetcar, crawled west along Queen Street. It stopped at the corner of Ossington outside the Columbia House, and Rice glanced over at the tavern, drummed on the wheel with his bruised thumb and breathed out a long slow breath. It almost sounded like a whistle. He looked at me. "And that's why the police were taken off the case."

"Someone didn't want you investigating," I said.

"Bingo. And we weren't happy about it. No detective likes it when he gets told not to do his job. We want to catch criminals and put them behind bars as much as the next guy. More."

"Except Cull."

He shook his head. "There's no need to run him down. There's more to him than you might think. Him and me, we said no, this is an open investigation and there were still plenty of leads for us to chase down. But we got the message straight: cease and desist. And it was coming from way up. You know what a police department's like — I remember you from the academy — it's all hierarchy. You do what you're told and that's the end."

I was surprised: I hadn't recognized Rice from my time at the academy. But then, getting turfed before I was halfway through for nearly killing a fellow cadet in a fight had probably given me a higher profile and clouded my memory of the experience. "But that's why I'm here," I said, "to offer you the opportunity to — well, if you can't work the case, you could at least share what you have to help me work it. And see justice done."

He sucked in air and shook his head. He was one of them: indoctrinated. They bled blue. They swore their oaths and signed their souls away and locked their hearts in safe deposit boxes at the beginning of each day. I was asking a lot. Too much. He swung into the right lane and took the streetcar on the inside on the stretch where we ducked under the rail bridge and emerged into Parkdale. Close to the Skyline, where Rosie worked.

"Let me put it to you another way: you know it wasn't a suicide. The police just swept that guy's life under the rug. He was no addict."

Rice didn't answer my question. "Where do you live? Where am I taking you?" He'd had enough of talking.

"I have my bike back at Fourteenth Division."

He swore. "A bike? So, dropping you in Mimico — that's where I'm going — doesn't work?"

"No."

"We'll split the difference. You can walk back from here." He turned the car north on Brock, pulled into the parking lot at the Brewer's Retail, killed the engine, and we sat and stared at the people coming in and out of the beer store that backed onto the train tracks. Rice rested his hands on the wheel even when the engine was off. "A couple of things," he said. "One is, in my short time of being a detective, I've never seen a call off a case like this one. We were just told to stand down: no questions asked, no explanation, no nothing. No one wanted to know where we were at, what we knew, how much progress — nothing. And if Cull and I weren't happy about it, neither was the lieutenant. No one liked it. There's no use looking for bad guys in the department. We're just foot soldiers following orders. If you want to take that and decide it lines up with FBI involvement — knock yourself out."

"Well what else would it be? At least you can tell me what you had so far."

"The call came early, so we'd barely started the investigation. I'm not holding back; there just isn't anything there. We were shut down before we could even get started." He paused for a moment, drumming his thumbs against the steering wheel, before making up his mind. "The biggest thing we got was the coroner's report. They pretty much need to work up their report regardless of an investigation or not — and the one part of it that was slightly strange was the toxicology report. Technically speaking, it was a drug overdose. But the drug they found in his body was not street-grade heroin. It wasn't like anything I'd ever seen here in Toronto. It looked like heroin, but it was characterized in the report as an opiate. It's not what's typically found in overdose cases. I'm not a doctor and I'm not a chemist, but my understanding of the way they wrote it was that it was described as pure. Closer to morphine than heroin. Medical grade."

"That could work. We both think it wasn't an overdose but administered to kill the victim."

"Yeah. It doesn't fully add up. The toxicology report also found barbiturates in the bloodstream, suggesting Turner was drugged and pacified before the opiate was injected. I mean, if you're going to murder someone, shooting them full of morphine doesn't seem the quickest or the most logical approach."

"But if it's what you had?" I said. "If you needed to make something happen quickly and that was what you had available. Make it look accidental — or at least open that possibility."

"Well, you're right there. Parts of the States might have that kind of heroin moving from their dirty little war in

Vietnam. By the time it reaches the streets, it's usually cut with all sorts of stuff, but if you've got connections and are getting your junk directly from the source, then it could be pure."

"Like someone on the inside, in the agency, might have the original uncut — pure stuff — if he had contacts back to Vietnam?"

"Possibly. That sounds more CIA than FBI to me. But it's not my department. I have no idea. I suppose it's possible. I don't move in that world of spies and shadows. I wouldn't have thought they'd be here in Toronto, but I wouldn't have thought James Earl Ray was here, either."

We sat for a while without speaking, two guys in a car in a parking lot. And in the silence, not really liking where my mind was going, but not being able to control it, I thought about Yusuf, the medical student in the house: maybe he had access to the drug that killed Jack. And there was Shirley, the nurse, who worked in the hospital downtown; she'd know her way around a syringe as well.

"How long do you think the body was there before you found it?" Checking what George had given me earlier, under the Flyer.

"It was put there overnight. No longer. And the time of death was sometime the day before. It was put there to be found, which again, doesn't completely add up. It doesn't seem the way a professional would do it."

I shrugged, struggling with the same question.

"I don't know," he said, as an entrepreneurial drifter with a bundle buggy full of empties pulled his wares into the store to cash out on the deposit. "Anything I could say would just be speculation. Maybe the goal was to hang the body on the city gates as a warning to anyone else who might be interested in this particular case — that's you, Bird, who should be getting that warning.

"Or maybe it's a question of arrogance," Rice continued. They're just so sure of protection, of having their backs covered, that it didn't matter to them where the body was dropped — or when it was found — as long as there was the possibility of an overdose they could lean on. They seem to be working with a level of arrogance that's scary. Not afraid of anything. They just took the closest and most convenient spot they could find. But with a little more effort they could have sunk the body in the lake, or taken it an hour north of the city and found an empty field to dig a grave in. It doesn't add up. On the one hand, it looks like a professional killing; on the other, it's pretty amateur hour."

A wiry guy with a thin moustache and two cases of Fifty passed close by the car, and a freight train pulled north along the tracks behind the store, making the distinctive clickety-clack of a railway.

"And another question," I said. "How come the chill came over the first investigation, on Ossington, but then they send the cavalry down to the house on Dundas. That doesn't make any sense to me."

"It adds up." The long freight was still rattling on the tracks behind the Brewer's Retail, but Rice spoke over it. "Ray's gone. They're happy enough to go through his rooms at the house on Dundas once he's left the country. It's all about Ray. No one else is involved."

"I get it," I said. "What they can't have is the connection to Turner's death. Ray had already bolted before that, and it points to only one thing, a second person's involvement. Someone covert. Unknown. If it's all tied in — and it must be — it shows their interest, that if nothing else — then the reason is that one of their guys is the killer. Their play is to cover up the handler and let Ray take the fall."

"Sounds like you got it all worked out." A trunk slammed across the parking lot and a car with an ailing muffler made a *vroom* before pulling away. "Time I was getting home. You, too." Rice smiled a sad smile that made me wonder what went on inside his head.

"You want to throw in with me?" I asked again.

"I just threw as much as I could. But no. No can do. I want to. But it isn't going to happen."

"All right, I'm off."

I closed the door, waved through the open window, and walked south to Queen Street. He gave two friendly taps on the horn as he passed and I felt the pull of Rosie, who worked just a block and a half away. The telephone was no way to solve a problem; it always seemed to choke the words off the moment they came into my throat. Maybe I could catch her at the restaurant and tell her I loved her, even if it still wasn't safe for her to come home. I ran the gauntlet of panhandlers that lined this stretch of sidewalk and made it to the plate-glass door. It opened outward before I could reach for the handle, and Rosie stood before me; we were both surprised and flustered as we stood facing each other, her on the threshold, and me standing on the street. She made a movement to get around me.

I stepped back. "Rosie?"

"What are you doing here?"

"I came to see you."

"You need some change from my tip jar? Is that what brought you down here?"

"No. I wanted to talk to you."

She walked west, weaving through a clump of shoppers hovering over baskets of fruit the greengrocers had stacked on the sidewalk. The beggars sensed her purpose and kept their eyes down as she swept past. But I, more the fool, was trotting behind her, trying not to break into a run, thinking about what I might say as I followed behind. Her determined stride had her hair bouncing on her shoulders. At the bus stop, she halted, turned, her face a rigid mask.

"You say you want to talk, but you've got nothing to say."

"I love you."

I'm not sure that anything changed on her face. An intensity lived behind her eyes; something physical passed through my body and I wavered. The Lansdowne bus pulled up in the pause; there was a shuffle of anticipation from those waiting, and the sigh of the doors opening to disgorge passengers. Rosie remained still, unaffected by its arrival and the bustle around us.

"I'm sorry —"

"Sorry?" she said. The heads that had discreetly turned away, the averted eyes, the housewives shopping, the crazies out on a day pass, the shopkeeper in her apron, and the father with his daughter on a tricycle, tried not to stare, but they weren't trying hard enough. "Sorry? Keep your sorries to yourself. And leave me alone."

I made a step toward her, to put my arm on her shoulder, to reassure her, to create contact, to bridge the divide.

"Don't touch me." Then louder. "Don't you dare touch me."

The crowd perked up, interested now, as they judged the situation. Rosie climbed the stairs into the bus. The bystanders took a last glance at me, before following her. She disappeared and I stood on the empty patch of the sidewalk. The doors wheezed closed and bus pulled out from the curb.

WAKING UP ALONE the next morning wasn't so fun. There was a job call-out from a contractor in the northwest of the city that I was supposed to be following up on, and I was dragging my feet. With no Rosie to push me out the door and make me go, it was too easy to find excuses.

The phone rang in the distant kitchen, and I thought about earlier in the week when I'd let it ring and then the dead click when I finally picked up. And I thought about Rosie and wondered if she'd had a change of heart since yesterday; maybe it was her and she wanted to talk. Maybe she wanted to come home. But it still wasn't safe here. The phone rang. And it stopped and started again. I thought about rushing down the stairs and into the kitchen; I thought about it some more and the ringing stopped.

It could've been Flavia. Or maybe Rice had a new idea he wanted to share. It could've been Danny, Yusuf, or even Shirley with some remembered tidbit of information that tipped the scales. It could've been anyone.

I put on my cleanest dirty shirt, tucked it in, found a pen and a couple of tokens for the subway, brushed my teeth and combed my hair and looked at myself in the mirror and didn't like what I saw too much, but couldn't do anything about it. I grabbed a jacket in the front hall, found my keys and wallet, and wondered how I could convince an employer to like me when I didn't even like myself. I needed a job, yes, but I wanted to finish this case first.

I could go back to the rooming house on Dundas and take another run at Shirley and Yusuf to determine what they knew about Jack and Bridgman; I could get the photos out and look at them again, turn them this way and that, and take a magnifying glass to them and stare harder at the third man. I needed to follow up with Amy and warn her about what was going on. There was plenty I could do, but I pulled the door shut behind me, turned the key in the lock, and started on my trek up to Weston to see about the construction jobs they were promising.

It was a long way there and a long way home with very little to show for it. The bus bumped and jolted as my mind still stuck on the mystery man Raul and that day he'd knocked on Amy's door. I worried about her. By the time the subway screeched into Ossington, I'd made up my mind that I'd give her a call and make sure. I walked to the far end of the platform, took the escalator up from underground, and was out the back exit and into the sunlight. What a strange world to rush under the city streets through the dark tunnels and arrive in a different place.

At home I was no sooner through the salmon door, prying my job search shoes off with the toe of one against the heel of the other — the laces could wait until I wore them again — when the phone started ringing. Did it ever stop? But its shrill insistence chased my early morning lethargy away and I was back in detective mode, rushing down the hall in my socks, to pull the receiver off the wall. "Hello."

"Patrick Bird?" inquired a sharp female voice.

"That's right," I said.

"This is Constance Turner."

"Good morning, Mrs. Turner."

"Good morning. Yes. I've tried you a couple of times today already, but you're not an easy person to reach."

"I've been busy." I didn't say doing what.

"That's what we like to hear. I'm calling for an update. What news do you have for us?"

News? "I'm doing a lot of legwork. I don't have anything to report right now, but I can tell you that the approach I'm taking is looking at photos Jack took, which might have compromised others and led them to —"

"To murder." She called it by its name, to make clear that the act had been done by another hand and banish the idea of an overdose.

"Yes, murder."

"Well, what are the photos of?" She was all business.

"I don't want to go into details right at this moment." I realized that in my haste I'd gone too far. "I need to tie up a few things first, but I'm moving forward. I think something will be breaking soon." Back at the agency, Sid had handled the clients. PR wasn't my department; all my life, I'd worn my inability to say the right thing as a badge of honour.

"That's all you've got for me?"

"That's all I've got right now."

"We're paying you by the day, so don't go taking any holiday on the beach on us. We're not living under a money tree out here." Everyone was getting cranky — but she wasn't far wrong. "We put our trust in you. You can have until Monday, but we'll need a report then at the very least."

"I'm working the case." It was only a half lie. "And it's coming along if you can just be a little patient."

"All right, Patrick, but it's hard to be patient with everything that's happened. We'll need a report with something to go on, or we'll have to close this off. Gregory and I have been talking, and it just doesn't seem that you've given us anything yet. There has to be something for you to tell us."

We said our goodbyes, and I was alone in the kitchen with the receiver in my hand. The client was pressing, and I thought I better do some work and figure out what I could tell them on Monday. I got the pictures from their hiding place and spread them on the table. That first photo, the one with the mysterious third man, a quarter of his face caught in the blur of the too-close shot. I squinted but couldn't bring him into focus; if I stared long enough, I'd convince myself I'd seen him somewhere before, but I couldn't get to the point where I believed it. He could have been anyone. I tried to force myself to look, but my heart wasn't in it. Connie's call had got me thinking about family, about kids and moms and dads. And me and Rosie. I took the phone list held on the fridge by a magnet, found Tina's number, and dialled. It rang four times and then I heard a voice that sounded close to Rosie's, except it wasn't. A baby was crying in the background.

"Hello."

"Hi Tina, it's Patrick."

"Oh, public enemy number one." The crying in the background went up in pitch and volume.

"I'm calling for Rose."

"About time, too." And then, not to me, but to someone in her house. "Here, take Gabby." A chair scraped against the floor on the other end of the line, and a deep voice sounded in the background. The teeming and tumultuous life squalling in that kitchen across the city made me aware of the cold silence in mine. The crying stopped abruptly.

"Is Rose there?" I tried again.

"No. She left for work. She's working the early shift today."

"Can you tell her I called?"

"Do you think that's going to help? You've got to do more than that."

"What time does she get home?"

"Home? Jesus Christ. Where's your head?"

"You know what I mean. To your house."

"You really are lost. Look, I have to go now. I'm busy."

"Okay. I'll try at four."

"Four-thirty." The phone clicked; the drone sounded. I hung it up on the cradle and looked at the photos again. Three men in that first image, the one in Montreal that Danny hadn't taken: two that I knew, and the blurred image in the foreground of the mystery man. Was he part of the group, or just a stray pedestrian, caught in the frame of the shot? That third man blurred beyond recognition, just a fraction of his face, one eye visible. I spun the picture slowly, looking at his cropped and grainy cheek from different angles to try and see some resemblance that could tweak my mind. Nothing clicked, but the harder I looked the more the possibility emerged.

A rap on the door interrupted my study. Was this Raul, just like I'd wanted, coming out into the open so I could play the hero? Was it happening already? I scooped the eight-by-ten glossies back into the envelope, dropped them into the album cover, and filed it back in the row of records beneath the turntable. The banging on the door kept up and, as had become commonplace in this new life, I felt the terror scaling up the back of my neck. I'd wanted Raul out in the open, and now it was happening, my bravado turned and ran. I had Rosie and the baby to live for. Sid had tried to warn me. And Cull. Why couldn't I be like Cull? Take the cheque and clock out and go home and rest up.

The metal frame of the mail slot made a few clicks, a clank, and a dead final clunk; I watched with horror, from my spot in the kitchen, as fingers pushed the aperture wide. They reached inside and were less than twelve inches from the door's interior knob. The wrist looked too thick to squeeze its way through, but I didn't want to wait to find out. I grabbed a knife out of the drawer and started down the hallway.

AS I APPROACHED, the hand withdrew, a pair of eyes appeared in the rectangular mail slot, and a voice came through the cut-out: "Bird. Open up. I know you're home."

It was Rice's clear baritone: the fear fell away. I ducked into the parlour, dropped the unneeded knife on the low table, and turned to unlock the door.

"Open up." Something in Rice's voice had changed; an urgency that was new rang in his sharp demand. Or perhaps, in our last two meetings, I'd been behind the curtain and heard his real voice, the man beneath the uniform, but now something had shifted again and the full-on cop-speak, the barking of orders before the door was kicked in was back. But there was no reason, I thought, with my hand on the deadbolt for the situation to have changed. I hesitated a second longer, snapped the bolt and swung the door open.

The screen was propped against his shoulder. “Did you hear the news?”

“What?”

“Cull. I thought maybe he called you.”

“Cull?”

“He had a heart attack. He’s in the hospital.”

“Shit.” I was sorry in a distant kind of way, but couldn’t figure what it had to do with me. “That’s not good news.”

“He wants to see you. Told me to bring you by his room.”

“What?”

“He didn’t say. I’ll wait in the car.” No one ever wanted in the house.

Lunch would have to wait. I laced my shoes and grabbed my notepad. My stomach said something sullen and demanding, which I ignored as I scooped up my keys and wallet and dropped them into my pocket. And out the door. The sun was up on the top of a blue sky. Rice had switched out the Grand Prix for an unmarked cruiser.

“What’s he want to see me for?”

Rice put the car in gear and pulled away from the curb. “He’s way up where he lives.”

“In hospital?”

“The new one. North York General.” I didn’t get north of Eglinton much.

“It was a heart attack? Not anything anyone did to him?” I asked.

“More what he did to himself.”

We rode in silence for a while, driving northward, up the rises in the land that lifted us above the city, away from the lake and the bustle of downtown.

"What's he want from me?"

"He wants to talk to you."

"About —"

"He isn't exactly what he seems. He has that …" Rice blinked twice as he put his foot on the accelerator and the car jumped through an amber light. "He was my partner," he said as if that explained something. "He's had a rough year. His wife, Cathy, died of cancer last summer. I think he'd be retired and with her if she were still alive, but then when …"

I grunted something noncommittal, trying to figure out the complicated relationship of their police brotherhood and where I might fit in it. "And now this."

"Now this."

"Is he … what are the doctors saying?"

"Doctors? They don't say anything to me."

"No, but to Cull. To his fam—"

"There is no family. I told you his wife died earlier this year. And there aren't any children."

I didn't say anything. Rice filled the empty air. "It's a lonely life."

"But how serious is it?"

"How the hell would I know, Bird? You can see for yourself when we get there." We took the cloverleaf onto the highway, the arc swung us three-quarters of the way around a circle, and then Rice hit the gas and the vehicle slung onto the great wide road, accelerating and merging into the traffic. The wind roared as it sheered through the window, and my hair lifted and danced in the gale. I cranked the glass up, my ears popped, and the interior of the car stilled and quietened, and there was just the high whine of the wheels on the concrete like a scream that wouldn't stop. At

Leslie, Rice slowed and took a long off-ramp that ended at a red light. He turned left and we went under the highway on a broad suburban avenue and there was the hospital, shining and new, in front of us. We found a parking spot in a big lot that was mostly empty and entered through a revolving door, him first, and then me, each of us in our own sealed pod that processed us into the building. It was all new; there wasn't even the hospital smell of stale urine, old people, and bleach.

"He's on the fourth floor," said Rice. We waited at the elevator bay, uneasy, not talking and I realized I'd be back at a hospital in seven months, bringing Rosie into one of these big, faceless buildings and dropping her off and wondering what would happen and worrying and fretting in the waiting room with its vinyl couches and old magazines until the nurse came to call me back to meet our brand-new baby and see Rosie, and everything would be okay. It was all so white and clean. So unlike our messy life at home, a strange place for a baby. The metal doors of the elevator split in two to welcome us. It purred as it rose to the fourth floor. I closed my eyes and could barely feel the movement. Rice touched my arm, and the doors were opening; there was a landing with a big window and the city in the distance through the glass.

"This way." Down a long hall, past the nursing station, past the racks of plastic lunch trays with their puréed delights, uneaten and unappetizing; past the spare beds floating unmoored; past the big-wheel wheelchairs and the tall, thin machines and monitors that looked like an alien race. Around a corner, another hallway, a door, a room, two beds, and in the first one, an old man in a blue gown with tubes coming out of his arm, and more tubes coming out of his nose. The other bed was empty. A smile broke the old man's face in two. It was Cull.

Rice sat in a chair the same shade of green as his car with his back to the window, and I dragged a second one over from where it rested beside the empty bed.

"Cull," I said. I didn't even know his first name.

He smiled his cracked grin again and took my wrist in his grey hand; the veins, red and blue, popped in relief. Tubes ran out the back of the wrist and up to a bag of clear liquid suspended above the bed. "Patrick Bird."

"Freddie said you wanted to see me."

"True." Even lying on his back, maybe dying, his grip was strong as he held me there and looked into my eyes.

The questions of life and death were too much and I looked away. "Here I am."

He nodded his head as if even speech was tiring. "Yeah. Something like this" — he used his free hand to indicate the hospital room, himself and his monitors, the whole set-up — "gets you to thinking. Puts things in perspective."

"I guess so."

His laugh turned into a cough. When he stopped, he lay back in his articulated bed and looked tired again. "That wasn't good." His raspy voice lost its scratch and just came out as a whisper.

Rice got up and looked both ways down the hall. "You want some water, Dave?"

"Yeah," said Cull.

"Let me see what I can find." He disappeared through the door.

Cull turned his gaze back to me, and something about the depths of his blue eyes was disarming; I shifted in my seat. "Sometimes," he whispered, "sometimes when you know something's wrong, even if you can't do anything about it at the time, you can ..." He paused and lay back on the angled bed and breathed a little. He squeezed the heel of my hand and said, "They've got this new gizmo down at the office. A Xerox machine. You ever heard of one of those? It can copy any piece of paper. You just put what you want to take a picture of on the glass, push the button, and it spits out a copy. Can you believe it?"

A nurse appeared in the room. "Dave, you're supposed to be resting." Cull gave her his weak smile, but it didn't have the intended effect. "Don't you go grinning at me, thinking you can charm me into changing my way of thinking. Rest is what the doctor ordered." She turned her efficiency on me. "And you. You the son? Your father needs rest."

Cull's laughter turned to coughing again.

"Do you see what you've done?" she said.

Rice was at the door behind the nurse. He sized up the situation and turned away out of the firing line.

Cull managed to stop coughing. "Brenda, I need some water."

"You need rest. Forget about water."

"If you could get me a cup of water, then I promise to rest."

"He promises," she looked at me. "Okay. I'll get you some water, then." She turned abruptly and almost bumped into Rice.

Cull's grip tightened on my wrist. "You'll find my keys in the jacket in the closet," he spoke quickly and harshly. "My apartment. Eleven-twenty-two Don Mills Road, number 203. Go get the keys." He released my wrist, and I found a narrow door to a narrow closet. His grey tweed was in there and in the right hip pocket a ring with four keys held together on a soft plastic fob from a car dealership. "A big file in the bookcase by the bed. Might be something for you in there. You should take a look." He lay back on the pillows, his eyes on the ceiling, looking more tired than before. "It looks like a cube, but it's a bookcase."

Brenda was back with the plastic cup she'd taken from Rice. She handed it to Cull, watched him sip at it, and when he was finished, took it from him, put it on his rolling tray, slid the tray away from the bed, and pushed a button on the side to lower Cull back to horizontal. I watched as the machinery took him back down, almost as if he were sinking beneath the surface. I moved closer to him and said, "Thanks, Cull. You didn't have to."

He nodded. "I wanted to."

"Out," said Brenda. "Mr. Cull needs his rest." The old cop lay flat on his back now, resigned, obedient, the patient, but she wasn't leaving until the room was cleared. "Out."

"Bye, Cull." I wasn't sure how final it was.

Rice was skulking in the hallway, successfully avoiding Brenda, smirking at me as I came past the nursing station. I lifted the key chain and jingled it. "Give me a ride over to his place?"

"Sure."

"Says he has a file on this case."

Rice shook his head. "You can know someone a long time and not really know him, if you know what I mean."

"Yeah."

And then we were back in Rice's unmarked car, touring through the new suburbs: flat, low bungalows with their expanses of lawns, spread out like green skirts, strip malls and gas stations, power lines and parks, young trees and two-door garages, humpback bridges over railway lines.

Opposite a shopping centre, his low-rise apartment complex was made of yellow brick. Rice slid the car into an empty space in the visitor parking and we stepped out into the sunshine.

"Poor bastard thinks he's going to die," he said.

"That what you think?"

"No idea. But at least this way, you're moving the evidence. Getting it out of the apartment before anyone else finds it." He laughed harshly. "Fucking tough old bastard. Too proud to die."

After a couple of false starts, I found the right key for the front door. Even though it was only to the second floor, we took the elevator because we didn't know where the stairwell was. It was a small box with mirrors on three walls, and it felt like maybe I could see eternity if I could just get out of the way. The second-floor hallway smelled of yesterday's cooking, liver and onions; the carpet was grey-and-brown stripes fading into one another in the windowless space.

I found the apartment key on the first try and we were inside. There were dishes piled beside the sink, but they were the anomaly and spoke of the interruption of an emergency. The rest of the living room and dining room was ordered and orderly: the table cleared, the sideboard dusted and home to a framed photo of Cull's wedding day. A TV on a low table, and a recliner facing it. Down a hallway, past a half-open door to a washroom, and then the darkness of the bedroom. I flicked the overhead light. The bed was made with a military crispness. The pillows didn't even have the dent of a sleeping head. There was a small wooden box to one side with a hook holding the two halves together. It was hinged on the back side, and when I lifted the latch, I pulled the two sides apart. Inside it was hollow; each half had a horizontal plank to make a hidden bookshelf. There were a couple of paperbacks, *The Call of the Wild* was one, and a manila file folder leaning on an angle. I lay it on the bed, closed the bookcase back up, and hooked the hook to hold it there. Once everything was back as I'd found it, I carried the folder into the living room. Rice was stretched out on the recliner.

Inisde the file was a page full of text and plenty of numbers, too, and in the top right-hand corner someone had glued Danny Blinken's mug shot.

"The rap sheet," said Rice, looking over my shoulder. Danny wasn't the most handsome guy to start with, and the police photographer had caught him at his worst, looking like an unwashed weasel: shirty, shitty, and shifty.

"You seen this?"

"I knew Cull was doing background checks on all the tenants, but we got called off it so quick that I didn't think he'd gotten around to pulling the records."

"Maybe he did it after you got called off."

"Possible. Like what I said before, sometimes people you think you know can surprise you." He pointed down to the list of arrests for Blinken at the bottom of the page. "A real piece of work."

I flipped the page to get to the court details. "Convictions, as well. Time inside."

"It doesn't exactly fit with your photos and your mystery man, Raul," said Rice.

But I barely heard him; I was trying to make sense of this new information. Behind the rap sheet there were more Xeroxes, the details of the police and court records. I was about to pop a paperclip off a sheaf of paper when Rice said, "Let's get out of here. This is yours now. Take it home and look at it there. I don't like the idea of us being caught here if some Samaritan from the force shows up to pick up a change of clothes for our old man in the hospital."

I grunted agreement and folded up the file. We locked up, found the stairwell and headed out, and all the time I wasn't sure what this new information meant.

Rice dropped me back home, which felt less like home than ever. I ate a lonely dinner, overcooked spaghetti and sauce straight out of the can; it was painfully clear that Rosie wasn't home. Cull's file was open on the table in front of me; Danny's mug shot was from a while back: shorter hair and no sideburns, the face narrower. I lost a bunch of strands of pasta from my fork, they landed back on my plate with a splash and a spatter of the red sauce jumped onto young Danny's forehead. The tomato-sauce wound didn't help his looks. I shovelled another mouthful in and turned the page. The rap sheet wasn't pretty: break and enter, assault, extortion. Arrests, two convictions, time inside, parole. But it was all back in time: the most recent arrest was in 1957, over ten years back. And while I wasn't trying to make excuses for Danny, it seemed like the kind of stuff that got him locked up was in the past. On the other hand, just a couple of days back, I'd squeezed him hard enough to get him to admit he was back in the extortion racket. Maybe it seemed less terrible this time around because he'd been putting the clamps on James Earl Ray and not some granny down the street. And who was I to judge extortion and coercion after some to the stunts Sid and I used to pull on the divorce circuit?

Did Cull have a theory he wasn't telling me? Or was he, like Danny, throwing the file at me and letting me do what I wanted with it? The old man wanted to help but he was out of touch with the case. He didn't know all the details about James Earl Ray and Raul. He didn't know about the photos. I slurped the last strand of spaghetti up and in and felt it slide down my throat, unsure what to think. I thought I'd had it all figured out — I still did — and now Cull's help wasn't helping much. His support boosted morale, but it didn't change my theory of the case.

Danny had fucked up when he was younger. So what? I knew someone else who fit that description pretty good, too. I took another look at the mug shot with its spaghetti-sauce wound leaking red on the forehead, and it stared back at me. I dug the other photos out from their hiding spot in the record sleeve and laid them on the table, covering Danny up. That photo of the three men — that grainy face so close it seemed to decompose the harder I looked: half a line of a craggy nose, the blurred arm of the glasses across the temple, and the sheen of light on corner of the forehead. They all began to suggest pieces of a composite that lived in another part of my brain, but I couldn't pull them together to make the picture complete and willing it to happen seemed to have the opposite effect. I had Ray and Raul. Wasn't that enough? I had Jack's killer. That's what I needed. If only I could draw him out into the open, I'd trust my luck to bring him in. I might be a hero yet.

I gave up staring and watched some TV with my eyes on the screen and my head somewhere else, gave up early, got into that big bed, and had a lonely sleep.

DOWNSTAIRS THE NEXT morning after sleeping late, I was making breakfast; two fried eggs, a pair of yellow eyes, frazzled and bubbling, stared up at me from the round face of the cast iron pan. Coffee was dripping through the filter, two pieces of bread were getting brown in the toaster, and Danny's file was still on the table when the phone rang.

I snatched the receiver from its perch. "Hello?"

"Patrick." It was my mother-in-law. A lie materialized in my mind at the first sound of her sharp accent; I was prepared to say Rose was at work — which wasn't an untruth — but wasn't the whole story, either. But Flavia surprised me: she didn't want Rose, or to know about the baby. She started right off with: "I saw him."

"Who?"

"The tenant. The one who ran away."

"He's dead, Flavia. They held the funeral."

"No, not him. The other one. The one who paid. Paul. He paid before he left. I saw him. But they give him a different name now. They call him something else."

"Okay." I could see where this was going. The troop of RCMP officers in street clothes that had raided the house on Dundas must have let the neighbourhood know; maybe they went door to door with the wanted poster. "Did the police —"

"No. You don't understand. I saw him on the TV this morning. They say he was arrested for killing that black preacher in Memphis. King. Dr. King, that was his name. He's in England at the airport. What's he doing there?"

"On TV?"

"Yes. On the TV. Right now." It wasn't a leaflet passed across a table, or a wanted flyer posted on a hydro pole: the story was out. Everywhere. I could imagine it already: "We are interrupting our regularly scheduled programming to bring you this breaking news on the arrest of the most wanted fugitive in …" And network television was pushing it around the world as fast as the cable lines would allow.

"Patrick?"

"Yes, I'm here."

"Not Paul. They call him a new name now. James. They call him James. That's not what he told me his name was. What did he lie to me for?"

What was there to say? Being deceived never feels good, even when you get paid upfront. Sometimes that makes it worse. "Yeah. He doesn't seem like such a good guy now. He's a killer. He killed Martin Luther King."

"I don't know if I can keep this house any longer. When people lie to you and don't tell you who they really are. They could be anyone. I don't want the police back at my house. Mr. Yusuf doesn't like them. Mr. Danny doesn't like them. Do you think he really did what the TV says? I can't trust anyone."

"It'll be okay." I didn't believe it, but I said it.

"Do you think so?" Her anger dialled back as if my bland reassurance really meant something. And then in one of those abrupt shifts that were such a part of her conversation style, she said, "And Rose. How's Rose and the baby? I can talk to her?"

"Sorry. She's at work."

"When does she get home?" I was grateful that the family grapevine hadn't reached her ears yet with news that the two of us were busted up.

"I'll let her know you called," I lied.

We said our goodbyes and I hung up.

The coffee had dripped, the toast had popped, and the eggs were getting cold, still staring up at me from the plate. I put my knife into the yolk and watched it bleed yellow.

Flavia's call changed things: now James Earl Ray had been arrested, the guilty, the handlers and backroom boys, the higher-ups and fixers and agents, would start to sweat. The moles and shadows would be covering their tracks. Tidying up loose ends. Perfecting their disappearing acts. Erasing memories the only way it could be done. Their boy was in custody now. He'd been taken alive, and not in their country; he wasn't in a Dallas holding tank with the doors open to all and the media milling in the hallway. There might be a new Jack Ruby yet, but it'd be harder to choreograph from across the ocean. I had the photos — right here on my kitchen table — the proof of the other man. Or men, if it came to that.

I needed to call Amy. I'd left her hanging in a dangerous place. A place she knew was tough, but just not how tough. Even tougher now. Raul was out there. The remnants of the egg yolks had dried hard and glued some crumbs from the toast onto the plate. I balanced it on top of the other dirty dishes in the sink, found my notebook, and dialled her number. The unanswered ringing of the phone reminded me of the call Rosie and I had taken just a couple of days earlier. But my waiting on the line, letting the phone ring without pause wasn't a threat: it was desperate hope. Maybe Amy was in the darkroom and it was taking her some time to get out to pick up the line. Maybe. But not this long. Maybe she was out getting an early lunch; maybe she had a shoot on location. And maybe it was all hope and nothing else.

The panic meter climbed a couple of notches. I added my empty mug to the Tower of Babel in the sink, laced up my shoes, and started north to the warehouse studio. It was grey and humid outside, and the streets were inexplicably quiet for a Saturday morning. The boys weren't convening one of their street hockey games, their mothers weren't dragging their daughters and shopping carts down the sidewalk to Bloor Street; the teenagers weren't smirking and preening for each other. Men weren't leaning against cars, lazy, shooting the breeze with the neighbours. Even the traffic was quiet today: the parked cars immobile on the side of the road, the central lane empty. Halfway up the street, a man sat shirtless on the sill of an open front door. A woman stood behind him in a shapeless black dress with one hand on her hip, and the other resting against the door frame. I could see their lips moving in conversation as they both faced forward, not looking at each other, and something about their pose seemed timeless and typical, and it was hard to believe I was rushing up the road to save a life and fighting forces that spanned the globe from Memphis to London and back again.

I felt the rush inside: it was coming closer. I knew Raul's name and face and had the photos to prove it; James Earl Ray was in custody. Wasn't that the provocation needed to force Raul to step out of the shadows and show himself? Then I'd have my chance at him. Through the gauze of grey, a bleary sun showed from behind the foliage of a front-lawn maple and got in my eyes; I tried to stare it down and send it back where it came from, but it ignored me and shone a little harder. I picked up the pace.

The rolled-up newspaper was gone and a little black rubber wedge on the concrete floor held the fire door today; the elevator waited calm and quiet at the end of the hall. It made its torture-chamber groans as it took me up to three. And then the too-quiet hallway and the echo of my fist pounding on the door and nothing. Sometimes silence can be the worst sound in the world. I twisted the knob and it held, clicking sharply on its truncated radius; I tried the door with my shoulder and it still held; I tried the lock with a few tools I kept in my pocket for occasions like these and got the knob to turn, but the door itself was held steady by the bolt and chain on the other side. Someone was inside.

And so it was back down the elevator, out past the sock factory, and I was staring at the outside of the building from the parking lot.

The last stage of the zigzag fire escape was hanging down, sweeping to touch the ground on the northeast corner of the building; someone had been careless, and I feared it was Raul. Almost like he wanted to make my job easier. My mind was racing, jumping to conclusions, getting ahead itself, but that was my job. It was a shaky climb up to the third floor, the rusty slats underfoot as tight and tense as guitar strings. The whole rickety structure was clamped to the side of the old building by a few untrustworthy bolts. Three floors up wasn't too much, but it felt like a long way, exposed to the world the way I was. The spider plant was thriving on northern exposure; the ashtray had dried out; the chair was folded and leaning against the siding. One of the panes in the matrix of the window had been smashed, and the whole panel hung halfway open on chipped hinges. I pushed the window wider and it croaked into the quiet as I stepped through into Amy's studio. There was none of the destruction I'd seen in Jack's rooms: it looked the same as when I'd last visited.

"Amy," I called, but I felt it. The unmistakable absence of life. I tried again. "Amy!" It was a studio apartment. One big open space. Nowhere to hide. Except for a standing screen with three sections — like actresses used in their dressing rooms in old black-and-white films — blocking off the back corner. This one showed a smiling dragon with a forked tongue, the body snaking behind it, onto the next panels against a background of soft mountains. Behind, there was a clawfoot tub. It was three quarters full of water coloured red with blood. Amy was there, half submerged, her wrists held up, resting on the rounded lip, all bled out. I was too late. There was a knife with the blade open and blood dried the colour of rust sitting on the lid of the closed toilet seat. It could have been a suicide, but I knew it wasn't. Raul had killed her, but it sure as hell felt like my fault. "Sorry," I said even though I knew she couldn't hear me.

I dipped a finger in the water: it was pretty cold, but maybe not all the way there. There wasn't a pulse to feel, just the raw wound of the severed artery. When I put my hand on her forehead, it felt colder than the water. The tap dripped and ripples fluttered across the tinted ocean, hit the porcelain wall at the end, thought about bouncing back, and gave up.

I'd jumped to conclusions and I'd been right. Right but late. Too late. And there was no consolation in being right; it was more the accusation of not acting fast enough. Raul was out tidying up loose ends and he'd tidied faster than I could get here. And I'd be next. I didn't like leaving Amy alone in the cold water, and I knew I needed to call it in, but it was time to get home and get ready for when Raul came calling for me.

I made a quick stop at the convenience store on the corner opposite the warehouse to see if the newspapers on the rack by the counter had anything on Ray. But neither the *Telegram* nor the *Star* had their afternoon editions out — and yesterday's news wasn't cutting it. The radio behind the counter, usually tuned to teeny-bop pop in stores like this, had been hijacked by a cultured voice discussing the Heathrow capture of James Earl Ray. The arrest was something, but it was a long way away and my work was here. From Memphis to London — it didn't seem like the radio had figured out yet that it'd been via Toronto.

Amy's death made things clear: Raul wasn't a shadowy figure lurking on the edges of the investigation. He wasn't a product of my paranoia, egged on by the warnings of others, he wasn't a hypothetical threat. He was for real. My fears had proven right. The warnings of others had been right. I was sick with what had happened to Amy, sick that there was more I could have done; but there was also, after all this time of speculating, a level of relief in the surety that I was closing in on Raul, that I'd get my showdown with him. It was time to be home. My fast walk broke into a trot as I came south on Delaware.

I turned the key, swung the door wide, and stepped inside my empty house. Except it wasn't empty: an unknowable shift in the way the air hung in the hallway; a half-sensed alien smell; squeaks heard or imagined — something was off. But the feeling was felt without producing action, like seeing a drinking glass in the air as it fell from the table to the floor — seeing it, but being unable to do anything to avert the coming crash — the water splaying in flight, the descent, the impact, the crystal shattering and scattering, the liquid loose and free and then flat and still on the floor. All my bravado about a showdown, all my desire to draw Raul out into the open evaporated in an instant. I stood inert, a passive witness, as the rogue agent, Turner's killer, Amy's killer, Ray's handler, Raul, who'd been stalking my footsteps all these days, slid out of the living room and stood facing me at the far end of the hallway.

XXIV

RAUL WAS HERE. In my home. Here: I'd drawn him out into the open. And all the warnings I'd heard from day one were coming true. Perhaps there was still time to turn and run, still a chance for escape. But why? This was what I'd wanted. This was what I was holding out for, waiting for. Raul had been called from his lair. A calm washed over me as I stared down the hallway at his thin figure framed in the kitchen archway. It was happening. I was here, face to face with him. He was here: the resolution to the case was close.

"Bird," he said, backlit from the light streaming through the kitchen window behind him. "How nice of you to come home. I've been waiting."

"Aren't you going to introduce yourself?"

"You know who I am. Raul. But you'll forgive me if we don't shake hands." My eyes adjusted to the light and I saw he'd given up his suit for a short-sleeved knit shirt. Casual for a summer day, less imposing than the first encounter, when I'd cowered behind the locked door of Amy's studio.

"You don't look much like a Raul."

"Jimmy said the same thing. James Earl Ray. We can say his name now. Everyone knows it. No more hiding behind aliases, pretending. I'd hoped he could have made it to Rhodesia like he wanted. He could've lived out his fantasies there. But he went and fucked it up. That's just like Jimmy. So much talent, but always the ability to fuck it up at the last moment. Come." He motioned me forward into the kitchen.

It didn't feel so good being invited into my own home.

"Come on. Move it. If you do what I tell you, this doesn't need to be painful. Or messy."

It was too late to bolt now. Mesmerized by his unblinking gaze, I drifted forward, without will, crossing the threshold into the kitchen, stepping closer and closer to death. The warning bells sounded, but too few, too slow, too far away — like hearing the neighbour's alarm clock through the wall. He walked backward, his eyes drawing me forward and I followed.

"Killing me won't help. Too many people know already."

"The funny thing is, killing usually does help. Take it from me." His smile showed his eye teeth. "Sit down." He indicated the seat between the table and the wall; he'd created a natural barrier and was penning me in behind it.

I sat on the chair in the yellow kitchen, conscious of how wrong things were going. Rosie was pregnant with our baby and here I was trying to negotiate with a psychopath. Not even fighting. "You should've killed Ray then. Right at the start. That would have solved everything."

"Do you think you're telling me something I don't know?" His face married the intensity of the moment with the calm of the professional. "I told them that at the beginning. But blood makes the bosses a little squeamish. And they have their rationale: they think it doesn't play well in the recruiting market if every time we hire a gunman they end up dead a week after the main event. But they don't understand that these drifters with an axe to grind who want to take a stand and be American heroes are a dime a dozen. They're as dumb as mules, these wannabe heroes — you could build an army of them and they'd do anything in the name of patriotism. They're so naive and idealistic it hardly seems fair to use them."

"And so you cast your net a little wider and kill the people a little further afield." I rose from the chair as I got myself worked up. "First Turner, and now —"

"Sit down." There was no room for discussion; a switchblade appeared in his hand and the blade snicked open. I dropped back into the chair.

"The funny thing is," he said, "I didn't kill Turner. Someone did it for me. Never had an assignment like this one. No one believes me — not the bosses, not you, not anyone, but it's true. I knew Turner had the photos. I tossed his apartment but couldn't find them. He was on my list: I was waiting for his return, but it didn't happen. He went and got found under the roller coaster, good and dead. Of course, a body in the open turns up the heat for everyone; I got blamed for that — 'What the hell were you thinking? How could you screw up so badly?' But it wasn't me. That's not my style. I'm not leaving a corpse out in plain sight."

"What about Amy?"

"Amy?"

"The photographer in the studio on Dupont."

"What about her?"

"You killed her."

"Oh really? I heard it was a suicide." He showed his teeth when he smiled to let me know he was joking. "It's different now," he conceded. "Now Jimmy went and got pinched in London."

"You're not innocent."

"Of Turner's death, yes. On my word." He held the switchblade, pointing down on the table, and eased the blade back into the housing and then clicked it back open. "Someone beat me to it."

We'd reached an impasse — and arguing about Turner didn't seem to matter at this stage. He broke the silence. "You have the photos. And you've seen them." The knife was pointing into the Formica table, it spun slowly in his hand, and the narrow window of the blade reflected the room and spun it around us. "Time to hand them over and we'll say goodbye. Clean and painless. Just like that suicide up on Dupont. And I'll be on my way. Let's do this the right way; no one needs to get hurt." Fiddling, he clicked the blade back into its home.

"What I don't get is how Ray came to choose that rooming house of all the ones in the city?" If I could keep him talking, if I could extend our time together, if I could find the break I was looking for.

"The photos, Bird. We don't have time for this. You should know by now that knowing things only leads to trouble. And don't deny you have the pictures. I'm sure you remember our first meeting at your friend Amy's where you got them printed."

"Why didn't you look for the pictures at her place?"

He shook his head. He wasn't about to be drawn into that discussion.

"And if I don't get the photos?"

Again I heard the spring and click of the knife and the blade popped back into sight.

"Then you die knowing I'm going to kill your wife as well. Your choice, Bird. Have it as you will. Not just you, but her also."

"Leave her out of it."

"That choice is yours, not mine."

Our eyes met across the table; the spell was broken, the chill flooded in.

"This is how it works." His voice was soft and calming; his eyes were hard and cold. "You get the photos for me, then we'll go upstairs, and you can lie in the bathtub and close your eyes, and I'll be there with you, and it'll happen fast without even a second of pain. And then you're free and your family's free, and no one need ever know. I'll tidy up everything and it's all taken care of."

He was selling me a funeral package; I'd be choosing the casket next. "You didn't tidy up at Amy's."

"Let's just say I was in a rush to come down here and see you."

I stood to get the photos, and my legs shook so much that I needed to put my hand on the table to steady myself. "That's right, Bird. Let's do this."

"But Turner was filled with pure heroin," I said. "If it wasn't you, who was it? You're lying to me."

"Was he?" he purred. "Pure? I have no idea who it was. That's your mystery, not mine. But you see the way I work. I'm not in favour of fancy locales, amusement parks, and flashy deaths. I keep it simple. Clean up after myself and disappear. Come on, we're getting somewhere. Get the photos, and we'll finish our business."

His words didn't reassure. The blood drained from my face, and as I came around the table, I felt my legs giving way. My hand stretched out grabbed the Formica in an effort to brace myself. Raul reached for me, and, in a reflex of self-defence, I jerked my hand from off the table to ward off his arm. My legs wobbled harder; my balance went, and I fell, my head snapping back against the kitchen tiles.

My eyes opened to the view of the stationary ceiling fan half hidden behind his narrow face. He slapped me twice on either cheek, "Jesus, Bird, what is this bullshit? I've never had a fainter before. It's like I walked into a soap opera. Sit up, man." He pulled on me and propped me against the cupboard where we stored the pots and pans.

"Give me a minute." I was woozy.

"Or how about you get your shit together, and you can have the rest of forever to have your dizzy spell? If you can't do it yourself, just tell me where the photos are and we'll finish this up." Impatience ruined his radio voice.

"You got a minute for me, don't you?" I tried to find something that wasn't hard and cold in his eyes and failed. "If I have a glass of juice, I'll be okay. There's some OJ in the fridge, and then I'll get the photos."

"Jesus Christ," he said. "I thought I worked with a bunch of losers. I do. But they have courage and conviction, you're just fucking pathetic."

"Juice."

"Juice," he said. "Fine. Juice it is. I'll get you a juice, and you'll get me the pictures and the negatives, and then we'll say our goodbyes." He crossed the kitchen, and my fingers explored the bump on the back of my head where it had met the tiles. The fridge door squeaked open, and its white light mixed into the yellow room. It was right then, while his head was in the insulated box, that I heard the click of the lock and the creak of the hinges as the front door swung inward. I couldn't see down the hall; I didn't need to. The only person with a key was Rosie. I pushed from the floor and got her in my sightline so I could warn her of the danger. I'd make the sacrifice and she could live.

"Are you even sure you have any fucking juice?" said Raul his head still in the fridge.

I lifted myself off the floor, took an unsure step, gathered what little strength remained, and shoved him as hard as I could into the open fridge.

Sprawling forward, his head hit the shelving, and knocked a carton of milk from the top rack. The knife popped out of his grasp and skittered across the tiles. A jar of raspberry jam tottered, fell, and shattered red on the floor.

"What the fuck?" He'd been hit, but he wasn't out. A tub of mayonnaise rolled in a semicircle and came to a stop. "I'm going to fucking kill you." He straightened up, still facing into the open refrigerator.

A second crude shove from behind had little effect; he was ready for this one, braced against the big appliance. Hope was fading as I tried to pin him against the open fridge; he ducked under my hold, swept his right leg out and around, and knocked me back to the floor. I went down, my hands breaking the fall this time, my face meeting the ceramic tiles in a gentle kiss, not a hard crack. He stood over me, panting, blood dripping down his forehead from where it'd collided with fridge's rack.

"I'm going to fucking kill you." His foot made contact just below my ribs. "And you're going to feel it. You're going to feel every inch of it. Every second of it. Trust is important. Trust is —" He stopped.

My breath was loud in my ears. My kidney throbbed. I rolled and saw Rosie's bare feet and ankles and the bottom of her pedal-pushers in the archway where the hall met the kitchen and the puddle of milk ended.

"And what have we here?" asked Raul.

Rosie didn't respond.

It didn't slow his friendly banter. "Cat got your tongue?"

I pushed my chest off the floor, trying to get a knee under me when I felt the sharp return of his pointed shoe in my side. I sunk back down.

"Come a little closer, darling. Don't be shy. We're all friends here. *En famille*, as they say in Montreal."

"Patrick," said Rosie. It was good to hear her voice, to hear my name. It was something to hold on to, but the price was high, and tears sprang to my eyes.

"Oh dear," said Raul. "I'm interrupting a family moment. Bit of a third wheel." He wandered, comfortable in his casualness, across the kitchen to where the knife lay on the floor. Using the distance between us, I pushed myself up to my knees and got a foot flat on the ground. "Don't be stupid, Bird. I hate these emotional scenes." The blade flashed in the light. "Let's stick to business, and it doesn't have to be awful." He wiped a hand across his brow and came away with a smear of red. "That hurt. Hurt my head. Hurt my feelings. You've lost my goodwill. My professionalism. Now it's personal." He smiled his cold smile.

I felt Rosie's hand on the inside of my elbow as she helped me back to my feet.

"And now the photos. I need the photos." Raul crossed to where we stood together, just inside the kitchen. He kicked the mayonnaise jar aside as he moved toward us. It rolled across the floor, hit the baseboard, and stopped. The open knife danced in his hand as he came closer. "You, come with me." He grabbed Rosie and her fingers slid from my arm. "My very own little motivator, to get Mr. Bird to work." His eyes met mine. "The photos."

Rosie stood pinned to Raul: his arm crossed above her chest, his hand clamped on her shoulder, the defiant angle of her chin, the fear in her eyes.

"I'll get the photos," I said.

AS SOON AS I turned away from the kitchen to retrieve the photos from the record stack, I heard a truncated intake of breath ending in a muted whimper. I spun back to Raul and Rosie: "What the hell's going on here?"

The knife was there, pushing Rosie's chin upward. Her eyes rolled in her head, scrabbling across the ceiling, avoiding mine, and I knew she knew this was the end.

"Feisty," said Raul. "Be still. Too much squirming'll cause an accident." His mirthless grin straightened out. "Let's get this done before I lose my fucking patience." His other hand had moved up her chest to her collarbone where it held her steady beneath the blade. "That's right. Hold still. When you're twisting this way and that, I can't help it if the blade slips."

"Let her go."

"Move it, Bird." A bead of blood popped through Rosie's taut skin, crimson on the pale flesh. It slid down her neck, trickling under her collar.

"You're cutting her, you bastard." I took a step back into the kitchen, feeling my anger.

But anger was all around: Raul had it, too. "The photos," he said.

Rosie's face stiffened, and the wheel of her gaze scraped past mine. We'd both heard it in Raul's tone.

"Just let her go. She'll sit quiet. Won't you, Rosie?"

"We're doing it my way, Bird. Get moving."

Rosie kicked a heel at his shins, and he cuffed her across the face with the knuckles of the hand that held the knife.

"Patrick."

Hearing her say my name held the same magic it always did. I loved her with all my heart. We were starting a family and this is where I'd gotten us. All the magic between us and there was nothing I could do. Nothing. There was no response. I couldn't even meet her eyes. In the living room beside the stereo on its low table, the records were still stacked in alphabetical order. I was working backward up the letters when Johnny Cash's *At Folsom Prison* showed up. I paused to look at the cover portrait: the sweat pouring off his face, the angle of his head, the fear and determination in his eyes. Johnny's face staring back at me, threatening to look away, but holding steady, asking a question that couldn't be put into words, but one I understood all the same; and it felt like he was saying something to me and only me, and everyone one of those unsaid words rang true and echoed inside.

"Bird?" Raul's voice broke my reverie. "Let's get this done."

I pulled the Blood, Sweat & Tears album out from its alphabetical home and returned to the kitchen.

"They're all here." I pushed the corners of the sleeve in, popped it open, and tipped the contents onto the yellow table. The manila envelope spilled out onto the surface, and the black disc of the record — the dust cover had been lost somewhere in the detritus of life — came tumbling out and landed beside it.

Raul made a crablike shuffle across the kitchen, dragging Rosie with him. "Here, Bird. Here."

I picked up the envelope and shook the contents onto the table. The pictures sprawled across the Formica.

"Wait," said Raul. "What's this one?" He held the anomaly, the picture Yusuf had identified as Montreal, between a thumb and forefinger.

With his attention captivated by the unknown picture, Rosie jerked forward, the knife blade scraping a red line on the underside of her chin. Raul's body turned as he was pulled, and the picture fell from his fingers. The record was already in my hand and I flung it as hard as I could. It caught him on his forehead where the first wound still oozed blood. Rosie broke free. Raul blinked twice, stunned, but still holding the knife. I grabbed a chair and swung it like a baseball bat, the legs catching him across the shoulders and deflecting up onto his head. The switchblade clattered on the tiles. He wavered, conceded to gravity, and slumped forward onto all fours. I kicked the blade away, swung the chair over my head, and brought it down across his back, determined to drive him into the ground. I swung it again and its leg splintered, the wood breaking across his hip. I reached for another chair, taking my eyes from him for a second. And when I turned back with the new one raised above my head, Rosie was there. Plunging the knife into his back. There was a gasp of pain, a grunt, a spasm, a momentary stasis, the full and final collapse, the red splotch leaking across the shirt, the crimson pool forming beneath. A gurgle. A rattle. Silence. We stood staring and panting across the last twitches of the body.

"Rosie," I said.

She didn't say anything.

"Rosie."

She raised her eyes to mine. "You almost got me fucking killed."

"I know. Both of us."

"Jesus Christ. I just came home to get some clothes." She felt at her neck and came away with a smear of red running down her forefinger to the webbing at the base of her thumb. "I killed someone. I just killed someone. Oh my God." Tears came. She looked at her reflection in the mirror hanging over the sink, and that made it worse. She wandered around the kitchen, looking for a chair to sit on, not finding one, standing on shaking legs, and collapsing to the floor to sit with her back against the stove. I felt tears coming, too, sat beside her against the oven, and we held each other until the tears stopped and our breathing slowed to somewhere close to normal.

"Stress isn't good for the baby," she said.

"Stress like that can't be good for anyone."

"I'm serious."

"So am I."

"What are we going to do?"

"I'm not sure." What were we going to do? A fly appeared from somewhere; it landed, pawing its furry feet across the sticky expanse of Raul's shirt. The afternoon was still going and light streamed through the back window where it felt like no light should be, making a rectangular spotlight on the figure lying face down on the floor.

"We should call the police." Rosie lifted her head, looked at the body, shuddered, and buried her face in my shoulder. "Something. Anything. We need to get this body out of here."

I pulled her tighter, trying to calculate the stresses of the call, the criminal trial, the uncertainty of a verdict, the political pressures brought to bear: the risk of it all. Not for Rosie, not for us.

"Let's get out of this room. We'll go upstairs, you can rest, and I'll figure it out. Something, so we never need to think about this again." We knew that was a lie. We'd never forget the moment, the struggle with Raul, the knife at the throat, the dead man on the kitchen tiles. I reached for her hands, took them in mine, and helped her up. We climbed a clumsy climb, side by side, up the narrow staircase; I sat on the toilet seat while she took a shower and washed her wounds clean, and the steam swirled around the room. I wrapped her in a towel and we walked together into the darkened bedroom. She crawled beneath the single white sheet and said, "I killed a man," and we both thought about that for a while. I lay beside her in the bed, holding her and thinking about Raul on our kitchen floor.

"It'll be okay."

"Do you think so?"

"Yeah." But I didn't know what I thought.

"The body?" she said.

"Yeah."

"What are you doing with the body?"

"I'm going to get rid of it."

"Are you calling the police?"

"I don't think so. I don't know."

"I killed him."

I could say I'd been the one who held the knife in my hands and committed the final act. I could say it, but once the lies started, they only multiplied until there were so many you were tripping over them. Who knew what questions would be asked, what analysis would be done, and what steps taken to challenge the story? Who knew how lawyers and prosecutors plied their trade and cut their deals? Who knew what powers would be unleashed, what retribution lay in wait, what forces would swirl and sweep around us? Nothing seemed impossible in this new world of blood and guns and knives; nothing seemed secure enough to trust.

"I killed him," she repeated, and I realized time had passed; the light from outside was fading, and the room was dark. I couldn't even see her face just inches from mine.

"It's going to be okay," I said, even though I didn't believe it. I lay by her side and after a while, I heard exhaustion overtake her and sleep settle on her body like a blanket. I crept through the darkness, squeaking on the floorboard that always squeaked, and slid through the door. I closed it slowly, turning the handle, settling it into the housing, and easing the latch into the plate. There was a soft click. I released the knob and started down the stairs.

In the kitchen I flicked the light switch; the fly had invited some friends over and their party was in full swing. They were having a good old time on Raul's back and on the crimson lake, getting their feet red and sticky, and I didn't care one bit. I got the phone book and dialled a number. The photos were still on the Formica, careless, spread in a fan like the winning hand slapped down on the felt.

It rang three times and a voice answered, "Diamond Taxi."

"I need a cab."

"What address?"

"Not just any cab. I need Danny Blinken. Is he driving tonight?"

"That's not how dispatching works."

"It's how I need it to work."

A sigh, followed by silence.

Cull had given me Danny's file and let me know all the news, all the terrible things he'd done, how I couldn't trust him this way or that, why he made the perfect suspect. But it just so happened that he was the kind of friend I needed right now. I could hardly call Rice for help burying a body.

"Danny Blinken," I said and gave him the address.

"This time only. I'll be talking to him about it, too."

"You do that."

"And another thing. I don't know where he is in the city or whether he's got a fare. What his situation is. You could be waiting a while."

"I can wait."

"All right, I'll pass on the message. But it's not my job to be your messenger boy."

"Thanks."

The line clicked in my ear and the drone of the signal sounded.

It was no fun in the kitchen with the light on and less fun with the light off. I found a beer in the back of the fridge and sat outside on the porch in the darkness to wait. The street was quiet, the night like any other — but not for me — cars passed, a couple out for an evening walk pushed a stroller, a cat strutted down the centre of the road; the bristled hunchback of a raccoon clambered onto a fence, where it stood in an eerie silhouette against the glow of the city. The cab, its top light lit, the red of the brake lights brightening when it passed the house, reversed into a parking spot. The engine died and I crossed the street and pulled on his door. It came open and a light went on inside the car.

"Howdy," said Danny.

Still on the sidewalk, I leaned into the car and said, "I've got a problem. I need your help." He looked as shifty as ever. So what? He'd done some things he shouldn't have, some of them not pretty at all, he wasn't a choirboy — and that's exactly what I needed right now.

"I never like conversations that start like this."

"I know." There was a beat of silence. "You got me into this: now I need some help getting out of it."

"No, no. Keep me out of that."

"You gave me the photos."

"Helped you out. What happened?"

"Come and see."

He looked like he was about to say something but closed his mouth when he saw the expression on my face.

"Why me?" It was a fair question. I couldn't shake my distrust of him, but he was the only one who could help me do what needed doing.

"I told you. You got me into this in the first place. You gave me the photos. You started the whole thing happening. Now you can help me out." And he had a car.

"Bird. A real fucking friend in need."

"I killed Raul." I needed his help, but it didn't mean I trusted him enough to tell him the truth.

"Good for you." When he saw I wasn't joking he said, "Jesus Christ."

"Yeah. Not good for me. He's on my kitchen floor right now."

"And ..." He drummed his fingers on the steering wheel. "And you're not calling it in; don't want to put that big target on your back. I hear you. You killed their guy; it must have been because he was coming for you — and he wouldn't do that without a reason. And then you get into the reasons why he was coming for you and the whole James Earl Ray conspiracy starts to unravel. Not good."

"Just help me get rid of the body. If we can rid of that ..."

"Yeah, yeah. If you make the body disappear, you solve your problem and their problem. If James Earl Ray ever says anything about the mysterious Raul, his handler, the man in the background who guided him into it, then no one knows anything; he doesn't exist." He turned his open face on mine. "You're smarter than I thought."

I didn't let him know I was only thinking of Rosie; once the body was gone forever, she'd be safe, too. But I wasn't about to interrupt while he talked himself into it.

"But the other side of it is ..." He could even argue with himself. "The other side is you still have a chance to change history: to let the world know who really killed Martin Luther King, to expose the racist bastards at the centre of the this for who they truly are. You could be the hero: on the right side of history. You call this in and there'd be a fucking media frenzy. First call, the police. Next, the press. You turn the photos over to the reporters. You expose the bureau, the government, and the whole corrupt system." He turned and flashed his bad teeth at me. "But there'd be danger in that approach. God, you'd be up against it."

He stepped up out of the cab, slammed the door, joined me on the sidewalk, gave me a friendly shove, and we were back in the present. "Best to bury him and bury him deep. You don't want to live the rest of your life looking over your shoulder, wondering when they're coming for you." He hadn't even seen the body on the kitchen floor yet. "Because they're coming if they think they owe you. They don't forget. If not you, your family, that pretty little wife of yours."

I'd had enough: he was right. I was no hero. I pulled away from him and started toward the house.

He followed behind me, the ugly excitement in his voice: "Let's see what you got."

I led him down the hallway and flicked the kitchen light. The knife still stuck out of Raul's back like the flagpole left by a forgotten explorer; the pictures, in their loose fan, still lay on the table; the flies still pawed their sticky feet in the blood.

"The friend in need." Danny was beginning to enjoy himself, and as his mood elevated, mine soured. "I'm not touching anything." He gestured at the knife.

I stooped, yanked it up and out of Raul's back, dropped it into the stainless-steel sink, and turned the tap on full. The water streamed, got red, came clear, and circled down the drain.

"You got a carpet we can roll this guy in?"

I picked the switchblade up with two fingers, shook a few drops off, dried it on the tea towel, not to dry it, but to make sure that Rosie's fingerprints were wiped clean and away forever, clicked the blade back inside, and lay it on the counter. "There's a rug in the front room we can use," I said. "We'll need to shift a few pieces of furniture."

"Won't be the first time I play moving man," said Danny. "Usually, I leave the meter running."

We tilted the loveseat off the floor and pulled the corners free from under the legs. I dragged the recliner into a corner to make some space to roll the rug in the darkness of the unlit room.

I grunted.

"You did it," said Danny. "You killed Raul. You beat their guy and came out the other side."

And I almost believed it was true.

XXVI

WE DRAGGED THE carpet, heavy and awkward even without a body inside, along the narrow hallway. I shoved the kitchen table into a corner, its metal legs doing a shuddering dance across the tiles, picked up the broken chair pieces, and lay them on its surface.

Through the chairs' spindles, Danny studied the array of photos of James Earl Ray. "So this was what all the fuss was about." He was careful not to touch.

"You should know. You're the one who took them."

"Glad this one bought it." He indicated the body on the floor. "After what he did to Jack."

I wasn't thinking about Jack at this stage; my mind was still fighting to push aside the memories of the knife against Rosie's throat, the look of terror on her face, the bead of blood on her neck.

Danny spoke again, pointing to the sticky mess on the floor: "I'm not kneeling on that."

"Give me a second." I went to the mudroom for the mop, had the handle in my hand, thought better of it, and reached for the rag bag instead, then returned to the kitchen.

On my knees I cleaned the blood up with an old T-shirt soaked in the sink. It took a few passes, with me wringing the full rag out into the drain, rinsing it out, and going back to work, before the worst of it was mopped up. The soiled rag and shards of glass from the broken jam jar made a garbage pile on Raul's back. The next rag, dampened under fresh water from the tap, cleaned the final smears and stains from the floor. I used an old towel, thin and full of holes, to dry the tiles. I added it to the pile building on the dead man.

"Beautiful," said Danny.

"Help me out." I unrolled the carpet until it lay flat on the clean floor, stretching from the body to the kickboard under the sink.

Danny wasn't helping at all; he was looking at the Blood, Sweat & Tears album cover with the picture of the band holding ventriloquist dummies of themselves on their knees. "This was your hiding spot?"

I didn't say anything; even now, I didn't like that he knew where I'd tucked the pictures away.

"Great place to hide them. Unless you're having a dance party." The record lay on the floor near Raul's head, the black vinyl cracked and smeared. I looked back at the cover and the image of my future flashed: bouncing a baby on my knee, responsible for the child who would become the adult. A lot of responsibility was pushing itself into my world.

Danny knelt at the far end of the body. "I'll take the legs." The end he'd left me, the head and torso was where the blood was. We rolled Raul onto the carpet.

"Nothing as heavy as a dead man." His talk grated as I wondered how many dead men he'd known. Cull's file only told me the times he'd got caught, but right now I needed his help and his car. We rotated the body farther onto the rug and the killer's face showed; it was calm and still, the eyes reflecting the light from the fixture overhead, but the spark that signalled life was missing. I threw the switchblade onto his chest. Without a word, working in unison, from either end, we pulled the corners of the carpet over the body and tucked them under. And then we rolled. It didn't look like much; but, most important, it didn't look like a body. I washed my bloodied hands at the sink.

"The pictures?" asked Danny. "Aren't we putting the pictures in with the body?"

I looked at them where they lay on the table; the photographs that had caused so much pain for Jack, for me, for Rose. Even Danny. A reluctance held me back. "Leave them."

"After all the trouble they caused?" And he'd given them to me.

"I'll figure out what to do with them later. Burn them if I don't want them." As long as I still had them, there was the possibility I could do right in my own small way.

"You're the boss. Easier to dispose of than a body, I guess." He lifted his eyes, glassy and protuberant, to meet mine. "You're not thinking of suddenly playing hero, are you? I thought we'd been through all that."

"No hero here."

"Good." He cuffed me on the back for the second time that night, leaning into a presumed brotherhood.

His touch was aversive; I could punch him in the face and put an end to his thoughtless cheer. I needed help, but it didn't mean I enjoyed his forced and flagrant friendliness. "Bring the car around the back. We're not carrying this out the front door."

He caught my tone and responded in kind: "Yes, sir."

"There's only one entrance to the alley. You have to go in off Dovercourt."

He nodded, silent and sullen. The door banged behind him on his way out; I bolted it, hoping Rosie hadn't been woken. The cab's engine revved in the quiet of the night, and its roar decrescendoed as it pulled up the street. In the kitchen thirst caught up to me, and I looked in the fridge where Raul's forehead had met the shelf. He'd been right: there wasn't any juice in the barren space, white and square like a modern vision of hell. The milk had all been spilled, so I gulped a glass of water from the tap. The red blur of the cab's tail lights appeared through the back window. I set the unwashed glass in the sink, grabbed the photos from where they lay on the table, and dropped them back in the manila envelope. Now that Danny had seen the hiding place, I resisted putting them back in the same sleeve. I snapped the broken record in two and dropped the halves into the trash. The cover of *Child Is Father to the Man* still lay on the table: the men with their children on their knees. Danny's footsteps in the mudroom forced the issue and in a rush I stuffed the envelope of photos back into the empty sleeve, opened the oven door, and slid it onto the top rack.

Danny pushed in through the back door; we found a couple of shovels in the mudroom, and he took them out to the car while I scribbled a note to Rosie and left it on the table. From either end we hoisted the carpet, heavy and awkward. Danny backed out of the kitchen, hunched while I pushed from the back, the load sagging in the middle.

"Wait." He lowered his end. "I'm losing my grip."

I dropped my side to the floor; we tried again, and this time made it out to the taxi. The roll wouldn't bend to fit in the trunk, so we shoved it halfway across the back seat. I circled the car, opened the back door, and pulled at the carpet from that end.

"Glad he wasn't any taller," said Danny, shoving Raul's feet clear of the door.

"Let's go," I said, panting and sweating.

I slammed the door shut on Raul in the back and slid into the front seat. The house was dark and quiet and still, and Rosie was asleep on the second floor. I didn't want to leave her now, but there wasn't any other way. I opened my mouth to ask Danny what he thought, to hear him reassure me, and didn't.

"Where to now?" he asked.

"I don't know. You have any ideas?"

"Construction site," he said. "Somewhere where they're pouring concrete soon. I have a couple of ideas." It was good thinking. Almost too good, I wasn't sure whether it was reassuring or unnerving to have help from someone who knew what they were doing in this situation.

Danny pulled out of the alley and we headed north under the street lights and the pale moon, the unmoving roll of carpet on the back seat. We drove in silence through the night, the meter off, the city gliding by outside the windows. North and farther north: the houses thinned and grew short and squat with wide patches of land around them, pedestrians disappeared, and at last even the street lights were gone. The darkness deepened, and the large, empty swaths grew wider and more frequent, and the housing thinner, sore-thumb apartment blocks, and the expansive wastelands of construction sites — the churned soil, the heavy machinery, the mounds of materials.

"One of these?" I asked.

"Somewhere around here."

I looked out the window, into the darkness, and saw my face in the glass, staring back at me. By now I'd convinced myself I'd killed Raul, believed it in my soul.

"Just a question," said Danny, "whether we're better off dropping the body under public housing or the new university?"

"I don't care. So long as it's never found."

"If we do it right, and it's not found in the next week, then it won't ever be found. We're just looking for the right spot." He swung the car off the main artery and we curled down a street with empty lots on either side. Fencing made of vertical slats of wood attached by wire appeared on our right, and Danny slowed the car. "This could be it." He killed the engine.

We walked the perimeter, looking through the fence to see what lay below in the murk of darkness at the bottom of the pit.

"Here," I said, finding the end of the fence and rolling it back, so we could step through. The early summer sun had baked the dirt under our feet to a hardpack. We peered into the construction site from where we stood at the top of an earthen ramp that led down one side of the massive foundation. Starting down the incline, we passed into the deep moon shadow as we descended into the pit, and it was difficult not to feel the eeriness of the experience as we went underground. At the bottom of the ramp, the ground was untouched by the diesel-powered tamping machines; the dirt was soft and fresh.

"This is it," said Danny. "We're not going to find a better place."

I grunted in agreement. We went back up the long ramp and came out of the night shadow into the grey glow of the city. At the car, with the silence of the night all around us, we dragged the carpet out of the back seat. This was the moment when we were vulnerable, when the stray pedestrian or lost driver might stumble upon us, catching us in the act.

"We'll move the body, you can grab the shovels, and then I'll park the car. We can't leave it up here like a signpost to anyone who passes," said Danny.

"All right." The carpet hung in a shallow arc between us, pulling against our fingers with each step.

We dragged it to the corner, and I pulled on my end, heading to the far side where the ramp led into the pit when Danny said, "Where the hell are you going? We're throwing it over the side."

Some vestige of decency resisted treating the body this way — even Raul. But Danny, in his callousness, knew how to do this. We swung the carpet hammock-style, a whispered one, two, three, and gave a final heave to lift it over the thin fencing circling the perimeter. The bundle rose up and over the vertical slats and dropped into the darkness. There was a beat of time — a beat too long — and the muffled thud echoed up out of the pit.

Back at the car, I pulled the two garden shovels from the trunk, one short and square, the other pointed and curved like a misshapen heart. Danny slid behind the wheel. "Once the cab's out of sight, we'll be home free. Give me fifteen minutes and I'll be back." The engine roared in the silence and the headlights brought colour back to the world. Danny pulled away from the curb and swung into a U-turn on the wide suburban street. The cab's beams swept the barren land; scrubby grass, piles of dirt, fresh white curbs, and a young maple, thin and lonely, held upright by a steel post and binding wire.

The red of Danny's brake lights flashed like an obscene gesture — a final fuck-you — at the end of the road, and I wondered if he was coming back.

Unlike Raul's body, I took the long way down, circling to find the earthen ramp; with each step the shadows grew thicker, and the light faded further until I hit level ground. It was pitch black as I began the search for the carpet roll. A creeping fear preyed on me as I stood in the darkness, not seeing Raul's shroud, imagining the impossible, that he was down here with me, alive, scuttering on the dirt floor, the knife I'd left in the roll now held tight in his bloody hand. My fears rose with each second that passed without finding him; rational thought stopped meaning much in the lightless pit. Without a point of reference, it was impossible to be systematic in the search. I tripped and went down, and the white noise of terror roared in my ears. And then I understood: I'd found Raul, fallen right over him. And now, lying next to him, knowing his body was here, where it had landed, my face flat on the cool dirt of the foundation floor, wasn't the best feeling, either. I crawled to the end of the roll and reached in. Just to make sure. My blind hand found a foot in a shoe that was stiff and still and the world felt halfway sane again.

Cursing Raul, I dragged the carpet roll into the middle of the pit, where the moonbeams made a pale illumination to work in. I lay the square shovel alongside it, picked up the spade, and began breaking the earth, outlining a hole about three feet by seven. I'd recovered from my moment of panic, but now, as time passed, I began to worry that Danny wouldn't return; maybe once behind the wheel, he'd decide that he didn't want any more of his friend in need and was getting the hell out of Dodge. I dug. And now I was in the grave, deeper, lifting the damp soil up and out, creating a pyramid of excavated earth off to one side. I felt the cramping in my hands and arms; the burning across my shoulders and back; the sound of my breathing; the steady beat of the shovel cutting through the soil; the thud of the earth landing on the growing cone.

"Bird." It was Danny's voice. Close by. "Took me some time. I parked at a strip mall out on Finch."

"Thought you'd called it a night."

"Now that's a good idea. Where's the shovel?"

"By the carpet."

We worked together, back to back, grunting and sweating, digging deeper into the ground. Panting and sweating and digging and aching and swearing. Plunging the shovel into the earth, jerking it free and throwing the meagre load up and out of the grave. A steady, endless rhythm. A night that would never end. When we got about four feet down, Danny said, "This is enough."

It seemed shallow. "All right." When they poured the concrete, our secret would be safe forever.

We took Raul's cocoon between us and gave it one last heave into the pit within a pit. And then filling the hole, taking all the dirt we'd pried out of the ground and putting it back in. It was easier work, more like coasting downhill, but still work — and we were that much more tired by this stage. And even when we'd filled the hole and completed our task, Danny wasn't prepared to call it a night. "We need to flatten the ground. Smooth it out." He took the square shovel, held it above his head, and brought it down hard on the earth. "Your job. I'm going to look for a real tamper."

He wandered off. After a bit I stopped slapping with the shovel and walked back and forth across the grave and jumped up and down in my boots on the fresh earth to push it back down. Danny returned with the tool he'd stolen from the construction site, a square plate on the end of a pole. He drove it onto the ground beside me, covering my footprints and flattening the earth. The moon's arc had taken it past the horizon of our pit and all we were left with was a faint glow, and before long, the first chirping of birds waking for the day. Traces of light followed, just in time for us to survey our work; it looked clean from where I stood.

Danny stopped his tamping to join me. "Let's get the hell out of here," he said.

XXVII

"I DON'T EVER want to think about that bastard again," said Danny as we started up the ramp out of the pit.

I opened my mouth to respond; it was dry and my throat sore.

He took my hesitation as uncertainty and jumped into the open space: "Not now. This isn't the time for doubts. I spent the night shovelling when I could have been driving."

"But —" I said.

"But nothing. We did what we did. Hopefully, by this time tomorrow, once the concrete is poured, it'll be like Raul never existed."

"But we could make the people responsible for this pay, we could expose their hypocrisy, show how the U.S. government was mixed up in the assassination, let the world know the truth." We emerged from the construction pit; a line of light that was almost green ran along the eastern horizon. It was easier to have doubts now the body was buried.

"You make things happen, Bird. I'll give you that. But you're not too smart. You see how they work: see Oswald, Jack Ruby. Dead before they could open their mouths. And those were their friends — the people on their side helping them out. And you want to get in front of them and wave the red flag. You're a fool. You'd be arrested on the spot, and while you're busy trying to hire a lawyer and make bail, some two-bit punk on the range sticks a shiv in your side, and that'd be the end. The end. We talked about this already."

Cull's file lent a credibility to his words. I thought about Rosie and how I'd seen her earlier in the night, Raul's arm pinning her to his body, the fight fading from me, and how I'd believed that was it for both of us. And I thought about the baby inside her that sometimes didn't even seem real and sometimes felt like the most important thing in the world. And I thought about what Danny was saying. What was history to me? "You're right."

The field was stripped of grass and the exposed earth ran right up to the fresh concrete of the curb. In the distance trees lined the edge of what had once been fields; others lay felled on their backs, staring into the dark sky, their roots exposed fingers straining upward, grasping at the thin light. We emerged onto the main road; his cab was across the wide street in a strip mall parking lot.

On the drive home, my eyes fluttered open and closed, and my head bobbed forward and snapped back on the hinge where it met the spine. The day was opening before us, the grey light coming slowly to colour like someone was fiddling with one of the knobs on the back of the TV. The early sun pierced the horizon off to the left; I squinted into it, gave up, relaxed, and released the muscles; my eyes drooped in fatigue, my mind drifted in the land between sleep and waking, my memories danced a frenzied dance, trading partners, swirling, coming together and subsiding to the shadows. I heard Raul's assertion that he hadn't killed Jack; saw the camera lying in Danny's room; and how his greed had caused his friend's death. I recalled the cabbie's shifting story, thought about that mystery of how Raul had been on to me and followed me to Amy's studio the very second I'd started on the case, before anyone had even known. I remembered Danny's prompt arrival in my time of need and thought about his readiness to leave history behind even when we stood on the wrong side of it — as if he wanted the body buried even more than I did. And maybe he did. I'd read Cull's file: Danny had had his run-ins with the law; he'd done time — and it wasn't just violence and anger, there'd been premeditation, coercion, and intent. His words about a shiv on the yard took on the wisdom of one who really knew. The images tumbled in my head, and, half-asleep, I had one of those lucid moments where the dream pieces, thoughts, and doubts snapped into place. I sat up in the cab, awake, sure that something wasn't right.

"Hey sleepyhead," he said. "You're jerking and twitching in your sleep. We had a dog like that when I was growing up."

"How come you showed up tonight? You didn't have to."

"No, I didn't." He slowed and stopped at a red light, the only car at the intersection.

Out the open window, the birds chirped and chirped, calling back and forth to each other, beginning their morning in glorious domestic dispute. I stared at the foliage, the buds and blossoms, but the sparrows, loud in my ears, were hidden in the thicket.

"You needed help, and you asked," he said.

"You could have just blown it off."

"I could have. But you were stuck. You don't even have a car of your own. What the hell were you going to do with the body?"

"But you didn't know it was a body when you came."

"No, I found out when I arrived. Let's say you helped me out when you took the pictures off me, and I'm paying you back now."

"I didn't know you were so helpful. You keep telling me how you like to mind your own business."

"Yeah. But no — not after what happened to Jack."

The light changed; Danny pulled through the intersection, and, staring at the open road, said, "This is what I get for helping you out? Now you're grilling me? The answer to your question is Jack was my friend. I feel like I owe him. And you took the pictures, and maybe I did you dirty there, and I owe you, too. Why the hell wouldn't I help?"

"I'm suspicious — getting a little paranoid."

"You can say that again."

"There's stuff that doesn't add up."

"And so it must be me." He took his eyes off the road and gave me a look that was part defiance, part pathetic self-pity. "Story of my fucking life."

The expression on his face pretty much convinced me of his innocence, but something inside turned once more. "But what about the lies you told me? When you gave the pictures to me, you said you'd never looked at them."

"Yeah, I lied. I already told you how I took the photos after I tried to hit Ray up for a payday. We had that conversation."

"You're a dangerous friend. Look what you did to Jack."

"You ungrateful bastard, you should shut up about what kind of friend I am until that concrete gets poured. When I lied to you about the photos, I was doing you a favour. Helping you figure out whatever it was you were looking for. You were working on the case. And helping out Jack, in his memory. It was the least I could do. And time proved me right. You evened the score. And I'm grateful for that." He flicked his indicator and pulled out around a bus that was slowing to a stop. "I got out of it, you solved the case, and Jack's killer got what was coming to him. Jack got killed. That's on me, and don't think I don't feel it. But since then, everyone got what they deserved."

"Except I almost got dead. And Rosie, as well."

"You want to be a detective, but you don't like blood? Come on."

"Stop the car. We need to talk."

We were coasting down a steep hill with the city spread out before us: the masses of trees sprouting up and over the houses, the straight gridlines of the streets, and the tall, new towers downtown. Traffic was picking up; the first of the commuters had kissed their wives goodbye and were on their way to work, oblivious of the hidden conspiracies Danny and I were rehashing in the cab.

"What do you want to stop for? Get home and see your wife. I need to get some sleep, too."

"We need to talk. You need to come clean. Someone must have followed me to the photographers — to where I got your photos printed. She was threatened. She was killed."

"What?"

"I went back up there and she was dead."

"Jesus."

"It was Raul."

"I assume so."

"But you led him to her. Led him through me. You're the only one who knew. You gave me the photos. And then Raul was trailing me right away. You must have put Raul on to me."

"What the hell are you talking about? I had the photos. I'd seen the photos. I took the fucking photos. If I wanted to give them to Raul, I'd have done that rather than giving them to you and then siccing Raul on you. You've fucking lost your mind."

"What did you know?"

"You want to know that story? I told you already, but I'll tell you again. From the first time I met Paul Bridgman, I made him for James Earl Ray. I can't believe no one else saw it. It was plain as day. Nothing about his story made sense: said he was a real estate agent. I wouldn't buy a bag of peanuts from him, let alone a house. His hours were all wrong. Stayed in his room the whole time, reading the newspaper. Had a sloppy drawl, plenty of money, and only one suit. And then there was him and Shirley and Yusuf; there was a hatred there right from day one. Like they knew it, too. Or they felt it. I don't know. I tried to figure out how I could turn it to my advantage. I got greedy. Pigs get fed; hogs get slaughtered. Isn't that the way it goes?"

"You should've turned him in. You could've done the right thing."

"I could have done the right thing and I didn't. No point in relitigating it now. It's over. I made my choices, and you made yours and they aren't so different. Sometimes it's easier to close your eyes and pretend it isn't happening." He hit the left turn signal and slowed into the turning lane. "Don't get so righteous; you're doing the same thing. And I didn't stick the knife in him; I didn't kill anybody; I just looked the other way when I saw what I saw."

"How many people did you get killed?"

"I told you already, I feel sick about what happened to Jack." We were circling the block now, coming at my house from Bloor, as it ran one-way north. It all looked the same as it had yesterday: trees stretching their limbs to the sky, a squirrel pirouetting on the powerline tightrope, grass pushing up out of the ground, and black windows in unlit houses reflecting the morning — except for one glowing with the unnatural blue of the television screen. Danny pulled onto the curb and braked hard.

I was jerked forward and my tired head brushed the windshield. "You could have blown the whistle on Ray any time — even after he'd disappeared."

"I could've. But it wasn't my business. I was staying out of it; I'd already put the clamp on Ray. I don't like the law so much and they don't like me. What more can I tell you? Ray disappeared, but he could always have reappeared. Things happen fast and when Jack went missing, I thought it better just to keep my head down." He chewed on his moustache; his face betrayed his fatigue. "I did what I did. And then you showed up, and everything was fixed. You were here to solve the mystery, and if I played my cards right, I could feed you the information you needed and everything could work out. Just like it did."

"You nearly got me killed." I'd said it before, but it was all I had left. It was hard to believe a word of Danny's, but there was a certain combination of cowardice, greed, and self-preservation that rang true. He'd helped me out, driving and digging — I never could have done it without his cab to transport the body and his conjuring of the construction site to bury it forever — but I tasted all the sour juices in my mouth that came from a night without sleep and knew I had to get out of the cab before I turned on him. I was too tired to think and too confused to act. "You bastard."

"Fuck you, Bird. Get out of my cab and fuck off."

I stepped out of the car into the long shadows, held myself back from slamming the door in the hush of morning, and crossed the street. I turned the key in the lock, entered the dark house, and saw the light at the far end of the hall, seeping onto the kitchen floor where Raul had lain the night before. The tiles were clean now, shining as if it had never happened.

I took the stairs two at a time; when I reached the landing I heard her voice, soft and tentative in the silence, call my name.

"Rosie," I said in response and pushed the door open into the darker darkness of the small bedroom.

She said my name again and my face got wet, and I was sitting on the bed beside her, and then we were both crying, so tired and terrified, and holding one another because we knew what we knew and how close it'd been.

"It's over now," I said. "It's all over."

She pulled me tighter, her arms across my back, pulling me as tight as she could. "Isn't someone going to come looking for him?"

"I don't think so. Everyone wants to pretend he never existed. Us, too."

"You're sure?"

"As sure as I can be."

"What did you do with the body? Won't somebody find it?"

"Danny had a good id—"

"Don't tell me. I don't want to know."

"It's gone for good. We got rid of it. Danny —"

"I wish it wasn't him. He's so …"

She didn't finish her sentence. But I knew what she meant. He'd helped me plenty, but I wasn't so sure I was happy being in his debt; having him hold our secret. "I think he's okay. It's done now."

"If you do something like that again," she said, "I'll kill you if no one else does. Don't you ever dare put our family in danger."

There were more tears. I tried to explain what had happened and why, but she put her hand over my mouth and told me enough was enough. My mistakes ached against my exhausted skin, and all I wanted was to tell her how much I loved her and needed her and would never do wrong again and fall asleep at her side. We lay in the darkness, the light forming a soft frame around the thick curtain, and I passed between sleep and consciousness with Rosie in my arms, my mind shunting between the present and the past. When I was awake, I was with her and my heart yearned with a depth that scared me; and when I was drifting, I kept hearing Raul's calm voice, telling me he hadn't killed Jack Turner.

XXVIII

ROSIE WAS SAYING my name.

My eyes opened, and the room was light, and she stood at the side of the bed, dressed, and I was blinking, and hot and sweaty, under the blankets.

"Patrick."

"What time is it?"

"It's after lunch if that's what you're asking."

I lay my head back on the pillow and groaned. Not at the missed meal, but because the memories were flooding back fast. "You're not at work."

"There's someone on the phone who wants to talk to you."

"Who?"

"They didn't say."

"Okay. I'm coming."

Our phone was in the kitchen, mounted on the wall; the receiver lay on the counter, the curly cord hung in a loose loop down the cabinet drawer. Stepping under the plaster arch that an intrepid drywaller had thought was a good idea fifty years ago took a burst of courage as the manic slideshow of memories flashed. Three speckled bananas lay in the fruit bowl, throwing off their musk; the cloying odour wasn't what I wanted to smell right then. I grabbed the phone, unsure who it might be.

"Hello?"

"Patrick? Patrick Bird?" It was Connie, Jack's mother, wanting to know about her dead son.

"Patrick here." Hadn't I just spoken to her yesterday? Or was it two days ago now? I couldn't remember. Had I promised I'd be back in touch to set up a final debrief?

"Constance Turner. I'm hoping for an update on the case. We've been waiting and we haven't heard from you. I don't mind saying, I'm beginning to get impatient. It's one thing not to know; it's another to believe that you're waiting on news that isn't coming. I'm ready to give up. Hoping for an answer just makes the time pass slower. We trusted you to do your best and —"

"And I have." More than my best if I were to tell the truth. I'd been up all night burying the body. I had to say something, if only to stop the tireless litany of her grief. "I'll come to you. Up where you live to provide a full report." I, too, wanted it to just end, for it to be done and over. "Are you in this evening?" I had the misguided hope that if I could speak to them in person, tell them a little of what I'd done, it would close this all off and I could call it the end and put it in a box and seal it tight and never think about it again. I couldn't tell them what had happened last night, but justice had been served. Retribution. An eye for an eye. Perhaps, if I wasn't half-asleep, and I was a little further out from last night's terror, I could have thought it out more clearly and figured an escape route, away from them and the accusation of their suffering, but that's not the way it happened.

"We're in every night. Just a second, young man. I need to sit down. You've suddenly made me believe you might have an answer." The muffled sounds of the phone being put down, a chair scraping on the floor, the phone being picked up again, the too-close sound of breath travelled across the wires.

Hope was a terrible thing, and I was responsible for it. And with nothing to tell them. Good for me. I jerked the phone from my ear. I'd already made the decision that every ounce of truth would stay buried with Raul; now, twelve hours later, I was slipping. If anyone deserved to know, it was them. I needed to be careful with what I promised. There was no room for a U-turn with Connie; I wasn't about to chop down the slender weeds she grasped at. "Give me a couple of hours to figure out my transportation and I'll call you back this afternoon."

"You do that. And thank you, Patrick. I'll let Gregory know."

We signed off. I needed a car, but even more desperately, to figure out what I could say. I'd gotten started in detecting because I had a certain respect for truth; and I'd gotten out of it, at least partially, because I couldn't stand the public relations side of the business, speaking out of the corner of your mouth and saying things coated in honey to hide the reality beneath. And now here I was. Maybe that was what growing up was all about, finding new and nice ways to lie. Becoming something you despised.

Rose came down the stairs behind me into the kitchen. "You're not going out again? Not today?" It was a question, but it wasn't a question.

Just five minutes ago, my eyes had been closed in dreamless bliss: and now here I was. "It was the client."

"I heard."

"They want to know what happened: how their boy was killed."

"I'm sure they do." Her eyes had that hardness I knew.

"And I want to end this case; to put this all behind us. Once and for all."

"And you think if you talk to them, then that'll be the end of it?"

"Maybe. It'd be a step in the right direction." It wouldn't stop my thoughts, but at least it would stop their phone calls.

She turned away. "And I don't want to be alone, not today of all days. This isn't what marriage is. I'm —"

"I know. I know." I was too fast and too loud; hearing someone else's truth was no fun, either. "This is just one last trip to tell them …"

"There's nothing to tell. Nothing. What can you say? You're going to say you got nowhere, that you failed, that there was nothing to discover. You don't need to drive all the way up there for that."

"I feel like I failed them. I took their money and I solved the case, sort of. It's just I can't tell them what I know."

"You feel guilty about the way you've treated them?" She shook her head and didn't say any more, and I understood what she meant.

"I just need to report to them, to close the case, and then I'm all yours. And no more detective business ever again. I promise. I'm cured. Forever. I'll go back to Massey Ferguson on my knees and beg them for that job."

She sat at the table and looked out the back window. There wasn't anything else to say, but I wasn't sure the conversation was over.

"I love you," I said.

"I love you, too," she said, and somehow I felt worse for it.

"Just today, and then it's over."

"Sure."

I picked up the phone, checked a number on the list on the fridge, and dialled.

"Tina?" The in-laws had inherited the old man's Ford when he'd passed, and I borrowed it occasionally.

"Yes, Pat? Is Rose with you? She told us she was just going home to pick up some clothes. For God's sake tell me she got home all right. You're not —"

"She's here."

"Well, thank God for that. What're you calling for, then?"

"The car, I need to borrow the car. Can I talk to Tony?"

Their house was silent today. Maybe the babies were napping.

"When do you need it? I don't know. He's over at Mama's, helping her. Try and get a hold of him there, will you? I've got the girls here." A cry came down the line right on cue.

They'd inherited the family car, and to them it was all theirs. I'd tried explaining that they could share it with us a little more, and Tony, a crease furrowing his brow, had let me know I wasn't part of the family when the inheritance was split, and I could just shut up.

"I'll try him at Flavia's, then." I could imagine Tina cringing at the sound of her mother's name. Tony called her Mama and spoke Italian to her; he was Flavia's family golden boy: had a job, a house, and two babies at home. "I'll let you go now — it sounds like the girls need your help." A parting shot before I went, cap in hand, to the Turners to tell them I hadn't found anything.

The phone at Flavia's rang and rang, and nobody picked up. I was surprised because she didn't leave her basement den too often. Maybe she was having Tony take her on a shopping tour at the supermarket; generally, she preferred the local shops where they knew her by name, spoke her language, and sold the kind of stuff that made her feel like she'd never left the old country.

I snuck a glance at Rosie, who had a magazine open on the kitchen table and showed no sign of having heard my conversation with her sister. What the hell was I going to say to the Turners? That I'd looked under a lot of stones, but there wasn't anything there; I'd talked to everyone in the rooming house; I'd been to the Flyer and spoken with the cabbies in its shadow. But nothing about the photos of James Earl Ray. Once I admitted to those photos, everything else would come rushing in with the floodwaters, and then there was the risk of drowning. Not the photos. I wouldn't admit to anything. I could lie like everyone else: like Danny, playing fast and loose, like Shirley hiding behind her door, and Yusuf with his easy smile and the nod of his head, which kept his thoughts locked up tight. And we could all go home and pretend Raul had never happened. The Turners could keep their money for all I cared, and I'd find a real job.

"Goodbye, Rosie — I'm going down to your mom's to see about borrowing Tony's car."

"All right."

"I'll call you and let you know when I should be home."

"Okay."

"I love you."

"I love you, too."

We were all liars, even Rosie. It didn't seem like anything was true. I left the house, my stomach empty, my head full, and my heart skipping a beat here and there as it tried to find the rhythm of the new day, the first day of the rest of my life. The only answer was to push the thoughts of Raul and Jack down and away. I'd done what I could. Raul was dead. I didn't need to say it out loud for it to have meaning.

The sky was overcast, the air hot and heavy, and I was working up a sweat as I came down Ossington, halfway between Dundas and the rooming house. Shirley appeared, walking toward me pulling a bundle-buggy, clothes and bedding spilling out of the garbage bag that lined its metal frame. At first it looked like laundry day, but then I realized something more was going on; the thoughts gained speed, spinning around in my head like one of those twirly rides they have at the Ex that some kids like, but only ever made me throw up. The load was too much for her little shopping cart, and she kept turning around and readjusting the bags laid across the top so they didn't tumble onto the sidewalk. I drew closer and she looked up and recognized me; a sullen look crossed her face before she snapped to and covered it up with a blank expression.

"Mr. Bird," she said, trying to push by me.

"Shirley." Her eyes were wet, but she had too much pride to let the tears out in front of me. "What's going on?"

"You pretend you don't know." This wasn't the same face I'd seen peering from behind the half-closed door; there was no fear in her expression now.

"I don't know."

"You and Mrs. Gentilini and Tony," she pretty much spat the last name, "see me out. Don't pretend you don't know. You're just a little late to the party; you miss their fun. 'Pack your bags and get out.' You feel good? You try to shame this girl. But you go down to the house and Tony tell you all about it. Maybe you and him have a beer to celebrate."

"What's going on?"

"You put me out. Don't pretend you don't know."

"But why, Shirley? What happened?"

She hesitated and her jacket fell open and I saw: the tiniest of bumps starting in her middle; her sharp face wasn't as sharp, her chest was heavier, straining at the floral print, her shape and movements reminded me of what was going on at my house. She was pregnant, just like Rose, except a month or two ahead. It wasn't enough to be sure, but it was enough.

She didn't say anything.

"How many months?"

"See, you do know." Her voice had a note of triumph that flared through her anger.

"I'm just seeing now. Just catching up."

"You go catch up and leave me alone."

"But who's the father?" The rooming house, home to Paul Bridgman, aka James Earl Ray, home to a death and a fugitive, home to the ever-suspicious Danny, as well as the enigmatic Yusuf, shifted and looked different.

"Who's the father? Who's the father? Everyone want to know my business. But no one help me; all they want is to shame me." She went to push by me and the motion upset the cart's equilibrium. Two bags tumbled onto the pavement. "Leave me alone." A pillow spilled out and lay on the concrete. "Look, you see what you cause. Leave me be. You throw me out of my home." She bent to pick up her belongings, the bright white shifts and sheets of her bedding.

"No, it's not that I want to know who the father is — I need to know. You remember Jack Turner. He was murdered. He —"

The raw expression on her face told me I'd hit the mark first try. She gave up holding the tears in, dropped her bundle back to the ground, and snapped, "Leave me alone. Look at me," she pointed to the bump under the flowered dress. "Look what that house has done: give me a baby and take his daddy."

Passersby were slowing to look at the scene that was us. A car heading north slowed and the passenger leaned out the window and shouted harsh and hateful words at Shirley and me. More at Shirley than at me but standing by and hearing it and doing nothing didn't feel good, either.

"You see?" said Shirley. "You see what my life is. And soon I can't work. No rent. No room. No house. And no one to help. Leave me alone. Don't think I don't see the way you look at me."

"What's that supposed to mean?"

She reverted to a silence.

"You think I'm against you? Is that what you're saying? I'm on your side. Your side and Jack's."

"And your mother-in-law's. Don't think I don't see."

"No," I said. But I didn't have anything else to say. Her words stung; and part of the sting was their truth. "What about Jack's family? The parents have some money. They could help."

She gathered her belongings from the pavement and loaded the buggy. When she straightened up, her lips were pursed in disgust. I pulled an old business card from my wallet, scratched the number out, wrote my home phone on the back, and pressed it on her. She ripped it in two, reset the halves, ripped again, and let the scraps fall on the street. I had a lot of questions, too many questions: the rooming house looked different now. She spat on the sidewalk as a final piece of punctuation, turned her back on me, and headed up the hill to Dundas. I didn't want to leave her there, to cut and run with her on the side of the road, but I did. I told myself she didn't want to talk to me, and maybe, just maybe there was someone at the house who could clear up the mystery of Jack's death now that I knew this much more.

XXIX

THE FRONT DOOR hung open, which wasn't the tight and tidy way my mother-in-law liked to keep her house, but what she thought of as rough and unclean, an invitation to the riff-raff off the street — everything and everyone she couldn't bear to have in her establishment. Voices were in conversation in the kitchen and as I shouted "Tony!" down the hall, the back door slammed. Shirley had been right: my brother-in-law sat at the table with a bottle of Black Label in his hand, his stubble blue on his face, his shirt unbuttoned too far and what looked like a furry animal sleeping in the nest of the open collar, "as *goombah* as hell" as he liked to describe himself.

"Well, look who's here. Just in time to miss the excitement." He said something to Flavia in Italian, and he laughed. She was more restrained, but a repressed smile flickered on her face. Out the window Danny, the only tenant who ever used the back door, was making his escape up the alley, walking calmly, not looking back, the innocence of the well-timed exit — there was always somewhere he had to go. He passed Tony's car, the one I wanted to borrow, an old Ford that had belonged to the man who would have been my father-in-law if he'd lived long enough. I was already the outsider in the family, and Tony didn't make it easier. His endless reminders that he was doing me a favour, lending his car — which in my mind should have been half Rose's — only stoked my resentment. I'd grown up alone with my mother and entering into the busy life of an extended family didn't come easy.

I ignored the pair in the kitchen, passed into the back alley, and trotted past the Ford. There was a new scrape on its fender. Danny was skulking up at the corner. I caught him with a hand on his shoulder and spun him around.

"Jesus, Patrick, don't you ever sleep? Last night was a late one. After I dropped you off, I had to return the cab to the yard, so I'm a couple of hours behind; just starting my day now."

"Cut the crap, Danny."

"And no, I don't have time for any more favours. Find someone else to be your chauffeur."

"What happened to Shirley?"

"Shirley? That's your family business. Ask your *paisano* brother-in-law and that old witch of a landlady. They put her out on the street. It wasn't pretty. Fucking noise woke me up. And in her condition."

"Because she's expecting?"

"I told you, ask your in-laws. What do I know about their thinking?" He looked over my shoulder and squinted at the clouds, which couldn't completely hide the sun.

"Forget what they think: what I need is what you know about it. The first time we met, you hinted there were fun and games going on up above. Who's the father?"

"Whoa." He smiled at me, but when he saw I wasn't smiling back, he took his cue from me and turned belligerent. "I've had about enough, Bird. Figure some of this out yourself and leave me out of it."

"But why the hell are you ducking and running? You can complain all you want about me leaning on you too hard, but if you told the truth the first time, I wouldn't need to chase you down. You keep feeding me lies, or forgetting half the story, and then running out the back when I show up."

A waif of a cat appeared on a fence rail, strutting above us, its tail straight up. The smell from garbage bins, fetid in the humidity, hung in the air; a can of tuna lay dented and empty on the pitted asphalt. The night creatures — raccoons, rats, and opossums — had licked it clean.

"You know who the father is."

"It's no secret."

"Tell me, then."

"Jack's the father." The confirmation of what Shirley hadn't said.

"So, why the running and hiding? I'm not the police."

He looked away, his gaze settling on the cat, down from the fence, sniffing around the empty can on the ground. He swung a leg half-heartedly at the tabby, and it made a hasty retreat.

"You're sure you didn't have anything to do with it?" Something about him made me question every story he told me; his confirmation that Jack was the father made it seem less likely, not more.

"Like I was half the father? What the hell? The trouble with you is you don't even listen when people help you."

"Ray?"

He snorted and laughed. "God, no. He couldn't stand her. He wanted her out. It almost killed him to live in the same house as Shirley and Yusuf. Use your head. He was too busy raging against —"

"Against who —"

"Whoever he could. He was a born victim, always complaining. He killed Martin Luther King, but everything in his world was someone else's fault."

The heavy sky, which had been threatening all morning, finally gave up holding it in; the first fuzz of a drizzle began.

"Yusuf?"

"Now there's an idea. Could be."

"I'm serious, Blinken."

"And so am I. I don't know about Yusuf. You'd have to ask him or Shirley. Now leave me alone."

"And you're telling me everything you know?"

"Nice day to put Shirley out." He looked back at the house where Tony could be seen watching us through the window. "God, you people." The cat, the same colour as marmalade, drifted back toward the empty can. "Jack's the father. I told you. I'm not about to stay out here talking in the rain."

"But Jack was murdered."

"I know that, too, and last night — or was it this morning — we buried the guy who killed him. And then you turn around and tried to tell me that it wasn't Raul when the guy's a professional killer. You don't need any more proof.

You've got everything but a signed confession. Let's hope the concrete's poured before the rain starts up at the university."

This time he let the cat be as it sniffed around the empty tin. "I think you're getting a case of nerves here. It's over: there isn't any mystery left. Raul killed Jack. It's simple: the story's over, and you're trying to make it into something else. So what if Jack was living his life, had a girl, got her pregnant — those things happen. Every fucking day. But it doesn't have anything to do with murder. It's just something that happens in life."

"But why didn't you tell me?"

"You have your killer. You don't need to know everything. And take a look at the way your fucking family treats people; what they did to that girl this morning, as soon as they knew. I've lived here long enough to see it coming. So don't ask me why I didn't tell you — for Shirley's sake — to give her another couple of weeks with a roof over her head."

"You think I'd throw her out?"

"Flavia would. And you don't keep secrets. You just find something out, smear it everywhere, and wait to see what happens — what sticks, what chaos can be created, what comes crawling out from beneath the baseboard, and who else gets killed. That's why I head out the back door when I see you coming. You're fucking chaos. It's too dangerous to be your friend. You called me last night, and I helped out, but we're done now. Take your help, be grateful, and fuck off."

The rain was a soft mist, and tiny globules of water clung to Danny's hair and moustache, and the knit of his sweater. "You're the fucking kiss of death. It's a miracle you didn't get yourself killed yesterday. And your little lady. No one wants to get too close to you. I've been a fool to help as much as I have."

He turned and started back to the house, but I had one last question for him: "What about the night Bridgman arrived? Did you see him come in?"

"I was out driving. Working. Didn't see anything," he said over his shoulder. I never knew whether to believe him or not. "Ask your mother-in-law; she's the one who rents the rooms."

Danny pushed past me, back into the house, through the kitchen, down the hall, and closed his door emphatically. Tony smirked across the table. He and Flavia talked in Italian, occasionally looking in my direction.

I interrupted the flow with my English: "Tony, I need to borrow the car tonight."

He turned to me, flashed a toothy grin, and looked back at Flavia as if playing to an audience. "The car? Tonight? Sorry. No can do, Pat. Not possible. Tina and me are going out on a date, just like before we were married. Mother's coming," he looked at Flavia, "over to watch the *bambinos* while we're out forgetting they exist. Live a little." He spread his arms wide apart and lifted his shoulders. "You know, I want to help you out, but you need to give me a little more warning if you want my car. You put me in these spots where it's impossible to say yes." He looked back at Flavia, the expression on his face continuing the unspoken conversation about my merits — and demerits — while I stood and watched.

"But —"

"Pat," he knew I hated being called Pat by anyone other than Rosie, "is what you've got going on so important it can't wait until morning? What about tomorrow night?"

I hated him: his self-satisfied air, his position in the heart of the family, his patronizing pose. But maybe he was right:

maybe it could all wait until morning. I mean, what was I in a rush to do? To run up to Midhurst and see the Turners and tell them I didn't have any news about their boy — I'd tried and failed. I knew nothing. I'd done nothing. They could keep their money. All that was left between us was "sorry" and "goodbye."

All this haste was about me. I wanted it over — to rush through the failure and put it behind me, to close the cover on this case, to put Raul and his knife, and the photographs, and the fear and the blood in the past, so we could start again; to forget about what might have been, the unknown story, the right thing I might've done. I could have blown the whistle and said look what we have here. I could have, but I didn't. And I wouldn't.

"You want tomorrow," said Tony. "I'd have to look at my schedule and check with Tina. It's a possibility — not like tonight, which is a straight no. Tina'd kill me if our night out went kaput."

I turned from Tony to Flavia, sitting quietly at the kitchen table, making arcane scratchings, a European seven with a line cutting it in half, a column of figures added to a total, the indecipherable handwriting in the spiral-bound account book that held her secrets. She must have felt my gaze, because her placid face looked up and met it.

"How did he get here?" I said.

"Tony? He drove. You see the car. You know that." She shook her head at my stupidity.

"Not Tony. James. James Earl Ray."

She looked momentarily blank, her mouth a straight line, her brows pulled tight over her eyes. "James?" Before I could explain, her mouth broke into a smile at the success of memory: "Paul? You mean Paul Bridgman?"

"Yeah, Bridgman."

"He came one evening. Let me look at the book." She wet a finger with her tongue and turned the pages until she found what she was looking for. "April six."

"But at what time?"

"The book doesn't say. But it was evening. It was dark."

"Did he call first to ask about a room?"

She frowned again. "No, he didn't call. He was just there at the door, in the hall. I don't remember. Someone came to get me. I don't even remember the bell ringing."

"But who got you?"

"It's a long time ago now."

"You're not still playing detective are you, Pat?" said Tony. "You need something a little more stable with a baby coming, eh?"

I wasn't to be deflected by his words. "But how did he know there was a room here? Did you have the sign up in the window?"

"Yes," said Flavia. "You're right. There was no sign in the window. There was no ad in the paper. I had just lost that Philippine girl a day or two before. She went back to where she came from without giving me any notice. Just up and left, so I had a spare room, and then like magic, he was there. Maybe that's why I liked him at first — not now I know what he did, but at first."

"But how did he know to knock on your door?"

"People know I have a rooming house and lots of times they just knock on the door and ask if there is a spare room." She closed her book, signalling that the conversation was over. And then she twigged. "Oh! I remember: it was Mr. Yusuf who came and got me. Maybe Mr. Yusuf told him."

I left Flavia and Tony in the kitchen, took the stairs two at a time, and banged on Yusuf's door. It swung open and there he was with his incurious expression.

"Patrick?"

"I need to ask you about the night Paul Bridgman arrived."

"Paul? You mean James Earl Ray?"

"Flavia said you let him into the house."

"That's right."

"How did it happen?"

We stood facing one another, me in the narrow hallway, he in the doorway of his tidy little room with its bed, desk and dresser, and little else. He didn't invite me in.

"I was coming home from the library one night at about nine o'clock, and as I came up to the house, I could see that a car was parked out front. The driver came out and opened the trunk and Paul — this James Earl Ray — he came around from the passenger side and got a bag and said something like, 'So is this the place?' And I had to squeeze by them to get to the steps to the house."

"But do you remember the car? Or the driver? Did you get a look at him?"

"The driver? He was a white man, older, maybe Mrs. Gentilini's age. He was losing his hair on the top and wore glasses. He shrank away when I approached to turn into the house. The other one, Bridgman, saw me going in and said, 'Jesus, you brought me somewhere where they let …'" His sentence died. "He called me a name I'd rather not repeat. I decided to steer clear of the two of them. The driver didn't say anything; he slammed the trunk and went back to his seat in the car and started the engine. I went into the house. But before I could —"

"But the car?"

"It was a Dodge, a Dodge Dart. It was dark outside, but the colour was yellow-brown, like mustard."

"Four doors?"

"The Dart is always four doors; the Swinger is the two-door model." He knew his cars.

"But how would they know there was an empty room here?"

"I don't know. But when I got in the hallway, the man, Bridgman, was already at the door before I could close it. He said, 'Hey roomie, get the landlady. I'm moving in.' I didn't like his tone, so I called Mrs. Gentilini and left."

"Did you tell the police all this?"

"They never asked." Because the Mounties had expended all their energy at the second rooming house and never made it the extra block and a half down to Flavia's. Because I'd never shared the photos.

His eyes met mine and again I couldn't read what his expression meant.

"Is that everything you wanted to ask?"

"Yes," I said, believing and not believing what was going on in my head. There was someone with a beige car; someone whose racial views seemed to line up pretty close with James Earl Ray's even when muted in the confines of polite conversation; someone who could have known there was an empty room in this house before the ad went up in the window; someone who'd been in on it from the very beginning, alerting Raul to my investigation even before it started; someone who had access to opiates; someone who fit the description of an older man with glasses. It just didn't seem possible. A lot of fucked-up things happen in this world, but this one seemed just too much.

THE BIG BRICK farmhouse swung into view as Rice, his foot on the brake, his hands releasing his grip on the wheel, let it spin itself to true, and the car eased off the dirt road and onto the long, straight lane. Loose gravel crunched under the tires as we drove up the slight incline, which made the house perched on the top of the rise, looming above us, seem even more imposing. We passed beneath its soft shadow in the grey afternoon and emerged behind the building to park on a scrap of grass scarred by muddy ruts. The rain had stopped — it had never really started, and the air hung heavy and still.

"You're sure about this?" said Rice. "I still have trouble seeing how a man could kill his own son."

"I'm telling you. I've told you."

"You just haven't convinced me."

"What the hell are we doing here, then?" Stuck in indecision, we hadn't left his Grand Prix yet. "There's the car, the one Yusuf told me about." The copper-coloured Dart was parked beside us behind the house.

"That's it. It's one thing to give a ride to James Earl Ray. It's another to kill your son."

I shook my head, disappointed that I hadn't made him see it my way, wanting him more on my side before we went through the door.

He broke the silence. "Let's get going and see if we learn anything. Maybe it's good I'm here. It could stop him from doing anything too stupid."

I paused, reaching for the handle; we'd already had this conversation. I was an unlicensed PI and Rice was a long way out of his jurisdiction; neither of us had any real authority. Maybe it was better that way. Once we were sure, we could make the call and have the provincial police come with their cuffs and booking papers.

"I still don't like it much," he said. "It's bold. Too bold. I've seen a few murders — murderers — and I've never seen this. Fathers don't kill sons."

"This is different. It happens. It's ideological. When belief is involved, anything can happen. Read your Bible. People do crazy shit when they believe something strongly enough."

Rice didn't say anything as he stared straight ahead, out the window across the big green field.

"You can't deny the evidence — what Yusuf said. The man who dropped Ray off: bald, glasses, thin frame. He saw them getting out of the car. You've driven all the way up here."

"Eyewitnesses are pretty useless at the best of times. The description might fit: glasses, white man, losing his hair, but that's a lot of people. Could be Cull."

"With the knowledge and access to pure morphine."

"Turner's a doctor. Yeah."

"Who knew about the rooming house, even knew there was a vacancy there."

"Okay, okay."

"And the way the body was dropped under the Flyer. It was so unprofessional. Why would you drop the body where it could be found?"

"But the psychology of it."

"I'm telling you, he's crazy. Has all these crazy ideas. These guys work themselves up to the point where their idea means more than any love they might have."

"You'd have to be crazy."

"He is fucking crazy. He's the third man in the picture." The photo lay between us on the bench seat. We'd both stared at the blurred fragment of face that loomed in a quarter profile on the right side of the image till we felt dizzy. It wasn't as definitive as I was making it. But for sure it could be him. "I'm telling you."

Rice picked up the photo and squinted at it again. "You keep telling me."

"Jack broke the family code," I said. "Went against everything they believed. And he wasn't willing to break it off; he loved Shirley and wanted to get married. That's why he left the city and came up here that week. To tell his parents and talk to them about it. To ask for their blessing for the marriage."

"And you think when they talked about him getting married to Shirley ..."

"He thought it would go one way, and it went the other. He thought he could talk them around, but the more they talked the worse it got —"

"That's all speculation."

"Isn't most murder this way? Love gone wrong? All in the family? Love that, when it can't have its way, flips on its head and becomes …"

"Love," said Rice in his low voice. "But why hire you if he killed his own son? He'd want the case to go away, the same as everyone else. If he sat quiet and looked the other way, it'd go away on its own."

"He never hired me. That was Connie. And he could hardly object — tell her no, he didn't want to find his son's killer. Plus, he had faith in Raul, that he would catch up to me sooner or later. He even put Raul on to me. That's how he showed up on day one. I talked to Connie and Gregory on the phone one night to say I'd take the case, and then Raul appears the next morning, tailing me up to the photographer's loft. I'd no sooner dropped the photos than he was knocking on her door." That one was on me. I hadn't told Rice everything — not about Amy's death. "In a sense it worked for Turner, having me on the case: he could keep tabs on the investigation and let Raul know what I knew."

"You think so?"

I didn't say anything, but at this stage it even seemed suspicious that Connie had phoned me that morning, right after the night Raul had come calling. Like her husband had put her up to finding out how Raul's visit had gone.

"Well, then, let's go in there and see what you can stir up. Maybe you'll get a signed confession."

But before we were all the way out of the car, Connie appeared from around the house, approaching the driver's side. "Detective Rice," she said, her face pinching in on itself. "What are you doing here?"

"Good afternoon, ma'am."

"But I don't understand. Mr. Bird, what's going on? Why is Detective Rice here?"

"He drove me up, Mrs. Turner." I stepped away from the car and into the big grassy space surrounding the house. A cow lowed on the other side of a split-rail fence; a group of them swivelled their stoic heads, their eyes locking on to our tableau as the conversation stalled.

"Let me get Gregory." Her narrow mouth drooped at the corners, and her face looked more tired and shrivelled than ever, its resting state a pure frown. "He's back in the barn. He knows you were coming this evening. Not you, Detective Rice. We weren't aware you would be here also." She turned back to me, fatigue and displeasure still dominating her face. "But you said that you had news, Mr. Bird. You sounded optimistic when we spoke, like you have an answer to all this."

Standing beside the car, with his unbuttoned jacket and white shirt, Rice looked out of place in the rural setting. The cows began to walk away, first one, then the others following, down the incline to a low patch where dogwood had taken hold and wouldn't let go. They moved slowly, their tails swishing behind.

"I grew up on a farm," he said.

"I can't understand what Gregory could be doing." Connie looked back at the barn and then at me. "He is always eager for news from you. To know how the investigation is going. As eager as I am. Maybe more so. He's always asking for your updates."

"Let's go inside," I said. "He'll join us when he's able."

Connie didn't look happy. "Yes. Excuse me. My mind is …" She glanced at Rice again and turned abruptly without telling us what was up with her mind. We followed single file as she led us to the door at the side of the house. A massive stone cut into a square step had sunken to a resting place that was not quite level under the aluminum screen. I took the door from Connie so she could pass in first, and held it for Rice, but he took it from my hand and insisted I follow next. We were all reluctant. No one wanted to enter and have the conversation we were going to have. None of us knew for sure: each of us held a few pieces of the puzzle, and once we put them together, we'd complete the picture we didn't want to see. And once we'd seen it, there'd be no doubt.

We stood in the kitchen: wooden wainscotting, plaster walls, the motionless ceiling fan, dishes drying in a rack, a counter wiped clean.

"Let's sit here." Connie gestured to the wooden chairs arranged around the wooden table. "But we should get Gregory. He said he'd just be a minute. He'll want to hear what you have to say."

There was a window out to the long drive, and we waited and looked, but Gregory didn't show.

"I have some questions for you first," I said.

"Why don't I go and get him?" she asked. "He'll want to hear what you have to say, too."

Rice rose from his chair.

"Let's wait," I said. "Maybe we can get started without him. We could ask you a few questions." When she lifted her head to meet my gaze, her glasses reflected the light coming through the window and hid her eyes and expression behind the glare. I'd seen that face before when they came to hire me, except then, it had been Gregory's glasses reflecting the light. They were similar even in their actions. Her fingers worried a button at her neck. "Questions? I thought you were here to tell us what you'd found."

There was no easy way to say it. "Things changed. My investigation has led me to the conclusion that your husband, Gregory, is responsible for Jack's death."

"Jonathan's death?" She was like a parrot that could mimic the words without understanding them. "Responsible?"

"We believe he killed your son." I included Rice this time round.

He pushed back slightly in his chair, like he was trying to put a little space between me and him.

"No," she said. She took her glasses off and rubbed her eyes. "Gregory loved Jonathan." She blinked and looked frightened and fought back with logic. "He loved him. What are you talking about? You were hired to find the killer, not this. This crazy theory. What are you talking about?" Her face began to collapse, the muscles twitched and failed, the expression of defiance melted slowly under a truth she might have already known — have known and not known, not allowed herself to know, somewhere back behind those small eyes, have intuited deep down and pushed it away and aside, refusing to believe it, unable to take it in. And even as her face fell, there was a twitch inside me that jagged the other direction: that said, as we sat in this quiet, middle-class kitchen, that it was impossible.

"He wouldn't kill Jonathan. No. He had so many dreams for him. Our boy." She was telling us she didn't believe, but the tears started in her eyes as if the part of her that believed what we said was gaining ascendancy. And in those tears maybe the truth was starting to show through.

"Your husband is a part of conspiracy of white supremacists. He's a racist." I tried to say it as straight and flat as I could, but I failed and there was a slight inflection at the end that might have made it sound more like a question than I'd intended.

Connie raised her head and looked at Rice, not me, as if I were the bystander in the conversation.

"Gregory?" It was too much for her. "Conspiracy? White supremacy? He doesn't like Negroes, if that's what you mean. Or foreigners. He never has. That's not our country. It's what he believes. You can't change a person's beliefs." Was that true? It scared me when she said it like that. "It's what I believe as well if it comes to that. It's why we didn't like it when Jonathan moved to the city. We knew we were losing him when we went. But we never thought we'd lose him so …" She clamped her mouth shut, not quite prepared to finish her sentence. "But what has that got to do with Jonathan's death?"

"And when he came up to see you in that last week, was there anything he wanted to talk to you and Gregory about?"

The tears were streaming down her face now. "No," she said. "It's not like that."

"It is. He came to talk to you about marriage to a girl. A girl who was going to have his child. Your grandchild."

"That has nothing to do with this. That … I want Gregory here. He can explain. He'll explain. You don't understand."

"Just wait. I have more questions for you."

"No." Connie stood from the table.

Rice stood also. "Let's get the father and see what he has to say."

She turned her head back to me, taking her glasses off to wipe her face, and dabbing her eyes with a handkerchief that had appeared from somewhere. Her eyes, without the prism of glass to enlarge them, were small and hard, like stones on a bed of snow. They blinked and changed; pain and confusion showed, and they sank deeper into the melting snow.

"He told us about the girl — I forget her name — when he came to see us that week. That's why he came up here. To tell us he wanted to get married. Gregory had to laugh. Boys will be boys, sowing their wild oats where they will — sometimes even ..." Her voice trailed off when she couldn't find the words. "Jonathan didn't see things that way. He thought he was in love. But of course, he wasn't. He was mistaken. He couldn't love that girl. It couldn't ever work. We told him that, explained it to him. He'd come to see we were right over time. We let him know that the marriage wouldn't take place."

"What did he say when you told him all that?" I asked.

"There were words. He was angry. But time can heal. He'd see it our way."

"And your husband, Gregory," said Rice. "He gave him a ride to Toronto later that day?"

"Gregory had paperwork to catch up on at the office that Sunday. So he took him to the bus station in Barrie."

Rice nodded his head like he understood.

"He was the last one to see Jack alive," I said.

"Jonathan." Her lips were pressed tight now, both a refusal to accept what I'd said, and an assertion that she was done talking. She clenched her eyes and squeezed some more water from those two pieces of hard gravel on the frozen field of her face. "That doesn't make him a murderer, though."

Rice walked to the window to look onto the drive.

"I wish he were here to explain for himself," she said.

Rice looked at me and I felt the accusation. "Let's go. We've waited too long already."

"Yes. Let's get Gregory," said Connie. "I can't think what he's doing. He can explain everything."

"Let's go," repeated Rice, pulling the door to the drive open.

"Did he tell you about his trip to Windsor?" I wasn't ready yet.

"Windsor? What are you talking about?" She blinked, disoriented, looking from Rice to me and back. "Why?" Her hands were knots fiddling with the buttons of her jacket, the fingers twisting and twining as her mind tried to understand the changes in her world.

"Come on," said Rice, glaring at me, from the outside where he propped the door for us.

"He was in Windsor on April sixth," I said, as Connie pulled her boots on.

"Ha!" She straightened up. "You're wrong there. He never went to Windsor. No." She turned back into the kitchen to the calendar hanging on the wall. There was a picture of a beach with white sand, palm trees leaning over the turquoise water, the sweep of the bay curling into the distance, deck chairs and umbrellas facing the horizon. She pulled it off the nail, flipped back a couple of months, looking for the date. There was a scrawl on the calendar. Connie squinted at the little square of information below another Caribbean beach. "He had to work that day; he was covering a shift at the emergency room. These small-town hospitals make demands on the family doctors. He couldn't have been in Windsor."

"But he wasn't here."

"He was at the hospital in Barrie."

"Rice already checked."

"How dare you."

"He wasn't there."

"They let me know he was there today as well," Rice said. "I checked on the opiate they found in Jonathan's bloodstream. I talked to the nurse there."

"You talked to the hospital?" She appeared to compute in her mind. "Today?"

"I spoke to the ER coordinator and the head nurse, not to Gregory."

She dropped the calendar and hurried to the door, where Rice still stood.

"Did he say anything when he arrived home?" Rice asked now, a tone of urgency in his voice. "Seem strange, different, anything?" He started walking up the drive.

"What have you done?" Connie was through the door now, catching up to Rice, and I was trailing behind.

Rice looked over his shoulder and shot me hard look. When I caught up to him, he said, "What the hell are you playing at, Bird, stalling us along?"

"Looks like the nurse told him of your call."

"I told her not to in no uncertain terms." But he picked up the pace.

Connie surged ahead. "Why has he been so long in the barn?"

I could only just catch Connie's words as she broke into an awkward trot and tried to run before reverting to a fast walk. And then Rice was running to overtake her and reach the barn door first, and I was running to catch him, and he pulled the door to the barn open. He went in, then me, then Connie.

It was dark. The sun had finally made an appearance and its beams, running parallel to the horizon, cut through the spaces between the boards and made slashes of light in the interior. I didn't see Gregory at first. Didn't see him until Connie pushed past us and I heard her moan. She reached back to grab my arm and squeezed it hard; harder than I would have thought possible. Her gaze directed mine upward and I saw him, too, up, up, above where the hayloft, which covered half of the barn, ended; the body still moving, twisting, this way and that, the toes pointed downward, a slow pirouette above us. The square bales up in the loft had been stacked into a rudimentary stairway. The rope wound and unwound, the face was purple, the body was still, and the neck rested at an angle that left no doubt. We all knew.

It was later, after Rice called it in, after the OPP had come to investigate, after they'd asked us all a hundred questions that none of us really answered, after they'd cut the body down and put it in the back of an ambulance and drove it away, after the sun went down and the day ended. I don't know what the others said, but I assume it wasn't much, because after a time, they let us go. By now it was night and the clouds had cleared, and you could see all the stars in the sky, cold and distant, twinkling away. They didn't care; the hugeness of space seemed like a challenge to anyone to care. Our world, our petty problems, our hatreds and fights, our wounds and hurts, were so small beneath that big dark sky with all those other worlds spinning off on their own trajectories.

"Get in." I'd been so lost in the night that I hadn't heard Rice come out of the house.

I got in.

He revved the engine and backed off the grass; it was crowded with cars now and they appeared red and ghostly behind us in the glow the Grand Prix's brake lights. And then we were pointed down the drive and back to the city.

"Well, you got what you wanted," he said.

"What I wanted?"

"The end to it all."

I didn't say anything.

"A little finality. One more death. Stalling us along. Keeping us from the barn for as long as you could, hoping …"

I didn't deny it.

"You were probably already playing this ending in your head when you wanted me to call the hospital and ask about opiates. And I thought we were working on this together."

I turned away to look out the window, but my reflection in the dark glass met me. That was my face I saw looking back at me, not the world outside and I didn't like what I saw. I turned to stare ahead out the windshield, and the ghost of my reflection was there, too. There was an awful lot not to like. And it wasn't just what had happened up there at Turners' farm. It was weeks and weeks of not liking who I was and now the mirror was there and wouldn't let me look away.

We got closer to the city, and the lights started appearing: other cars, truck stops, street lamps, billboards, and the yellowed windows of houses; and, as the lights of the city came up all around us, the face in the glass faded, but I knew it'd still be me in the mirror tomorrow morning. And when Rice dropped me on Delaware, the stars had mostly disappeared, the night was as grey as ash, and I could barely remember that moment before I'd gotten in the car when the sky seemed so big with all those other worlds.

ACKNOWLEDGEMENTS

MANY THANKS TO those who read early drafts of *Opposite Sully's Gym*.

Thank you to my partner, Lara, for all her support and feedback on this book and all my writing.

To Jingshu Yao for her thoughts on pacing and credibility; to Ted Fines for his knowledge of a historical Toronto and his unerring editorial eye; to Deborah Brewster for all her insights into character and Toronto. And to all my writing friends at No Way Gary and the Junction Writers.

Thank you to the team at Dundurn, who supported the editorial process. To Shannon Whibbs for sharing her family stories about Toronto in the sixties and her incredible help in leading me to the edits needed to make this book the best it can be. To Meghan Macdonald for her support of my work and my writing. And to Janna Green for shepherding this process to its final stages.

Thank you so much to Julia Kim, my agent at The Rights Factory, for her generous editorial support.

Thank you to the Ontario Arts Council and the Government of Ontario for their financial support in the writing of this book.

So much help from so many people, but any mistakes found in these pages are mine alone.

ABOUT THE AUTHOR

Photo by Lara Stefanovich-Thomson

ALEXIS STEFANOVICH-THOMSON WRITES a wide variety of crime and crime-adjacent fiction. *Opposite Sully's Gym* is the second novel in the Patrick Bird Mystery series. The first book in the series, *The Road to Heaven*, was nominated for an Edgar Award (2025) in the Best Paperback Original category and a Shamus Award (2025) in the Best First PI Novel category. Alexis is a past winner of the Black Orchid Novella Award (2021) and the CWC Best Crime Novella Award (2023). He won third place in the *Toronto Star*'s Short Story Contest in 2022. Before writing, Alexis worked as a special education teacher, primarily with students with intellectual disabilities and autism. Alexis lives with his partner in Toronto.

BOOK CLUB QUESTIONS

1. The author has described this novel as "maple noir." What features do you think make it noir, and what parts seem distinctly Canadian?
2. *Opposite Sully's Gym* might seem like a strange title for this book. Why do you think the author chose it, and what could it mean?
3. What is your impression of the private investigator as a family member? Can you think of other detectives with partners and children? How do you think Patrick Bird will fare as a husband and father?
4. Rooming houses were once common in Toronto, but there are now fewer and fewer of them. Danny Blinken, who lives on the first floor of the rooming house in the novel, is an erratic character. Do you have any memories

or stories — good or bad — of unpredictable roommates and the challenges of communal living?

5. Patrick Bird isn't the world's best detective: he isn't even Toronto's best detective. But he's now solved two mysteries almost despite himself. What are his strong points as an investigator? What are his weaknesses?
6. Some characters in *Opposite Sully's Gym* are overtly racist and part of the conspiracy to assassinate Dr. Martin Luther King Jr., while other characters demonstrate a different, sometimes more subtle, racism through their words, actions, or bias. What examples of racism can you find in the novel?
7. Did you know before reading this book that James Earl Ray was in Canada for six weeks after assassinating Dr. King? If not, did it surprise you? Why isn't this story better known?
8. *Opposite Sully's Gym* is a work of fiction based on a conspiracy to assassinate Dr. King. The character of Raul is not the author's invention but a figure Ray named in his trial. Dr. King's family believed Ray's claims that he had not been acting alone, and in 1999, they won a wrongful death claim against a Memphis restaurateur and "other unknown co-conspirators." Where do you think the history ends and the fiction begins in the book?
9. The action in this novel takes place almost sixty years in the past. What has changed since that time, and what remains the same?
10. What do you see in Patrick Bird's future? Are there any events from Toronto's history that you think would be perfect for the next book in the Patrick Bird Mystery series?